JACK OF NEWBURY

JACK OF NEWBURY

Thomas Deloney

a *Broadview Anthology of British Literature* edition

Contributing Editor, *Jack of Newbury*:
Peter C. Herman, San Diego State University

General Editors,
Broadview Anthology of British Literature:
Joseph Black, University of Massachusetts, Amherst
Leonard Conolly, Trent University
Kate Flint, University of Southern California
Isobel Grundy, University of Alberta
Don LePan, Broadview Press
Roy Liuzza, University of Toronto
Jerome J. McGann, University of Virginia
Anne Lake Prescott, Barnard College
Barry V. Qualls, Rutgers University
Claire Waters, University of California, Davis

broadview press

BROADVIEW PRESS – www.broadviewpress.com
Peterborough, Ontario, Canada

Founded in 1985, Broadview Press remains a wholly independent publishing house. Broadview's focus is on academic publishing; our titles are accessible to university and college students as well as scholars and general readers. With over 600 titles in print, Broadview has become a leading international publisher in the humanities, with world-wide distribution. Broadview is committed to environmentally responsible publishing and fair business practices.

The interior of this book is printed on 100% recycled paper.

Library and Archives Canada Cataloguing in Publication

Deloney, Thomas, 1543?-1600, author
        Jack of Newbury / Thomas Deloney ; contributing editor, Peter C. Herman ; general editors, Joseph Black, Leonard Conolly, Kate Flint, Isobel Grundy, Don LePan, Roy Liuzza, Jerome J. McGann, Anne Lake Prescott, Barry V. Qualls, and Claire Waters.

(Broadview anthology of British literature editions)
ISBN 978-1-55481-210-3 (paperback)

        1. Winchcombe, John, -1520—Fiction. I. Herman, Peter C., 1958-, editor II. Title. III. Series: Broadview anthology of British literature (Series)

PR2244.D2J33 2015   823´.3   C2015-905241-6

Broadview Press handles its own distribution in North America
PO Box 1243, Peterborough, Ontario K9J 7H5, Canada
555 Riverwalk Parkway, Tonawanda, NY 14150, USA
Tel: (705) 743-8990; Fax: (705) 743-8353
email: customerservice@broadviewpress.com

Distribution is handled by Eurospan Group in the UK, Europe, Central Asia, Middle East, Africa, India, Southeast Asia, Central America, South America, and the Caribbean. Distribution is handled by Footprint Books in Australia and New Zealand.

Broadview Press acknowledges the financial support of the Government of Canada through the Canada Book Fund for our publishing activities.

Developmental Editors: Laura Buzzard and Jennifer McCue

PRINTED IN CANADA

Contents

Introduction

I.

We do not know very much about Thomas Deloney's life. He was probably born between 1540 and 1560, probably in Norwich (approximately 117 miles north of London, very near the North Sea coast); his surname suggests a French origin and many French Protestant refugees settled there over the course of the sixteenth century. Many of these people were involved in the cloth trade, which may have influenced Deloney's decision to become a silk-weaver. Clearly, Deloney learned how to read and write English, and it is possible that he knew Latin, although most if not all of the learned references in *Jack of Newbury* come from a poor man's encyclopedia, Pedro Mexía's *The Forest*,[1] rather than original sources. His first publication—a translation of a jest-book (a collection of funny tales) by Bonaventure Des Périers—indicates that he knew French, although we do not know how he learned the language. The baptism of his son Richard at the church of St. Giles Cripplegate (situated just outside of London's northern wall) on 16 October 1586 indicates that he had moved to London by then and married, although when and to whom remains unknown.[2] We also do not know if he had any other children. The only reference to his death is a comment by Will Kemp, the great clown for Shakespeare's company, at the end of his pamphlet, *Kemp's Nine Day's Wonder: Performed in a Dance from London to Norwich* (1600). Kemp, unhappy at the "abominable" ballads written about his stunt, wants to know who wrote them:

> I was told it was the great ballad-maker *T.D.*, alias Tho[mas] Deloney, chronicler of the memorable lives of the 6 yeomen of the west, Jack of Newbery, the Gentle-craft, and such like honest me[n] omitted by Stow, Holinshed, Grafto[n], Hall, Froissart, and the rest of those well-deserving writers: but I was given

---

1 See Appendix 4 of the contextual materials.
2 Sadly, on 21 December, the parish register records the burial of "Richard, the son of John Deloney (weaver)," "John" in all likelihood being an error for "Thomas."

since to understand your late general Tho[mas] died poorly, as ye all must do, and was honestly buried.

So we can assume that by 1600 Thomas Deloney had died, but when exactly, and under what financial circumstances, is unknown. There is no surviving will, and there are no portraits.

The biographical record, however, is not completely blank. We know that Deloney was a silk-weaver and he belonged to the silk-weavers' guild, the London Weavers' Company. We also know that he was not shy about championing their commercial interests when he considered them threatened. In June 1595, Deloney and several others wrote an open letter to the Elders of the French Church.[1] The gist of their complaint was that "strangers" (i.e., foreigners) refused to abide by the guild's rules for controlling the number of people in the trade:

> [They] exceed and keep more looms and servants than any free-man dare do, and rather than they will be bridled of their will, they run into the country five or six miles from the city out of our liberties, and there maliciously keep and do what they list.

The "strangers," in other words, were taking money out of the pockets of English silk-weavers by not observing any limits on the numbers of weavers and looms, thus diluting the market for silk goods. Deloney and his co-authors grant that "strangers ought to be cherished and well-intreated [well-treated]," but only insofar as "their life may not be our death, nor their welfare our woe.... In all well-governed commonwealths, the native-born are preferred before the stranger," the authors conclude, and the stranger should not take advantage of the "native" country's hospitality.

But Deloney and his co-authors misjudged the sympathies of London's authorities. The Elders of the French Church complained to London's mayor, who threw the letter's authors into jail. The prisoners, however, successfully petitioned Sir John Popham, Lord Chief Justice of England, repeating their complaint that "the Company of

---

1 According to the Lord Mayor's subsequent report, Deloney et al. planned to print forty copies, then deliver eleven to the French and Dutch Churches and one apiece to the Lord Mayor and the aldermen.

silk-weavers in the city of London [find] themselves greatly decayed and injured."

The complaint against immigrant weavers reveals a few salient details about the author of *Jack of Newbury*. First, Deloney expresses a keen sense of English identity, albeit one that veers very close to what some today would call jingoism. In his mind, "strangers" are guests in his country, and they ought to act like guests, remembering that the host should always come first. Instead, they, "like the viper ... seek to destroy their nourishers." Second, Deloney extends his patriotism to his guild, conflating the interests of the silk-weavers with the welfare of the commonwealth. The letter accuses foreign workers of seeking "their own private lucre without any Christian regard of the native born of our country ... to the great and amazing endamaging of the commonwealth and to the utter spoil and beggary of the Queen's liege people of this faculty." What is good for the guild, in other words, is good for England, and the reverse is equally true: anything that threatens the guild's interest also threatens the commonwealth. (Deloney will return to these principles in his prose fiction.) Third, while Deloney adopts a deeply respectful tone toward the French ministers and to the Lord Chief Justice, he has no difficulty speaking plainly and bluntly to those in authority, a propensity that informs *Jack of Newbury* and that also landed Deloney himself in serious trouble.

If weaving was Deloney's vocation, literature was his avocation. Several contemporary references in addition to Kemp's testify that he had become if not, as one critic writes, "London's premier balladeer," then certainly one of the most prominent. In 1592, Robert Greene, playwright and author of several "cony-catching" pamphlets (descriptions of London's underworld, its methods, and slang), used Deloney as an example of the typical balladeer, referring to him not by name but by his initials: "such trivial trinkets and threadbare trash had better seemed T.D., whose brains beaten to the yarking up of ballads." The more conventional Gabriel Harvey (scholar and friend to Edmund Spenser) in 1593 included Deloney among "the common pamphleteers of the city."

To be named London's chief balladeer was not necessarily a position of high repute. Ballads may have been incredibly popular, but the ballad was not a highly respected form. In fact, as Greene's comment suggests, it was at the very bottom of the early modern hierarchy of genres. In 1586, William Webbe, author of *A Discourse of English Poetrie*, condemned "the unaccountable rabble of rhyming ballad-makers and compilers of senseless sonnets, who be most busy to stuff every stall full of gross devices and unlearned pamphlets." The seventeenth century was hardly kinder. In 1620, during the reign of King Charles I, the playwright Thomas Middleton referred to ballads as "fashions, fictions, felonies, fooleries."

But while critics might have complained, ballads—really, narrative poems set to known tunes or melodies—were astonishingly popular. According to one count, there are 10,000 surviving examples from the sixteenth and seventeenth centuries, and probably many more have been lost. Printed on one side of a sheet of paper, selling for less than a penny, and covering about as wide a swath of topics as one could imagine, from current events to sensational murders to prodigies to political crises and scandals, ballads filled (some said "stuffed") London's bookstalls and were widely sold in the countryside by peddlers. In *The Winter's Tale*, Shakespeare nicely represents the low reputation of ballads and ballad sellers—as well as of their consumers, seen as unsophisticated rubes who cannot distinguish fact from fiction:

CLOWN. What hast here? Ballads?
MOPSA. Pray now, buy some. I love a ballad in print, alife [on my life], for then, we are sure they are true.
AUTOLYCUS. Here's one to a very doleful tune, how a usurer's wife was brought bed of twenty money bags at burden, and how she longed to eat adders' heads and toads carbonadoed [grilled].
MOPSA. Is it true, think you?
AUTOLYCUS. Very true, and but a month old. (4.4.250–57)

Deloney's efforts are nowhere near as fantastic as those sold by Autolycus. Only a few of his original broadsides are now extant, but the two collections of his ballads, *The Garland of Good Will* (entered into the Stationer's Register in 1593, though the earliest surviving edition dates from 1631), and the posthumous *Strange Histories of Kings, Princes, Earls, Lords, Ladies, Knights, and Gentlemen* (1602) presumably represent most, if not all, of his efforts. Taken together, Deloney's ballads show a clear interest in English history, and particularly in the doleful ends of English monarchs, as evidenced by these titles from *Strange Histories*: "The Imprisonment of Queen Elinor," "The Death of King John Poisoned by a Friar," and "The Murthering [Murdering] of King Edward the Second, Being Killed with a Hot, Burning Spit."

More unusually, Deloney's ballads demonstrate considerable sympathy towards women.[1] Almost all of the twenty-seven ballads printed in *The Garland* are either written in a woman's voice (e.g., "A Song of Queen Isabel"), concern famous women (e.g., "The Overthrow of Proud Holofernes, and the Triumph of Virtuous Queen Judith"[2] and "Of King Edward III, and the Fair Countess of Salisbury, Setting forth Her Constancy and Endless Glory"), or describe the victimization of a woman (e.g., "A Mournful Ditty on the Death of Rosamund, King Henry the Second's Concubine," who was forced to drink poison by King Henry's wife). In the second ballad in the collection, "A New Sonnet containing the Lamentation of Shore's Wife," Jane Shore, who was Edward IV's mistress and fell into misery after his death, complains bitterly about her end. Though this story was often used as an opportunity to moralize about the perils of adultery, Deloney's Jane reminds us that while she ruled like a queen, "many poor men's suits / By me was obtained," and the seizing of her possessions by the Duke of Gloucester (later King Richard III) was "against all law and right."

Deloney also wrote a ballad called "The Widow's Solace," in which he first commends the widow to God, if her husband was good to her, but says, if her husband did not love her, "Then give God praise and glory, / That he is dead and gone. / And mourn no more." If the widow chooses to remarry, Deloney counsels her thus:

> Receive such suitors friendly,
>   As do resort to thee;
> Respect not the outward person,
>   But the inward gravity,

---

1 While one can find any number of misogynistic texts and statements in this period, it would be a mistake to assume that the entire culture was unreflectively and reflexively anti-women.

2 In the Book of Judith, included in some versions of the Bible, Judith (a wealthy widow, not a queen) saves her city by tricking the Assyrian general Holofernes into sleeping in her tent. While he sleeps, she beheads him—a popular subject in early modern art.

And with advised judgment
   Choose him above the rest
Whom thou by proof hast tried
   In heart to love thee best.

We will see how the Widow in *Jack of Newbury* follows this advice.

In terms of politics, the ballads are always conventionally patriotic. Deloney clearly loved all things English—he included in *The Garland* a paean to the English rose—and he especially loved those who defended England against its enemies. After the English victory over the Spanish Armada in 1588, Deloney contributed three celebratory songs to the outpouring of nationalist sentiment.[1] Whenever he sees an opportunity, Deloney lays on the flattery. For example, at the end of the Holofernes ballad, he moves from praising Judith to praising Elizabeth as a contemporary Judith:[2]

How often hath our Judith saved
   And kept us from decay
'Gainst Holofernes, Devil and Pope,
   As may be seen this day.

And Deloney concludes his ballad on the 1586 Babington Plot[3] by making the conventional assertion that the Queen enjoys God's protection:

But, sovereign Queen, have thou no care,
   For God, which knoweth all,
Will still maintain thy royal state
   And give thy foes a fall.
And for thy Grace thy subjects all
   Will make their prayers still,
That never traitor in the land
   May have his wicked will.

---

1 One of these, "The Queen's Visiting of the Camp at Tilbury," is included in this volume; see Appendix 1.

2 Comparing the Queen to Israelite heroines was common in early modern writing.

3 A group of English Catholics planned to assassinate Queen Elizabeth and put Mary, Queen of Scots on the throne. The attempt ultimately led to Mary's execution in 1587.

Deloney's attitude toward rebellion, however, is interestingly split. In "A Song of the Banishment of the Two Dukes," he retells the story of Richard II's interrupting the joust between the Dukes of Hereford and Norfolk to send them both into exile (Shakespeare dramatizes this incident at the start of *Richard II*). As Deloney's audience certainly knew, the Duke of Hereford, Henry Bolingbroke, would later return, remove Richard from the throne, and become King Henry IV. But rather than terming this act rebellion—let alone making the conventional claim that for this crime, God would punish England with years of civil strife—Deloney endeavors to justify it:

> The Lords of England afterward
>   Did send for him [Bolingbroke] again,
> While that King Richard at the wars
>   In Ireland did remain,
> Who through the vile and great abuse,
>   Which through his deeds did spring,
> Deposed he was, and then the Duke
>   Was truly crowned king.

But rebellion against Richard receives a very different treatment in *Strange Histories'* final ballad, about the Peasants' Revolt of 1381: "How Wat Tyler and Jack Straw Rebelled against King Richard the Second." "The vile and great abuse" that caused the uprising, Deloney tells us, is "the tax the which our king / Upon his commons then did bring." However, Deloney unqualifiedly condemns the rebels, calling them "rude, disordered, frantic men" and "villains void of awe" who loot, set fires, and destroy all in their path. While "A Song of the Banishment" has no sympathy at all for Richard, whose "vile and great abuse" of the law justifies his deposition, "Wat Tyler" accuses the rebels of intending "much evil to him." The political stance is even more explicit in the prose epilogue, "A Speech between Ladies, Being Shepherds on Salisbury Plain." The rebels' larger purpose, according to "the Lady of Oxenbridge," is to destroy England's hierarchy: "their intent was, if they could have brought their vile purpose to pass, to have murdered the King and his nobles, and to have destroyed so near as they could all the gentilities of the land." Deloney's attitude towards Richard seems to depend on the nature of the opposition.

When faced with a rabble, Deloney takes Richard's side, never mind his extortionate taxation policies. But Bolingbroke and the nobles, who follow a legal process that ultimately leads to Richard's deposition, are not themselves a force for disorder and chaos, so Deloney can safely condemn Richard.

There is thus nothing extraordinary or unconventional in Deloney's extant ballads (except perhaps for their overt sympathy towards women). As "The Queen's Visiting of the Camp at Tilbury" (1588) demonstrates, Deloney both shared and contributed to the wave of patriotism following the Armada victory, and the attitude toward rebellion expressed in his ballads tracks perfectly with the affirmation of hierarchy and the condemnation of rebellion as Satanic in the officially authorized "An Homily against Disobedience and Willful Rebellion" (1570).[1] His rough treatment at the hands of London's authorities seems to have left no trace in his ballad-writing.

2.

Had Deloney died before 1596, his career would have amounted to little more than a footnote. What transformed Deloney from a popular, largely conventional balladeer into a revolutionary writer of prose fiction? The short answer is the Crisis of the 1590s.

In many ways, the Armada victory was the high point of Elizabeth's reign, but the accompanying groundswell of unity and national pride did not last. Very quickly, cracks began to appear (or reappear) in the façade of English unity. Despite the destruction of the Spanish fleet, the threat of invasion did not dissipate, and every year brought another invasion scare. Growing concerns about the government's competence also added to the underlying anxiety. Every year brought more and more vacancies to the Privy Council as Elizabeth's original councilors died off, and the combination of the Queen's age with her deliberate refusal to name a successor exacerbated the pervasive sense of insecurity. Contradicting the fulminations against rebellion in the "Homily against Disobedience" (issued by Elizabeth's government after a rebellion in 1570) and the picture of a happy, stable hierarchy in the Edwardian homily, "Exhortation

---

1 See Appendix 3 in this volume.

Concerning Good Order" (both included in this volume's appendices), anger against a social structure that seemed to care only for the rich started to burst out again.[1]

1591 seems to have been a very bad year. A group of sailors were arrested for publicly insulting their admiral: "Hang him, villain, for he hath cast away a number of men better than himself." They were not alone in their refusal to happily participate in the country's wars, notwithstanding the fear of a new Spanish invasion. Elizabeth decided to send troops to Brittany to help keep Spain at bay, but attempts to collect troops and ships to fight the Spanish in France ran into significant resistance. The invasion's commander Sir John Norris asked the Privy Council for permission to "press" one hundred more men "to fill up the default of the runaways," and to punish the runaways and anyone who helped them, "to give the country better minds than to hinder the soldiers and assist them to escape." Discovering an insufficiency of ships at Southampton that were suitable for military transport, Norris asked the mayor of the nearby town of Poole if anything was available, and the mayor responded with an offer of ships. But rather than jumping to serve their Queen, the ships' operators "disobediently and contemptuously took down their masts and rigging, for which the Mayor committed them; they have used very bad language, and threaten revenge."

Anger over the inequities in the social structure often ran high. In 1591, the unfortunately named Thomas Blaby delivered a sermon "against authority" and found himself prosecuted for sedition. The same year, the Privy Council heard about a man in Great Wenden (a small town about forty miles north of London) who bluntly denounced the gap between the "haves" and the "have-nots": "The Queen is but a woman and ruled by noblemen, and the noblemen and gentlemen are all one, and the gentlemen and farmers will hold together so that the poor can get nothing."

Matters exponentially worsened starting in 1594, when extreme weather caused a series of disastrous harvests. Terrible storms led to crop failures, which in turn led to dearth and severe inflation. The price of wheat doubled after the disastrous harvest of 1594, and rose even higher in 1596–97. "The period 1594–97 experienced," writes

---

1 Earlier instances include the Peasants' Rebellion of 1381, which gave us the rhyme, "When Adam delved and Eve spun / Who then was a gentleman?" and Kett's Rebellion (1549).

the historian M.J. Power, "the most sustained and severe inflation of prices in the sixteenth and seventeenth centuries, and culminated in the lowest real wages in English history." As one might imagine, the combination of scarcity and poverty did not breed generosity of spirit. "Small quantity of corn [grain] is brought to market," recorded one Philip Wyot in 1596, adding that "there is but little comes to the market and such snatching and catching for that little and such a cry that the like was never heard."

It would be wrong to say that Elizabeth and her government were indifferent to the misery caused by dearth. The "Exhortation Concerning Good Order" (better known today as the "Homily on Obedience") portrays the early modern convention of a divinely instituted hierarchy in which "every one have need of other," and England's rulers acknowledged that occupying the top rung of the ladder meant that they had a responsibility to relieve the suffering of the poor, to stop the hoarding of grain, and to control the profiteering of unscrupulous merchants. Between 1594 and 1600, Elizabeth issued at least four proclamations and one book trying to address the situation; each stresses the queen's full understanding of the problem's magnitude. The title, for example, of the 1595 proclamation is "For remedy whereof to the relief of the great multitude of her poor loving subjects lacking corn for their food." Also in 1595, Elizabeth's government published a short pamphlet with very specific instructions on who could buy and sell grain, when they could do it, and for how much: *A New Charge Given by the Queen's Commandment to All Justices of the Peace, and All Mayors ... for Execution of Sundry Orders Published the Last Year for Stay of Dearth of Grain, With Certain Additions Now this Present Year to Be Well Observed and Executed.*

But the order and the proclamations were not "well observed and executed." In fact, they were completely ignored. The same year that Elizabeth issued her *New Charge*, the mayor and justices of Norfolk received a libel demanding "What are these edicts and proclamations, which are here and there scattered in the country, concerning kidders [corn transporters], corn-mongers and those devilish cormorants, but a scabbard without the sword, for neither are those murthering [murdering] malsters nor the bloody corn-buyers stayed." The government could issue however many proclamations it desired, but nobody, it seems, paid them any mind.

The Crisis of the 1590s shredded the sense of mutual obligation expressed in the "Exhortation." According to the chronicler John Stow, as the price of grain rocketed, the poor started complaining that greed, not weather, had caused the shortages: "which dearth happens (after the common opinion) more by means of overmuch transporting [exporting], by our own merchants for their private gain than through the unseasonableness of the weather passed.... [T]he poor did feel ... whatsoever was sustenance for man was likewise raised without all conscience and reason." In 1596, the printer John Windet published *Three Sermons or Homilies, To Move Compassion towards the Poor and Needy in these Times.* This book, set forth, as the title page has it, "by Authority," admonishes the wealthy not to spurn the poor: "when thou meetest a poor man in the streets, consider that he is a man, created after God's image: though he be poor, naked, and miserable, yet beware thou despise him not, such as he is, take heed thou smite him not, take heed thou drive him not away." The Homilist also turns his attention to the magistrates, who he says have failed in their charge. After discussing how "this office of distributing is not only private, but public, and appertaineth to the Magistrate, as well as to other rich men," the author acidly suggests that they "take a view of a little book entitled *The Regiment of Poverty.*[1] I doubt not but they shall be greatly directed thereby."

Faced with the indifference of the rich and the impotence of the government, some turned to violence. London's apprentices rioted at least six times starting in June 1595, when a silk-weaver showed up at the Mayor's house and delivered "some hard speeches in dispraise of his government." William Cecil, Lord Burghley, who served as Elizabeth's chief councilor, blamed the riots on the food crisis, and both to contain the large number of arrested persons and to serve as a deterrent, London's authorities set up cages in various parts of the city to house and display "disordered persons." The Norwich Libeler threatened the authorities with revolution: "There are 60,000 craftsmen in London and elsewhere, besides the poor country clown [rustic, peasant], that can no longer bear [endure], therefore their draught is in the cup of the Lord which they shall drink to the dregs, and some barbarous and unmerciful soldier shall lay open your hedges, reap

---

1   Andreas Hyperius, *The Regiment of Poverty*, trans. Henry Tripp (London, 1572). I am grateful to Professors Geoffrey Chew and Robert Fehrenbach for identifying this book.

your fields, rifle your coffers, and level your houses to the ground." He ended his missive with these chilling words: "Necessity hath no law." In early fall, 1596, Bartholomew Steere of Oxfordshire tried to organize an uprising because, according to one participant's deposition, Steere had tired of the poor being treated "like dogs"; this man also testified that he "commonly heard the poor people say that they were ready to famish for want of corn, and thought they should be forced by hunger to take it out of men's houses." The rebellion fizzled, but the authorities nonetheless took all such threats deeply seriously.

Deloney stepped into this combustible context with a ballad complaining "of the great want and scarcity of corn." Provokingly—as Stephen Slany, London's mayor, reports in an agitated letter to Lord Burghley[1]—in the ballad the queen "speak[s] with her people in dialogue in very fond and undecent sort, and prescribeth orders for the remedying of the dearth of corn, extracted (as it seemeth) out of the book published by your Lordship the last year" (doubtless the book is *A New Charge* [see above]). Sadly, the ballad is no longer extant, so we do not know exactly what Deloney said. But clearly, the authorities were not pleased; Slany reports that while he has the ballad's printer in custody, Deloney himself seems to have gone missing.

3.

Deloney was never found, or perhaps the authorities lost interest and he resumed his life. Either way, we have little record of Thomas Deloney's activities until 1600, when Will Kemp reported the famous balladeer's recent demise. While the archive reveals nothing about the details of Deloney's post-1596 life, evidently he kept writing, although he made a significant change in his literary output. In addition to ballads, Deloney turned to prose fiction, producing four proto-novels between 1597 and 1600: *Jack of Newbury*; *The Gentle Craft, Part 1*; *The Gentle Craft, Part 2*; and *Thomas of Reading*. The first, *Jack of Newbury*, was entered in the Stationer's Register on 7 March 1597, and was frequently reprinted afterward. The earliest extant edition dates from 1619; presumably all the others were so popular that they were shared until the books fell apart.

---

1   See Appendix 8 in this volume for the full letter.

Jack of Newbury is not a novel according to contemporary defini-
tions in that it neither presents a unified story "whose primary crite-
rion [is] truth to individual experience" (as Ian Watt describes in *The
Rise of the Novel*) nor reflects "an epistemological crisis," (as described
by Michael McKeon in *The Origins of the English Novel*). However,
there are some similarities to the kind of books pioneered by Daniel
Defoe and Henry Fielding. For one thing, like later novels, Deloney's
work follows the central character through time. The story of Jack's
rise in economic status is handily dealt with in the first chapter, and
after that we have chapters on Jack's subsequent marriage and his
contribution to homeland defense during the 1513 Scottish invasion
of England. The later chapters seem to take place later in Jack's life,
although the only specific indicator of date comes in Chapter 6, when
Jack and his fellow clothiers protest the economic fallout of Henry's
brief 1528 war with the Holy Roman Empire. Though some chapters
(4, 5, and 7, for instance) are self-contained and could be placed almost anywhere in the book's chronology, other chapters (such as 10)
build on events in previous chapters, contributing to a sense of the
book as a coherent whole.

While *Jack of Newbury* does not embody many present-day defini-
tions of the novel, the book does exemplify Terry Eagleton's definition
of the novel as a genre that contains elements of just about everything:

> You can find poetry and dramatic dialogue in the novel, along
> with epic, pastoral, satire, history, elegy, tragedy and any num-
> ber of other literary modes.... The novel quotes, parodies, and
> transforms other genres....

Similarly, in *Jack of Newbury*, Deloney blends together history, the
ballad, the jest book, romance, hagiography (in, e.g., Jack's generosity to the bankrupt Randolph Pert in Chapter 9), and realism (in
recording the rhythms of actual speech)—in other words, nearly all
the fictive and prose traditions available to him—into a story that is
altogether original.

But to grasp the full range of Deloney's achievement, we need to
return to the ideas espoused in such works as the "Exhortation Concerning Good Order" that depict a rigid, hierarchical social structure
that mirrors the structure of the universe. Those above rule those

below: God rules the universe just as monarchs rule their subjects, parents rule their children, and husbands rule their wives. Each may "have need of other," but there is no movement allowed between stations, and there is no doubt where authority lies and obedience is due.

Yet as we have seen, this sense of order was more often disregarded than followed without question. The source for Chapter 5 of *Jack of Newbury*—in which the narrator gives us a tour of Jack's collection of portraits depicting poor people who rose to great heights, thereby implicitly contradicting the "Exhortation"'s view of a static society—is Pedro Mexía's *Silva de varia lección* (A Miscellany of Several Lessons). First published in 1540 and then reprinted across Europe until it reached England in 1571, the popularity of Mexía's text suggests that the discourse of social mobility was quite prevalent in the sixteenth century. More generally, the development of the public theater in the late sixteenth century, with playwrights producing works aimed at pleasing a paying audience that largely came from the middling sort contributed to the rise of a literature that reflected their values. These sometimes overlapped with those of aristocratic culture but nonetheless differed in key respects, such as an emphasis on the value of merchants to the commonwealth. The conflict between contradictory political perspectives took on a much sharper point during the Crisis of the 1590s, when more than one person blamed the troubles on the aristocracy, not on rebelling peasants. Deloney's *Jack of Newbury* incisively contributes to these developments by providing an alternative to the aristocratic view of English society animating such government authorized texts as the "Exhortation" and the "Homily against Obedience"—an alternative that retains the monarchy but privileges the merchant class over the aristocracy.

Deloney first signals his anti-aristocratic, pro-merchant class position in the book's dedication. Usually, authors and printers used dedications to gain some sort of preferment (hoping that the person so honored would send money), and so the dedicatee was almost always a member of the wealthy aristocracy. To give a few admittedly arbitrary examples, Edmund Spenser dedicates *The Faerie Queene* (1596) to Elizabeth; William Shakespeare dedicates *Venus and Adonis* (1594) to Henry Wriothesley, Earl of Southampton; and *Holinshed's Chronicles* (1577) is dedicated to William Cecil, Lord Burghley. While some authors forego dedications and others address themselves to "learned gentlemen," Deloney does something (to my knowledge) unique: he dedicates his book to an entire artisanal class. "To All Famous Cloth-workers in England," he writes, using the body of his dedication to praise cloth-workers as essential to the commonwealth because they not only practice "the most necessary art of clothing," but they provide employment and "nourishment of many thousands of poor people"—unlike, perhaps, the aristocracy in this time of dearth.[1]

More abstractly, but equally importantly, Deloney rejects the conventional protocols for writing history, which in this period was mainly written "from above"—with a focus on the acts of the great and powerful. Alternatives to this perspective did exist. John Foxe's massive and massively popular *Acts and Monuments of the Church*, popularly known as the *Book of Martyrs* (1563; revised and expanded in 1570, 1576, and 1583), gave example after example of non-elite Protestants destroyed for their faith, and certainly, the major chroniclers of the period (Edward Hall, John Stow, and the contributors to *Holinshed's Chronicles*) paid some attention to the sufferings of the poor. But while these works occasionally attend to the concerns of the middle and lower classes (for example, Hall and Holinshed positively record the protests over Henry VIII's taxes to pay for his wars), the monarchy and the aristocracy constitute the center of gravity of their narratives. No history of England yet existed that placed the doings of great merchants at the center of the narrative. Deloney, however, bases *Jack of Newbury* on the lives of two notable Newbury clothiers: John Winchcombe the Elder (d. 1520) and his son, also named John Winchcombe (c. 1489–1557). *Thomas of Reading*, set in the reign of Henry I, is likely also based on an actual person. Deloney's use of people who really lived but are excluded from the grand historical narratives set out by Hall and Holinshed contributes to the creation of an alternative history of England, one that puts the merchant class at the center.

Jack of Newbury's first chapter introduces the reader to the book's larger themes through the story of Jack's economic rise. His master's widow (who is never given a name) decides to marry Jack and he becomes her husband, rising from an apprentice to a master as a result. Upon the widow's death at the chapter's end, Jack inherits the

---

[1] The second part of the 1619 title stresses how Jack "set continually five hundred poor people at work, to the great benefit of the commonwealth, worthy to be read and regarded."

business. While one might expect this plot to serve as a vehicle for parodying lusty widows and unscrupulous apprentices, that is not the case here. Instead, the chapter illustrates how economic virtues lead to tangible results, and Deloney ties his pro-merchant class agenda to an arguably proto-feminist viewpoint.[1] The widow's romantic interest in Jack is not superficial or predatory, but motivated by an appreciation of Jack's "good government and discretion," "diligent labour," and "obedience" to her. When the widow dies, Jack's choice of wife is guided by similar principles: he chooses a woman of no means but much quality who he believes to be "careful in her business, faithful in her dealing, and an excellent good housewife."

Jack promises never to "forget [his] former estate," and throughout the text he is true to his word. Even when he is offered the great honor of a knighthood, he remains loyal to the working and merchant classes. He declines what he calls "the vain tilts of gentility" to remain one of those "who labour in this life"—or, in other words, refuses to join the aristocracy, dismissing it as a group of wasteful parasites who consume everything and produce nothing. In the book's final chapter, Jack forces a nobleman to marry the servant he impregnated, and in the process once more asserts the moral superiority of the working classes over the aristocracy, telling the nobleman that he "'account[s] the poorest wench in my house too good to be your whore, were you ten knights.'"

Deloney pairs such assertions of class loyalty with a sharp critique of the monarchy. Much of this critique concerns Henry VIII's departure from England in 1513 to conduct a war in France, which Deloney condemns as leaving England open to the invasion from Scotland that occurred later the same year. (Scotland's attempted invasion was brief and met a dismal end, but this fortunate conclusion for the English does not appear to excuse the king's irresponsibility.) This judgment is given most scathingly in Chapter 3, via an invented meeting between Henry VIII and Jack. When Henry VIII makes a progress into Berkshire, Jack decides that he will encounter his monarch by setting up an allegorical tableaux: "knowing the King would

---

1 Throughout the chapter, idleness is linked to misogyny; for example, when the "wild youths of the town" try to entice Jack to leave work, they couch their temptation in explicitly anti-woman terms: "'Doubtless,' quoth one, 'I doubt some female spirit hath enchanted Jack to her treadles, and conjured him within the compass of his loom, that he can stir no further.'"

come over a certain meadow near adjoining to the town, [he] got himself thither with all his men, and repairing to a certain ant-hill, which was in the field, took up his seat there, causing his men to stand round about, the same with their swords drawn." Standing in the king's path with swords out is a very dangerous move on Jack's part, but Jack's explanation of his behavior seems to defuse any violently subversive intent:

"it is poor Jack of Newbury, who being scant marquis of a mole hill, is chosen Prince of Ants, and here I stand with my weapons and guard about me to defend and keep these my poor and painful subjects from the force of the idle butterflies, their sworn enemies, lest they should disturb this quiet commonwealth, who this summer season are making their winter's provision."

It is not the monarch who is the enemy, but the "butterflies," which threaten the commonwealth through their idleness (their identity we will return to below).

The king commands Jack to appear before him, and, shockingly, *Jack refuses* and asks the king to come to him instead, claiming that to leave his post would make him as irresponsible as Henry VIII: "while I am away, our enemies might come and put my people in hazard, as the Scots did England while our king was in France." Needless to say, in sixteenth-century England, subjects are expected to comply when the monarch beckons—and not to criticize the monarch's policies— but, in this imagined encounter, the king obeys Jack's summons and Jack gets away with criticizing him to his face.

Deloney will return to the theme of the war in Chapter 6, where he describes the deleterious effect of the "wars our King had with other countries" on the economy. While Deloney understands a direct link between trade embargoes and economic loss, he also perceives the indirect costs of halting trade:

By means of the wars our King had with other countries, many merchant strangers were prohibited for coming to England, and also our own merchants (in like sort) were forbidden to have dealing with France or the Low Countries. By means whereof, the clothiers had most of their cloth lying on their hands, and that which they sold was at so low rate that the money scarcely paid for the wool and workmanship. Whereupon they thought to ease themselves by abating the poor workmen's wages, and when that did not prevail, they turned away their people— weavers, shearmen, spinners and carders—so that where there was a hundred looms kept in one town, there was scant fifty, and he that kept twenty, put down ten.

By preventing trade, war causes reduced wages and then unemployment. Unemployment causes hunger, and hunger causes "great woe in most places in England," resulting in a society divided against itself: "The poor hate the rich because they will not set them to work, and the rich hate the poor because they seem burdensome." Consequently, Jack forms what might be the first trade lobbying group: he sends a letter to "all the chief clothing towns in England" suggesting that each send "two honest discreet men" to present their petition to Henry VIII. The king of course agrees to their requests and issues an order proclaiming that "merchants should freely traffic with one another."

In *Jack of Newbury*, Deloney rewrites the very structure of English society so that the merchant and manufacturing class *replaces* the landed aristocracy as the source of the nation's wealth and cultural value. Chapter 2 commences with a ballad describing the microcosm of Jack's massive clothing factory, in which women and men, children and adults, together form a harmonious mini-commonwealth dedicated to the production of cloth (but also including the butchers, brewers, and bakers who feed his employees). The ballad declares at its conclusion that the person responsible for this epitome of wealth-producing labor is "a gallant clothier sure, / Whose fame for ever shall endure." "Fame" and "gallant" are terms more usually associated with chivalric feats, such as Henry's attempt at retaking France. But Deloney appropriates these adjectives for a new sort of economic hero, one whose glory, as we are told repeatedly, lies in providing relief to the poor, not in conquering lands or dragons.

Significantly, Jack's nemesis in this story is not a member of the aristocracy, but the Lord Chancellor, Cardinal Thomas Wolsey, who rose from humble beginnings (his father was a butcher) to become Henry's right hand man. The actual Wolsey made himself truly hated in England, partly because he funded Henry's foreign ventures through various "loans" (that were never repaid), and partly because he was as greedy as he was competent. According to Edward Hall, Wolsey was "very eloquent and full of wit, but for pride, covetous[ness], and ambition, he excelled all others." It is Wolsey who is the main target of Jack's allegory in Chapter 3. Unlike the Grasshopper and the Caterpillar, who for the crimes of idleness and living "upon the labours of other men" are banished from the kingdom, the Butterfly remains (even though he is "very much misliked") because:

> few durst say anything to him because of his golden apparel, who, through sufferance grew so ambitious and malapert that the poor Ant could no sooner get an egg into her nest but he would have it away.

Jack's enmity against Wolsey, aside from drawing on historical dislike of the man, arises for two related reasons. First, Wolsey does not embrace his non-aristocratic, working-class lineage—an attitude that leads him to throw the clothiers in jail when Jack makes a disparaging remark about his father's profession. Second, and most importantly, Wolsey is the one held responsible for Henry's anti-merchant policies and for the economic woe besetting England:

> This Cardinal was at that time Lord Chancellor and a wonderful proud prelate, by whose means great variance was set betwixt the King of England and the French King, the Emperor of Almaine, and divers other princes of Christendom, whereby the traffic of those merchants was utterly forbidden, which bred a general woe through England, especially among clothiers, insomuch that having no sale for their cloth, they were fain to put away many of their people which wrought....

The landed aristocracy may be idle. They may live off the labor of other men. But Wolsey is bad for business, and that Deloney cannot forgive.

Jack of Newbury takes cultural norms that many assume were unquestionable during the early modern period and turns them on their head. While Deloney's vision retains the monarch as a figurehead, its truly valuable subjects are not the nobility, but the merchant class:

people who provide the opportunity for labor. Industry is the nation's strength, not chivalry. And women are to be respected, not used and discarded. It would, however, be a mistake to assume that Deloney's challenges came from the extreme margins of the culture. No book sells as many copies as this one did without offering something that a great many people want to hear. *Jack of Newbury* thus allows us to recover a more intellectually diverse, challenging, and complex early modern culture, one in which it is conceivable for the poor to become rich and for those who work to be valued more than those who consume.

JACK OF NEWBURY

TO ALL FAMOUS
Cloth-workers in England, I wish
all happiness of life, prosperity and
brotherly affection.

Among all manual arts used in this land, none is more famous for desert,[1] or more beneficial to the commonwealth, than is the most necessary art of clothing. And therefore, as the benefit thereof is great, so are the professors of the same to be both loved and maintained. Many wise men, therefore, having deeply considered the same, most bountifully have bestowed their gifts for upholding of so excellent a commodity, which hath been, and yet is the nourishing of many thousands of poor people. Wherefore to you, most worthy clothiers, do I dedicate this my rude work, which hath raised out of the dust of forgetfulness a most famous and worthy man, whose name was John Winchcombe, alias Jack of Newbury, of whose life and love I have briefly written, and in a plain and humble manner, that it may be the better understood of those for whose sake I take pains to compile it, that is, for the well-minded clothiers, that herein they may behold the great worship and credit which men of this trade have in former time come unto. If therefore it be of you kindly accepted, I have the end of my desire, and think my pains well recompensed; and finding your gentleness answering my hope, it shall move me shortly to set to your sight the long hidden history of Thomas of Redding, George of Gloucester, Richard of Worcester, and William of Salisbury, with divers others, who were all most notable members in the commonwealth of this land, and men of great fame and dignity.[2] In the mean space, I commend you all to the most high God, who ever increase, in all perfection and prosperous estate, the long honoured trade of English clothiers.

Yours in all humble service,
T.D.

---

1   *more famous for desert*   More deservedly famous.
2   *it shall move me … fame and dignity*   Deloney would publish *Thomas of Reading* on 19 April 1602, although the first extant edition dates from 1612.

Chapter 1: The most pleasant and delectable history of John Winchcombe, otherwise called Jack of Newbury, and first of his love and pleasant life.

In the days of King Henry VIII, that most noble and victorious prince, in the beginning of his reign, John Winchcombe, a broadcloth weaver, dwelt in Newbury,[1] a town in Berkshire, who, for that he was a man of a merry disposition and honest conversation, was wondrous well-beloved of rich and poor, especially because in every place where he came, he would spend his money with the best, and was not at any time found a churl of his purse.[2] Wherefore, being so good a companion, he was called of old and young Jack of Newbury, a man so generally well-known in all his country for his good fellowship that he could go in no place but he found acquaintance. By means whereof, Jack could no sooner get a crown but straight he found means to spend it. Yet had he ever this care: that he would always keep himself in comely and decent apparel, neither at any time would he be overcome in drink, but so discretely behave himself with honest mirth and pleasant conceits that he was every gentleman's companion.

After that Jack had long led this pleasant life, being (though he were but poor) in good estimation, it was his master's chance to die, and his dame to be a Widow, who was a very comely ancient woman and of reasonable wealth. Wherefore, she having a good opinion of her man John, committed unto his government the guiding of all her workfolks for the space of three years together. In which time she found him so careful and diligent that all things came forward and prospered wondrous well. No man could entice him from his business all the week, by all the entreaty they could use,[3] insomuch that in the end some of the wild youths of the town began to deride and scoff at him.

"Doubtless," quoth one, "I doubt some female spirit hath enchanted Jack to her treadles,[4] and conjured him within the compass of his loom, that he can stir no further."

---

1 *Newbury* Town nearly equidistant between Bristol and London.
2 *was not ... purse* Was never cheap or stingy.
3 *by all the entreaty they could use* No matter how much they tried.
4 *treadles* Pedals used to work a loom.

"You say truth," quoth Jack, "and if you have the leisure to stay 'til the charm be done, the space of six days and five nights, you shall find me ready to put on my holy day apparel, and on Sunday morning for your pains, I will give you a pot of ale over against the maypole."

"Nay," quoth another, "I'll lay my life that as the salamander cannot live without the fire,[1] so Jack cannot live without the smell of his dame's smock."

"And I marvel," quoth Jack, "that you being of the nature of the herring (which so soon as he is taken out of the sea straight dies) can live so long with your nose out of the pot."

"Nay, Jack, leaving thy testing," quoth another, "and go along with us, thou shalt not stay a jot."

"And because I will not stay, nor make you a liar," quoth Jack, "I'll keep me here still, and so, farewell!"

Thus then they departed, after they had for half a score times tried him to this intent, and saw he would not be led by their lure, they left him to his own will. Nevertheless, every Sunday in the afternoon, and every holiday, Jack would keep them company, and be as merry as a pie,[2] and having still good store of money, in his purse, one or other would ever be borrowing of him, but never could he get any penny of it again. Which when Jack perceived, he would never after carry about twelve pence at once in his purse, and that being spent, he would straight return home merrily, taking his leave of the company in this sort:

My masters, I thank you, it's time to pack home,
For he that wants money is counted a mome,[3]
And twelve pence a Sunday being spent in good cheer,
To fifty-two shillings amounts in the year,
Enough for a craftsman that lives by his hands,
And he that exceeds it shall purchase no lands.
For that I spend this day, I'll work hard tomorrow,
For woe is that party that seeketh to borrow.[4]

---

1 *salamander ... fire* According to popular legend, salamanders lived in fire.
2 *pie* Magpie.
3 *wants* Lacks; *mome* Fool.
4 *For woe ... borrow* Compare Polonius' advice to his son, Laertes: "Neither a borrower nor a lender be" (*Hamlet* 1.3.75).

My money doth make me full merry to be,
And without my money, none careth for me.
Therefore, wanting money, what should I do here?[1]
But haste home, and thank you for all my good cheer.

Thus was Jack's good government and discretion noted of the best and substantiallest[2] men of the town, so that it wrought his great commendations, and his dame thought herself not a little blessed to have such a servant that was so obedient unto her, and so careful for her profit, for she had never a prentice[3] that yielded her more obedience than he did, or was more dutiful, so that, by his good example, he did as much good as by his diligent labour and travail. Which his singular virtue being noted by the Widow, she began to cast very good countenance to her man, John, and to use very much talk with him in private. And first, by way of communication, she would tell unto him what suitors she had, and the great offers they made her, what gifts they sent her, and the great affection they bare[4] her, craving his opinion in the matter.

When Jack found the favour to be his dame's secretary, he thought it an extraordinary kindness,[5] and guessing by the yarn it would prove a good web, began to question with his dame in this sort.

"Although it becometh not me your servant to pry into your secrets, nor to be busy about matters of your love, yet for so much as it hath pleased you to use conference with me in those causes, I pray you let me entreat you to know their names that be your suitors, and of what profession they be."

"Mary,[6] John," sayeth she, "that you shall, and I pray thee take a cushion and sit down by me."

"Dame," quoth he, "I thank you, but there is no reason I should sit on a cushion 'til I have deserved it."

"If thou hast not, thou mightest have done," said she, "but faint soldiers never find favour."

---

1 *wanting money ... here?* Since people want my money, what should I do?
2 *substantiallest* Most substantial.
3 *prentice* Apprentice.
4 *bare* Bore.
5 *he thought ... kindness* The position of secretary in early modern England was one of great trust and prestige.
6 *Mary* An exclamation, as in "By the Virgin Mary."

John replied, "that makes me indeed to want favour, for I durst not try maidens because they seem coy, nor wives, for fear of their husbands, nor widows, doubting their disdainfulness."

"Tush, John," quoth she, "he that fears and doubts womankind cannot be counted mankind, and take this for a principle: all things are not as they seem. But let us leave this and proceed to our former matter. My first suitor dwells at Wallingford,[1] by trade a tanner, a man of good wealth, and his name is Craftes, of comely personage and very good behaviour, a widower, well thought of amongst his neighbours. He hath proper land, a fair house and well-furnished, and never a child in the world, and he loves me passing well."

"Why then," quoth John, "you were best to have him."

"Is that your opinion?" quoth she. "Now trust me, so it is not mine. For I find two special reasons to the contrary. The one is that he being over-worn in years makes me over-loathe to love him, and the other, that I know one nearer hand."[2]

"Believe me, dame," quoth Jack, "I perceive store is no sore, and proffered ware worse by ten in the hundred than that which is sought.[3] But I pray ye, who is your second suitor?"

"John," quoth she, "it may seem immodesty in me to bewray[4] my love secrets, yet seeing thy discretion, and being persuaded of thy secrecy, I will show thee. The other is a man of middle years, but yet a bachelor, by occupation a tailor, dwelling at Hungerford,[5] by report a very good husband, such a one as hath crowns good store, and to me he professes much good will, for his person,[6] he may please any woman."

"Aye, dame," quoth John, "because he pleaseth you."

"Not so," said she, "for my eyes are unpartial[7] judges in that case, and albeit my opinion may be contrary to others, if his art deceive not my eyesight, he is worthy of a good wife, both for his person and conditions."

---

1 *Wallingford* Town approximately fifteen miles north of Newbury.
2 *nearer hand* Nearer at hand.
3 *proffered ware ... sought* Proverb meaning that we much prefer the ideal we are seeking over the choices actually before us.
4 *bewray* Betray, reveal.
5 *Hungerford* Town approximately nine miles east of Newbury.
6 *crowns good store* Many crowns, a lot of money; *for his person* Concerning his looks.
7 *unpartial* Impartial.

"Then trust me, dame," quoth John, "for so much as you are without doubt of yourself that you will prove a good wife, and so well persuaded of him, I should think you could make no better a choice."

"Truly, John," quoth she, "there be also two reasons that move me not to like of him: the one, that being so long a ranger, he would at home be a stranger. And the other, that I like better of one nearer hand."

"Who is that?" quoth Jack.

Saith she, "the third suitor is the parson of Speenhamland,[1] who hath a proper living, he is of holy conversation and good estimation, whose affection to me is great."

"No doubt, dame," quoth Jack, "you may do wondrous well with him, where you have no care but to serve God and to make ready his meats."

"O John," quoth she, "the flesh and the spirit agrees not, for he will be so bent to his books that he will have little mind of his bed. For one month's studying for a sermon will make him forget his wife for a whole year.

"Truly, dame," quoth John, "I must needs speak in his behalf, and the rather for that he is a man of the Church, and your near neighbour, to whom, as I guess, you bear the best affection. I do not think that he will be so much bound to his book, or subject to the spirit, but that he will remember a woman at home or abroad."

"Well, John," quoth she, "I wis[2] my mind is not that way, for I like better of one nearer hand."

"No marvel," quoth Jack, "you are so peremptory, seeing you have so much choice. But I pray ye, dame," quoth he, "let me know this fortunate man that is so highly placed in your favour?"

"John," quoth she, "they are worthy to know nothing that cannot keep something. That man, I tell thee, must go nameless, for he is lord of my love, and king of my desires. There is neither tanner, tailor, nor parson may compare with him. His presence is a preservative to my health, his sweet smiles my heart's solace, and his words heavenly music to my ears."

"Why then," quoth John, "for your body's health, your heart's joy, and your ear's delight, delay not the time, but entertain him with

1 *Speenhamland* Suburb just north of Newbury.
2 *I wis* I believe.

a kiss, make his bed next to yours, and chop up the match in the morning."

"Well," quoth she, "I perceive thy consent is quickly got to any, having no care how I am matched so I be matched. I wis, I wis, I could not let thee go so lightly, being loathe that any one should have thee, except I could love her as well as myself."

"I thank you for your kindness and good will, good dame," quoth he, "but it is not wisdom for a young man that can scantly keep himself to take a wife. Therefore, I hold it the best way to lead a single life, for I have heard say that many sorrows follow marriage, especially where want remains. And beside, it is a hard matter to find a constant woman, for as young maids are fickle, so are old women jealous, the one a grief too common, the other a torment intolerable."

"What John!" quoth she, "consider that maidens' fickleness proceeds of vain fancies, but old women's jealousy of superabounding love, and therefore the more to be born withal."

"But dame," quoth he, "many are jealous without cause, for is it sufficient for their mistrusting natures to take exceptions at a shadow, at a word, at a look, at a smile, nay, at the twinkle of an eye, which neither man nor woman is able to expel! I knew a woman that was ready to hang herself for seeing but her husband's shirt hang on a hedge with her maid's smock."

"I grant this fury may haunt some," quoth she, "yet there be many other that complain not without great cause."

"Why, is there any cause that should move jealousy?" quoth John.

"Aye, by St. Mary, is there," quoth she, "for would it not grieve a woman (being one every way able to delight her husband) to see him forsake her, despise and condemn her, being never so merry as when he is in other company, sporting abroad from morning 'til noon, from noon 'til night, and when he comes to bed, if he turn to his wife, it is in such solemnness, and wearisome drowsy lameness, that it bring rather loathsomeness than any delight. Can you then blame a woman in this case to be angry and displeased? I'll tell you what, among brute beasts it is a grief intolerable, for I heard my grandmother tell that the bellwether of her flock, fancying one of the ewes above the rest, and seeing gratis the shepherd abusing her in an abominable sort (subverting the law of nature),[1] could by no means bear that abuse. But

---

1 *abusing her ... nature* Engaging in bestiality.

watching opportunity for revenge, on a time found the said shepherd sleeping in the field, and suddenly ran against him in such violent sort that by the force of his wreathen[1] horns, he beat the brains out of the shepherd's head and slew him. If then a sheep could not endure that injury, think not that women are so sheepish to suffer it."

"Believe me," quoth Jack, "if every horn-maker[2] should be so plagued by a horned beast, there should be less horns made in Newbury by many in a year. But dame," quoth he, "to make an end of the prattle, because it is an argument too deep to be discussed between you and I, you shall hear me sing an old song, and so we will depart to supper":

A maiden fair I dare not wed
For fear to have Acteon's head.[3]
A maiden black is often proud,
A maiden little will be loud,
A maiden that is high of groath[4]
They say is subject unto sloth.
Thus, fair or foul, little or tall,
Some faults remain among them all.
But of all the faults that be,
None is so bad as jealousy.
For jealousy is fierce and fell,[5]
And burns as hot as fire in hell.
It breeds suspicion without cause,
And breaks the bonds of reason's laws.
To none it is a greater foe
Than unto those where it doth grow.
And God keep me both day and night,
From that fell, fond,[6] and ugly spright.
For why? Of all the plagues that be,

---

1   *wreathen* Twisted.

2   *horn-maker* Person who makes cuckolds of others.

3   *Acteon's head* Acteon was a hunter who looked at Diana while bathing. The goddess turned him into a stag and he was torn apart by his own hounds. The reference here is to having horns, and thus being a cuckold.

4   *groath* Girth.

5   *fell* Evil.

6   *fond* Foolish.

The secret plague is jealousy.
Therefore I wish all womenkind
Never to bear a jealous mind.

"Well said, John," quoth she, "thy song is not so sure, but thy voice is as sweet. But seeing the time agrees with our stomachs, though loath yet, we will give over for this time, and betake ourselves to our suppers."

Then calling the rest of her servants, they fell to their meat merrily, and after supper, the goodwife went abroad for her recreation to walk awhile with one of her neighbours. And in the mean space John got him up into his chamber, and there began to meditate on this matter, bethinking with himself what he were best do to, for well he perceived that his dame's affection was great toward him. Knowing therefore the woman's disposition, and withal that her estate was reasonably good, and considering beside that he should find a house ready furnished, servants ready taught, and all other things for his trade necessary, he thought it best not let slip that good occasion, lest he should never come to the like. But again, considering her years to be unfitting to his youth, and that she that sometime had been his dame would, perhaps, disdain to be governed by him that had been her poor servant, that it would prove but a bad bargain, doubting many inconveniences that might grow thereby, he therefore resolved to be silent rather than to proceed further. Wherefore he got him straight to bed, and the next morning settled himself close to his business.

His dame coming home and hearing that her man was gone to bed, took that night but small rest, and early in the morning, hearing him up at his work merrily singing, she by and by arose, and in seemly sort attiring herself, she into the workshop, and sat her down to make quills.[1]

Quoth John, "Good morrow, dame, how do you today?"

"God a mercy,[2] John," quoth she, "even as well as I may, for I was sore troubled in my dreams. Methought two doves walked together in a cornfield, the one, as it were, in communication with the other, without regard of pecking up anything to sustain themselves, and after they had with many nods spent some time to their content, they

---

1   *in seemly sort attiring herself* Dressing in pretty clothes;   *quills* Spools of thread or yarn.
2   *God a mercy* God have mercy.

both fell hard with their pretty bills to pick up the scattered corn left by the weary reaper's hand. At length, finding themselves satisfied, it chanced another pigeon to light in that place, with whom one of the first pigeons at length kept company, and after, returning to the place where she left her first companion, perceived he was not there, she kindly searching up and down the high stubble to find him, lighted at length on a hog fast asleep, wherewith methought the poor dove was so dismayed that presently she fell down in a trance. I, seeing her legs fail and her wings quiver, yielding herself to death, moved with pity ran unto her, and thinking to take up the pigeon, methought I had in my hands my own heart, wherein methought an arrow stuck so deep that the blood trickled down the shaft and lay upon the feathers like the silver-pearled dew on the green grass, which made me to weep most bitterly. But presently methought there came one to me crowned like a queen, who told me my heart would die except in time I got some of that sleeping hog's grease to heal the wounds thereof. Whereupon I ran in all haste to the Hog with my heart bleeding in my hand, who, methought, grunted at me in most churlish sort, and vanished out of my sight. Whereupon coming straight home, methought I found this hog rustling among my looms, wherewith I presently awaked, suddenly after midnight, being all in a sweat and very ill, and I am sure you could not choose but hear me groan."

"Trust me, dame, I heard you not," quoth John, "I was so sound asleep."

"And thus," quoth she, "a woman may die in the night before you have the care to see what she ails or ask what she lacks. But truly John," quoth she, "all is one,[1] for if thou shouldst have come, thou couldst not have got in because my chamber door was locked. But while I live this shall teach me wit, for henceforth I will have no other lock but a latch 'til I am married."

"Then, dame," quoth he, "I perceive though you be curious in your choice, yet at length you will marry."

"Aye, truly," quoth she, "so thou wilt not hinder me."

"Who, I?" quoth John, "on my faith, dame, not for a hundred pounds but will further you to the uttermost of my power."

---

1   *all is one*   It doesn't matter.

"Indeed," quoth she, "thou hast no reason to show any discourtesy to me in that matter, although some of our neighbours do not stick to say that I am sure to thee already."

"If it were so," quoth John, "there is no cause to deny it or to be ashamed thereof, knowing myself far unworthy of so high a favour."

"Well, let this talk rest," quoth she, "and take there thy quills, for it is time for me to go market."

Thus the matter rested for two or three days, in which space she daily devised which way she might obtain her desire, which was to marry her man. Many things came in her head, and sundry sleights in her mind, but none of them did fit her fancy, so that she became wondrous sad and as civil as the nine sibyls.[1] And in this melancholy humour she continued three weeks, or a month, 'til at last it was luck upon a Bartholomew day (having a fair in the town) to spy her man John give a pair of gloves to a proper maid for a fairing, which the maiden with a bashful modesty kindly accepted, and requited it with a kiss, which kindled in her[2] an inward jealousy. But notwithstanding very discreetly she covered it, and closely passed along unspied of her man or the maid.

She had not gone far, but she met with one of her suitors, namely, the tailor, who was very fine and brisk in his apparel, and needs he would bestow the wine upon the Widow. And after some faint denial, meeting with a gossip[3] of hers, to the tavern they went, which was more courtesy than the tailor could ever get of her before, showing herself very pleasant and merry. And finding her in such a pleasing humour, the tailor, after a new quart of wine, renewed his old suit. The Widow with patience heard him, and gently answered, that in respect of his great good will long time borne unto her, as also in regard of his gentleness, cost and courtesy, at that present bestowed,[4] she would not flatly deny him.

---

1   *sleights* Tricks; *as civil as the nine sibyls* As grave or as serious as the nine sibyls (women who could prophesy the future, according to Greek and Roman mythology).

2   *Bartholomew day ... the town* On the feast of St. Bartholomew, 24 August, a fair was held at Smithfield, just outside London's north walls, at the old site of the monastery of St. Bartholomew. It was known as England's most important cloth fair, although it also featured horses, cattle, and leather goods; *fairing* Present given or purchased at a fair; *her* Jack's dame.

3   *gossip* Female friend.

4   *at that present bestowed* Given at that time (by treating the Widow and her friend to drinks at the tavern).

"Therefore," quoth she, "seeing this is not a place to conclude of such matter, if I may entreat you to come to my poor house on Thursday next, you shall be heartily welcome, and be further satisfied of my mind," and thus preferred to a touch of her lips, he paid the shot and departed.

The tailor was scant out of sight when she met with the tanner, who, albeit he was aged, yet lustily he saluted her, and to the wine she must, there was no nay. The Widow, seeing his importunacy, calls her gossip and along they walked together. The old man called for wine plenty,[1] and the best cheer in the house, and in hearty manner he bids the Widow welcome. They had not sitten long, but in comes a noise[2] of musicians in tawny coats, who (putting off their caps) asked if they would have any music.

The Widow answered no, they were merry enough.

"Tut," quoth the old man, "let us hear, good fellows, what you can do, and play me 'The Beginning of the World.'"[3]

"Alas," quoth the Widow, "you had more need to hearken to the end of the world?"

"Why, Widow," quoth he, "I tell thee the beginning of the world was the begetting of children, and if you find me faulty in that occupation, turn me out of thy bed for a bungler, and then send for the sexton."[4]

He had no sooner spoke the word, but the parson of Speen with his corner-cap[5] popped in at the door, who, seeing the Widow sitting at the table, craved pardon and came in.

Quoth she, "for want of the sexton, here is the priest, if you need him!"

"Mary," quoth the tanner, "in good time, for by this means we need not go far to be married."

"Sir," quoth the parson, "I shall do my best in convenient place."

"Wherein?" quoth the tanner.

"To wed her myself," quoth the parson.

---

1   *wine plenty*   Plenty of wine.
2   *sitten long*   Sat for a long time;   *noise*   Group or band of musicians.
3   *'The Beginning of the World'*   Song popular in the sixteenth century.
4   *sexton*   Church official tasked with overseeing funerals.
5   *Speen*   Speenhamland;   *corner-cap*   Hat with three or four corners worn by academics and clergymen.

"Nay, soft," said the Widow, "one swallow makes not a summer, nor one meeting a marriage. As I lighted on you unlooked for, so came I hither unprovided for the purpose."

"I trust," quoth the tanner, "you came not with your eyes to see, your tongue to speak, your ears to hear, your hands to feel, nor your legs to go."

"Brought my eyes," quoth she, "to discover colours; my tongue to say 'no' to questions I like not; my hands to thrust from me the things that I love not; my ears to judge 'twixt flattery and friendship, and my feet to run from such as would wrong me."

"Why then," quoth the parson, "by your gentle abiding in this place, it is evident that here are none but those you like and love."

"God forbid I should hate my friends," quoth the Widow, "whom I take all these in this place to be!"

"But there be divers sorts of loves," quoth the parson.

"You say truth," quoth the Widow. "I love yourself for your profession, and my friend, the tanner, for his courtesy and kindness, and the rest for their good company."

"Yet," quoth the parson, "for the explaining of your love, I pray you drink to them you love best in the company."

"Why," quoth the tanner, "have you any hope in her love?"

"Believe me," saith the parson, "as much as another."

"Why then, parson, sit down," said the tanner, "for you that are equal with me in desire shall surely be half with me in the shot, and so, Widow, on God's name,[1] fulfill the parson's request."

"Seeing," quoth the Widow, "you are so pleasantly bent, if my courtesy might not breed contention between you, and that I may have your favour to show my fancy, I will fulfill your request."

Quoth the parson, "I am pleased, howsoever it be."

"And I," quoth the tanner.

"Why then," quoth she, "with this cup of claret wine and sugar,[2] I heartily drink to the minstrel's boy."

"Why, is it he you love best?" quoth the parson.

"I have reasons," said she, "to like and love them best that will be least offended with my doings."

---

1   *be half with me in the shot* Pay half the bill;   *on God's name* In God's name.

2   *claret wine and sugar* Claret, also known as sack, is a rough Spanish wine often further sweetened with sugar.

"Nay, Widow," quoth they, "we meant you should drink to him whom you love best in the way of marriage."

Quoth the Widow, "You should have said so at first. But to tell you my opinion, it is small discretion for a woman to disclose her secret affection in an open assembly. Therefore, if to that purpose you spake, let me entreat you both to come home to my house on Thursday next, where you shall be heartily welcome, and there be fully resolved of my mind, and so, with thanks at this time, I'll take my leave."

The shot being paid, and the musicians pleased, they all departed, the tanner to Wallingford, the parson to Speen, and the Widow to her own house, where in her wonted solemnness[1] she settled herself to her business.

Against Thursday she dressed her house fine and brave, and set herself in her best apparel. The tailor, nothing forgetting his promise, sent to the Widow a good, fat pig and a goose. The parson, being as mindful as he, sent to her house a couple of fat rabbits and a capon, and the tanner came himself and brought a good shoulder of mutton, and half a dozen chickens. Beside, he brought a good gallon of sack and half a pound of the best sugar. The Widow, receiving this good meat, set her maid to dress it incontinent,[2] and when dinner-time drew near, the table was covered, and every other thing provided in convenient and comely sort.

At length, the guests being come, the Widow bade them all heartily welcome. The Priest and the tanner, seeing the tailor, mused what he made there; the tailor, on the other side, marvelled as much at their presence. Thus looking strangely one at another,[3] at length the Widow came out of the kitchen in a fair train gown stuck full of silver pins, a fine white cap on her head with cuts of curious[3] needlework under the same, and an apron before her as white as the driven snow. Then, very modestly making curtsey to them all, she requested them to sit down. But they, straining courtesy the one with the other, the Widow with a smiling countenance,[4] took the parson by the hand, saying:

---

1   *wonted solemnness* Usual seriousness.

2   *dress it incontinent* Quickly prepare it for cooking.

3   *one at another* At each other; *curious* Artistic, finely wrought.

4   *But they, straining ... smiling countenance* While something seems missing in this sentence, the overall sense is clear: the suitors, barely able to be courteous to each other, remain standing after the Widow's invitation to sit down. She then invites each one individually to sit.

"Sir, as you stand highest in the Church, so is it meet you should sit highest at the table, and therefore, I pray you sit down there on the bench side. And sir," said she to the tanner, "as age is to be honoured before youth for their experience, so are they to sit above bachelors[1] for their gravity," and so she set him down on this side the table, over against the parson. Then coming to the tailor, she said: "Bachelor, though your lot be the last, your welcome is equal with the first, and seeing your place points out itself, I pray you take a cushion and sit down. And now," quoth she, "to make the board equal, and because it hath been an old saying that three things are to small purpose if the fourth be away, if so it may stand with your favours, I will call in a gossip of mine to supply[2] this void place."

"With a good will," quoth they.

With that she brought in an old woman with scant ever a good tooth in her head, and placed her right against the bachelor. Then was the meat brought to the board in due order by the Widow's servants, her man John being the chief servitor. The Widow sat down at the table's end between the parson and the tanner, who in very good sort carved meat for them all, her man John waiting on the table.

After they had sitten awhile, and well-refreshed themselves, the Widow, taking a crystal glass filled with claret wine, drunk unto the whole company and bade them welcome. The parson pledged her, and so did all the rest in due order, but still in their company the cup passed over the poor old woman's nose, insomuch that at length[3] the old woman (in a merry vein) spake thus unto the company: "I have had much good meat among you, but as for the drink, I can nothing commend it."

"Alas, good gossip," quoth the Widow, "I perceive no man hath drunk to thee yet."

"No, truly," quoth the old woman, "for churchmen have so much mind of young rabbits, old men such joy in chickens, and bachelors in pig's flesh take such delight, that an old sow, a tough hen, or a gray coney[4] are not accepted. And so it is seen by me, else I should have been better remembered."

---

1 *bachelors* Young, unmarried men.
2 *if so it may stand with your favours* If you will permit it; *supply* Fill.
3 *pledged her* Drank in her honor, toasted her; *at length* Eventually.
4 *coney* Rabbit.

"Well, old woman," quoth the parson, "take here the leg of a capon to stop thy mouth."

"Now, by St. Anne, I dare not," quoth she.

"No? wherefore?" said the parson.

"Mary, for fear lest you should go home with a crutch," quoth she.

The tailor said, "Then taste here a piece of goose."

"Now God forbid," said the old women, "let goose go to his kind. You have a young stomach, eat it yourself, and much good may it do your heart, sweet, young man."

"The old woman lacks most of her teeth," quoth the tanner, "and therefore a piece of tender chick[1] is fittest for her."

"If I did lack as many of my teeth," quoth the old woman, "as you lack points of good husbandry, I doubt I should starve before it were long."

At this, the Widow laughed heartily, and the men were stricken into such a dump that they had not a word to say. Dinner being ended, the Widow with the rest rose from the table, and after they had sitten a pretty while merrily talking, the Widow called her man John to bring her a bowl of fresh ale, which he did.

Then said the Widow: "My masters, now for your courtesy and cost, I heartily thank you all, and in requital of all your favour, love, and goodwill, I drink to you, giving you free liberty when you please to depart."

At these words, her suitors looked so sourly one upon another, as if they had been newly champing of crabs.[2] Which when the tailor heard, shaking up himself in his new russet jerkin, and setting his hat on one side, he began to speak thus: "I trust, sweet Widow," quoth he, "you remember to what end my coming was hither today. I have long time been a suitor unto you, and this day you promised to give me a direct answer."

"'Tis true," quoth she, "and so I have. For your love, I give you thanks, and when you please, you may depart."

"Shall I not have you?" said the tailor.

"Alas," quoth the Widow, "you come too late."

"Good friend," quoth the tanner, "it is manners for young men to let their elders be served before them. To what end should I be here if

---

1   *chick*   Chicken.

2   *champing of crabs*   Eating crab apples, which are notably tart.

the Widow should have thee? A flat denial is meet[1] for a saucy suitor. But what sayest thou to me, fair Widow?" quoth the tanner.

"Sir," said she, "because you are so sharp set,[2] I would wish you as soon as you can to wed."

"Appoint the time yourself," quoth the tanner.

"Even as soon," quoth she, "as you can get a wife, and hope not after me, for I am already promised."

"Now, tanner, you may take your place with the tailor," quoth the parson, "for indeed, the Widow is for no man but myself."

"Master parson," quoth she, "many have run near the goal, and yet lost the game, and I cannot help it though your hope be in vain. Besides, parsons are but newly suffered to have wives,[3] and for my part, I will have none of the first head."

"What," quoth the tailor, "is our merriment grown to this reckoning? I never spent a pig and a goose to so bad purpose before. I promise you, when I came in, I verily thought that you were invited to the Widow to make her and me sure together, and that the jolly tanner was brought to be a witness to the contract, and the old woman fetched in for the same purpose, else I would never have put up so many dry bobs[4] at her hands."

"And surely," quoth the tanner, "I knowing thee to be a tailor, did assuredly think that thou wast appointed to come and take measure for our wedding apparel."

"But now we are all deceived," quoth the parson, "and therefore as we came fools, so we may depart hence like asses."

"That is as you interpret the matter," said the Widow, "for I ever doubting that a concluding answer would breed a jar[5] in the end among you every one, I thought it better to be done at one instant, and in mine own house, than at sundry times and in common taverns. And as for the meat you sent, as it was unrequested of me, so

---

1 *meet* Appropriate.

2 *sharp set* Eager.

3 *parsons are but newly suffered to have wives* This is historically inaccurate. Henry VIII may have separated the English church from Rome, but he remained a firm believer in a celibate priesthood. Clergy were allowed to marry under Edward VI, but the next monarch, the Catholic Mary I, revoked the privilege. Elizabeth allowed Anglican priests to marry, but with restrictions.

4 *put up so many dry bobs* Put up with so many tricks or insults.

5 *breed a jar* Cause dissension.

had you your part thereof, and if you think good to take home the remainder, prepare your wallets[1] and you shall have it."

"Nay, Widow," quoth they, "although we have lost our labours, we have not altogether lost our manners. That which you have, keep, and God send to us better luck, and to you your heart's desire," and with that, they departed.

The Widow, being glad she was thus rid of her guests, when her man, John, with all the rest sat at supper, she, sitting in a chair by,[2] spake thus unto them: "Well, my masters, you saw that this day your poor dame had her choice of husbands, if she had listed[3] to marry, and such as would have loved and maintained her like a woman."

"'Tis true," quoth John, "and I pray God you have not withstood your best fortune."[4]

"Trust me," quoth she, "I know not, but if I have I may thank mine own foolish fancy."

Thus it passed on from Bartholomewtide[5] 'til it was near Christmas, at what time the weather was so wonderful cold that all the running rivers 'round about the town were frozen very thick. The Widow, being very loath any longer to lie without company, in a cold winter night made a great fire, and sent for her man, John. Having also prepared a chair and a cushion, she made him sit down therein, and sending for a pint of good sack, they both went to supper.

In the end, bed time coming on, she caused her maid in a merriment to pluck off his hose and shoes, and caused him to be laid in his master's best bed, standing the best chamber, hung round about with very fair curtains. John, being thus preferred, thought himself a gentleman, and lying soft, after his hard labour with a good supper, quickly fell asleep.

About midnight, the Widow, being cold on her feet,[6] crept into her man's bed to warm them. John, feeling one lift up the clothes, asked who was there.

"O good John, it is I," quoth the Widow, "the night is so extreme cold, and my chamber walls so thin that I am like to be starved in

---

1 *wallets* Bags for holding provisions.
2 *by* Nearby.
3 *listed* Wanted.
4 *withstood your best fortune* Missed your best opportunity.
5 *Bartholomewtide* Feast of St. Bartholomew.
6 *being cold on her feet* Having cold feet.

my bed, wherefore rather then I would any way hazard my health, I thought it much better to come hither and try your courtesy, to have a little room beside you."

John, being a kind young man, would not say her nay, and so they spent the rest of the night both together in one bed. In the morning, betime she rose up and made herself ready, and willed her man, John, to run and fetch her a link[1] with all speed, "for," quoth she, "I have earnest business to do this morning."

Her man did so. Which done, she made him to carry the link before her until she came to Saint Bartholomew's Chapel, where Sir John the priest, with his clark[2] and sexton, stood waiting for her.

"John," quoth she, "turn into the chapel, for before I go further, I will make my prayers to Saint Bartholomew, so shall I speed the better in my business."

When they were come in, the priest, according to his order, came to her, and asked where the bridegroom was?

Quoth she, "I thought he had been here before me. Sir, (quoth she) I will sit down and say over my beads, and by that time he will come."

John mused at this matter, to that his dame should suddenly be married, and he hearing thereof before. The Widow rising from her prayers, the priest told her that the bridegroom was not yet come.

"Is it true?" quoth the Widow. "I promise you, I will stay no longer for him if were as good as George a Green, and therefore dispatch,"[3] quoth she, "and marry me to my man, John."

"Why dame," quoth he, "you do but jest, I trowe."[4]

"John," quoth she, "I jest not, for so I mean it shall be, and stand not strangely, but remember that did promise me on your faith not to hinder me when I came to the church to be married, but rather, to set it forward. Therefore, set your link aside and give me your hand, for none but you shall be my husband."

---

1   *betime* Early;   *link* Pitch torch used for guiding people along dark streets.

2   *clark* Clerk.

3   *George a Green* The proverbial best of men. A play detailing his life sometimes attributed to Robert Greene, *A Pleasant, Conceited Comedy of George a Green*, was published in 1599;   *dispatch* Go quickly.

4   *trowe* Assume.

John, seeing no remedy, consented, because he saw the matter could not otherwise be amended, and married they were presently.[1] When they were come home, John entertained his dame with a kiss, which the other servants seeing, thought him something saucy. The Widow caused the best cheer in the house to be set on the table, and to breakfast they went, causing her new husband to be set in a chair at the table's end, with a fair napkin laid on his trencher.[2] Then she called out the rest of her servants, willing them to sit down and take part of their good cheer. They, wondering to see their fellow John sit at the table's end in their old master's chair, began heartily to smile and openly to laugh at the matter, especially because their dame so kindly sat by his side. Which she perceiving, asked if that were all the manners they could shew[3] their master. "I tell you," quoth she, "he is my husband, for this morning we were married, and therefore hence forward look you acknowledge your duty towards him."

The folks looked one upon another, marvelling at this strange news. Which, when John perceived, he said: "My masters, muse not at all, for although by God's providence and your dame's favour, I am preferred from being your fellow to be your master, I am not thereby so much puffed up in pride that any way I will forget my former estate.[4] Notwithstanding, seeing I am now to hold the place of a master, it shall be wisdom in you to forget what I was, and to take me as I am, and in doing your diligence, you shall have no cause to repent that God made me your master."

The servants hearing this, as also knowing his good government beforetime, passed their years with him in dutiful manner.

The next day the report was over all the town, that Jack of Newbury had married his dame, so that when the woman walked abroad, everyone bade God give her joy. Some said that she was matched to her sorrow, saying that so lusty a young man as he would never love her, being so ancient. Whereupon the woman made answer, that she would take him down in his wedding shoes, and would try his patience in the prime of his lustiness, whereunto many of her gos-

---

1 *presently* Immediately.

2 *trencher* Plate.

3 *shew* Show.

4 *puffed up ... former estate* Much of the hatred for Cardinal Thomas Wolsey came from the sense that he had grown so proud that he had forgotten his common origins.

sips did likewise encourage her. Every day, therefore, for the space of a month after she was married, it was her ordinary custom to go forth in the morning among her gossips and acquaintance to make merry, and not to return home 'til night, without any regard of her household. Of which, at her coming home, her husband did very oftentimes admonish her in very gentle sort, shewing what great inconvenience would grow thereby, the which sometime she would take in gentle part, and sometime in disdain, saying:

"I am now in very good case, that he which was my servant but the other day will now be my master. This it is for a woman to make her foot her head. The day hath been when I might have gone forth when I would and come in again when it had pleased me without controlment, and now I must be subject to every jack's check. I am sure," quoth she, "that by my gadding abroad and careless spending I waste no goods of thine. I, pitying thy poverty, made thee a man, and master of the house, but not to the end I would become thy slave. I scorn, I tell thee true, that such a youngling as thy self should correct my conceit, and give me instructions, as if I were not able to guide myself. But yfaith, yfaith,[1] you shall not use me like a babe, nor bridle me like an ass, seeing my going abroad grieves thee, where I have gone forth one day I will go abroad three, and for one hour I will stay five."

"Well," quoth her husband, "I trust you will be better advised," and with that he went from her about his business, leaving her swearing in her fustian[2] furies.

Thus the time passed on, 'til on a certain day she had been abroad in her wonted manner, and staying forth very late, he shut the doors and went to bed. About midnight, she comes to the door and knocks to come in. To whom, he looking out of the window, answered in this sort.

"What, is it you that keeps such a knocking? I pray you, get hence and request the constable to provide you a bed, for this night you shall have no lodging here."

"I hope," quoth she, "you will not shut me out of doors like a dog, or let me lie in the streets like a strumpet."

---

1 *yfaith* In faith, truly
2 *fustian* Bombastic.

"Whether like a dog or a drab," quoth he, "all is one to me, knowing no reason but that as you have stayed out all day for your delight, so you may lie forth all night for my pleasure. Both birds and beasts at the night's approach prepare to their rest, and observe a convenient time to return to their habitation. Look but upon the poor spider, the frog, the fly, and every other silly worm, and you shall see all these observe time to return to their home. And if you being a woman will not do the like, content yourself to bear the brunt of your own folly, and so, farewell."

"Alack, husband, what hap[1] have I? My wedding ring was even now in my hand, and I have let it fall about the door! Good, sweet John, come forth with the candle and help me to seek it?"

The man incontinent did so, and while he sought for that which was not there to be found, she whipped into the house, and quickly clapping to the door,[2] she locked her husband out. He stood calling with the candle in his hand to come in but she made if she heard not. Anon[3] she went up into her chamber, and carried the key with her. But when he saw she should not answer, he presently began to knock as loud as he could at the door.

At last, she thrust her head out at the window, saying, "Who is there?"

"'Tis I," quoth John, "what mean you by this? I pray you come down and open the door that I may come in."

"What, sir," quoth she, "is it you? Have you nothing to do but dance about the streets at this time of night, and like a spirit of the buttery, hunt after crickets?[4] Are you so hot that the house cannot hold you?"

"Nay, I pray thee, sweetheart," quoth he, "do not gibe any longer, but let me in."

"O sir, remember," quoth she, "how you stood even now at the window, like a judge on the bench, and in taunting sort kept me out of my own house. How now, Jack, am I even with you? What, John my man, were you so lusty to lock your dame out of doors? Sirra,[5]

---

1 *hap* Fortune, luck.

2 *incontinent* Incontinently, quickly; *clapping to the door* Slamming shut the door.

3 *Anon* Later.

4 *buttery* Storehouse for food; *hunt after crickets* The exact meaning of this is unclear, although the general sense is "have you nothing better to do?"

5 *Sirra* Highly contemptuous term of address.

remember you bade me go to the constable to get lodging, now you have leisure to try if his wife will prefer you to a bed. You, sir sauce,[1] that made me stand in the cold 'til my feet did freeze and my teeth chatter, while you stood preaching of birds and beasts, telling me a tale of spiders, flies, and frogs. Go try now if any of them will be so friendly to let thee have lodging. Why go you not, man? Fear not to speak with them, for I am sure you shall find them at home. Think not they are such ill-husbands as you, to be abroad at this time of night."

With this, John's patience was greatly moved, insomuch that he deeply swore that if she would not let him in, he would break down the door.

"Why John," quoth she, "you need not be so hot, your clothing is not so warm, and because I think this will be a warning unto ye against another time how you shut me out of my house, catch, there is the key, come in at thy pleasure, and look you go to bed to your fellows, for with me thou shalt not lie tonight."

With that, she clapped to the casement,[2] and got her to bed, locking the chamber door fast. Her husband that knew it was in vain to seek to come into her chamber, and being no longer able to endure the cold, got him a place among his prentices, and there slept soundly. In the morning, his wife rose betime, and merrily made him a caudle,[3] and bringing it up to his bed, asked him how did.

Quoth John, "troubled with a shrew, who the longer she lives, the worse she is, and as the people of Illyris[4] kill men with their looks, so she kills her husband's heart with untoward conditions. But trust me, wife," quoth he, "seeing I find you of such crooked qualities, that (like the spider), ye turn the sweet flowers of good counsel into venomous poison, from henceforth I will leave you your own willfulness, and neither vex my mind nor trouble myself to restrain you, the which if I had wisely done last night, I had kept the house in quiet, and myself from cold."

"Husband," quoth she, "think that women are like starling, that will burst their gall before they will yield to the fowler, or like the fish

---

1 *sauce* Saucy, insolent toward superiors.
2 *clapped to the casement* Slammed shut the window.
3 *caudle* Warm drink of thin gruel mixed with wine.
4 *Illyris* Illyria, an ancient region in eastern Europe.

scolopendra,[1] that cannot be touched without danger. Notwithstanding, as the hard steel doth yield to the hammer's stroke, being used to his kind, so will women to their husbands, where they are not too much crossed. And seeing you have sworn to give me my will, I vow likewise that my willfulness shall not offend you.[2] I tell you, husband, the noble nature of a woman is such that for their loving friends, they will stick, like the pelican,[3] to pierce their own hearts to do them good. And therefore, forgiving each other all injuries past, having also tried one another's patience, let us quench these burning coals of contention with the sweet juice of a faithful kiss, and shaking hands, bequeath all our anger to the eating up of this caudle."

Her husband courteously consented, and after this time, they lived long together in most Godly, loving and kind sort, 'til, in the end, she died, leaving her husband wondrous wealthy.

Chapter 2: Of Jack of Newbury, his great wealth and number of servants, and also how he brought the Queen Katherine one hundred and fifty men[4] prepared for the war at his own cost against the King of Scots at Flodden Field.

Now, Jack of Newbury, being a widower, had the choice of many wives, men's daughters of good credit and widows of great wealth. Notwithstanding, he bent his only like to one of his own servants, whom he had tried[5] in the guiding of his house a year or two, and knowing her careful in her business, faithful in her dealing, and an excellent good housewife, thought it better to have her with nothing than some other with much treasure. And besides, as her qualities were good, so was she of very comely personage,[6] of a sweet favour

---

1 *the fish scolopendra* Legendary one hundred foot long fish that afflicts anyone who touches it with an extreme itch.

2 *I vow ... shall not offend you* Compare the Widow's response to the ending of Chaucer's *Wife of Bath's Tale*.

3 *like the pelican* According to legend, the mother pelican fed her young by piercing her breast with her beak and giving them her blood.

4 *one hundred and fifty men* The original chapter summary gave the number as "two hundred and fifty," differing from Deloney's ballad. This suggests that the summaries were added at some later date.

5 *bent his only like* Gave his sole affection; *tried* Tested.

6 *very comely personage* Very beautiful.

and fair complexion. In the end, he opened his mind unto her and craved her good will. The maid, though she took this motion kindly, said she would do nothing without consent of her parents. Whereupon a letter was writ to her father, being a poor man dwelling at Aylesbury[1] in Buckinghamshire, who, being joyful of his daughter's good fortune, speedily came to Newbury, where of her master he was friendly entertained, who, after he had made him good cheer, showed him all his servants at work, and every office in his house:

Within one room being large and long,
There stood two hundred looms full strong.
Two hundred men, the truth is so,
Wrought in[2] these looms all in a row.
By every one, a pretty boy,
Sat making quils with mickle[3] joy.
And in another place hard by,
An hundred women merrily
Were carding[4] hard with joyful cheer,
Who singing sat with voices clear.
And in a chamber close beside,
Two hundred maidens did abide,
In petticoats of stammel red[5]
And milk-white kerchers[6] on their head.
Their smock sleeves like to winter snow,
That on the western mountains flow,
And each sleeve, with a silken band,
Was featly[7] tied at the hand.
These pretty maids did never lin,[8]
But in that place all day did spin.
And spinning so with voices meet,[9]

---

1 *Aylesbury* Town approximately fifty miles northeast of Newbury, twenty-five miles due east of Oxford.
2 *Wrought in* Worked at.
3 *quils* Hollow stems on which to wind yarn; *mickle* Much.
4 *carding* Preparing wool for spinning by combing out dirt and straightening the fibers.
5 *stammel red* Coarse woolen cloth dyed deep red.
6 *kerchers* Kerchiefs.
7 *featly* Neatly, elegantly.
8 *lin* Stop, leave off.
9 *meet* Proper, in harmony.

Like nightingales they sung full sweet.
Then to another room came they,
Where children were in poor array,
And every one sat picking wool,
The finest from the coarse to cull.
The number was seven score and ten,[1]
The children of poor, silly[2] men.
And these, their labours to requite,
Had every one a penny at night,
Beside[3] their meat and drink all day,
Which was to them a wondrous stay.[4]
Within another place likewise,
Full fifty proper men he[5] spies,
And these were shearmen[6] every one,
Whose skill and cunning were shown,
And hard by them there did remain
Full four-score rowers taking pain.[7]
A dye-house likewise had he then,
Wherein he kept full forty men,
And likewise in his fulling[8] mill
Full twenty persons kept he still.
Each week ten good fat oxen he
Spent in his house for certainty,
Beside good butter, cheese, and fish,
And many another wholesome dish.
He kept a butcher all the year,
A brewer eke[9] for ale and beer,
A baker for to bake his bread,
Which stood his household in good stead.
Five cooks within his kitchen great,

---

1   *seven score and ten*   One hundred and fifty.
2   *silly*   Simple.
3   *Beside*   In addition to.
4   *stay*   Support. Given that these children are employees, not apprentices, Jack's terms of employment are actually very generous.
5   *he*   Jack's future father-in-law.
6   *shearmen*   Workers who cut woolen cloth with scissors.
7   *Full four-score rowers taking pain*   Eighty spinners carefully working.
8   *fulling*   Process of cleaning and thickening cloth by washing and beating.
9   *eke*   Also.

Were all the year to dress his meat.
Six scullian[1] boys unto their hands
To make clean dishes, pots and pans,
Beside poor children that did stay
To turn the broaches[2] every day.
The old man that did see this sight
Was much amazed, as well he might:
This was a gallant clothier sure
Whose fame forever shall endure.

When the old man had seen this great household and family, then he was brought into the warehouses, some being filled with wool, some with flocks, some with woad and madder, and some with broadcloths and kersies, ready dyed and dressed, beside a great number of others, some stretched on the tenters,[3] some hanging on poles, and a great many more lying wet in other places.

"Sir," quoth the old man, "Iwis che zee you bee bominable rich, and cham content you shall have my daughter, and God's blessing and mine light on you both."[4]

"But father," quoth Jack of Newbury, "what will you bestow with her?"[5]

"Mary, hear you," quoth the old man, "I vaith cham but a poor man, but I thong God, cham of good exclamation among my neighbours, and they will as zoone take my vice for any thing as a richer man's: thicke I will bestow, you shall have with a good will because che hear very good condemnation of you in every place, therefore chill give you twenty nobles and a weaning calf, and when I die and my wife, you shall have the revelation of all my goods."[6]

---

1   *scullian*   Scullery, kitchen.

2   *broaches*   Spits on which meat roasts over a fire.

3   *woad and madder*   Plants used for making blue and red dye respectively; *kersies*   Rough, woolen cloths;   *tenters*   Frames for drying cloth.

4   *Iwis che zee ... both*   I see that you be abominably rich, and am content you shall have my daughter, and God's blessing and mine alight on you both. Deloney writes in dialect to reproduce the old man's country accent, and he will misuse words to demonstrate his rusticity.

5   *bestow with her*   Give me as a dowry.

6   *Mary ... all my goods*   Mary, hear you, in faith, I am but a poor man, but I thank God, I am of good exclamation [reputation] among my neighbors, and they will as soon take my advice for anything as they would a richer man. That which I will bestow, you will have with my best wishes because I hear very good condemnation [commendation] of you in every

When Jack heard his offer, he was straight content,[1] making more reckoning of the woman's modesty than her father's money. So the marriage day being appointed, all things were prepared meet for the wedding, and royal cheer ordained. Most of the lords, knights, and gentlemen thereabout were invited thereunto, the bride being attired in a gown of sheep's russet, and kertle of fine worsted, her head attired with a billiment of gold,[2] and her hair yellow as gold hanging down behind her, which was curiously combed and pleated. According to the manner in those days, she was led to church between two sweet boys with bride-laces and rosemary tied about their silken sleeves, the one of them was son to Sir Thomas Parry, the other to Sir Francis Hungerford.[3] Then was there a fair bride-cup of silver and gilt carried before her, wherein was a goodly branch of rosemary gilded very fair, hung about with silken ribbons of all colours. Next was there a noise of musicians that played all the way before her. After her came all the chiefest maidens of the country, some bearing great bride-cakes, and some garlands of wheat finely gilded, and so she passed into the church.

It is needless of me to make any mention here of the bridegroom, who being a man so well-beloved, wanted no company, and those of the best sort, besides divers merchant strangers of the Steelyard[4] that came from London to the wedding. The marriage being solemnized, home they came in order as before, and to dinner they went, where was no want of good cheer, no lack of melody. Rhenish wine at this wedding was as plentiful as beer or ale, for the merchants had sent thither ten tunnes[5] of the best in the Steelyard.

This wedding endured ten days, to the great relief of the poor that dwelled all about, and in the end the bride's father and mother came

---

place, therefore I will give you twenty nobles [gold coins last minted in the 1550s] and a weaning calf, and when my wife and I die, you shall have the revelation [reversion] of all my goods.

1 *straight content* Immediately happy.

2 *sheep's russet* Coarse woolen cloth; *kertle of fine worsted* Skirt of fine, lightweight cloth; *billiment of gold* Head adornment made of gold.

3 *bride-laces* Pieces of gold or silk used to bind up sprigs of rosemary (for remembrance); a form of wedding favor; *Sir Thomas Parry ... Sir Francis Hungerford* Local gentry.

4 *merchant strangers* Foreign merchants; *Steelyard* Building for foreign merchants on the north bank of the Thames above London bridge.

5 *Rhenish wine* Dry, sweet wine from Germany; *tunnes* Large barrels.

to pay their daughter's portion,[1] which when the bridegroom had received, he gave them great thanks. Notwithstanding, he would not suffer them yet to depart, and against[2] they should go home, their son-in-law came unto them, saying: "Father, and Mother, all the thanks that my poor heart can yield, I give you for your good will, cost, and courtesy, and while I live make bold to use me in anything that I am able, and in requital of the gift you gave me with your daughter, I give you here twenty pound to bestow as you find occasion. And for your loss of time and charges riding up and down, I give you here as much broadcloth as shall make you a cloak and my mother a holiday gown, and when this is worn out, come to me and fetch more."

"O my good zonne," quoth the old woman, "Christ's benison bee with thee evermore, for to tell thee true, we had zold all our kine[3] to make money for my daughter's marriage, and this zeaven year we should not have been able to buy more. Notwithstanding we should have zold all that ever we had before my poor wench should have lost her marriage."

"I," quoth the old man, "chuld have zold[4] my coat from my back and my bed from under me before my girl should have gone without you."

"I thank you, good father and mother," said the bride, "and I pray God long to keep you in health." Then the bride kneeled down and did her duty to her parents, who, weeping for very joy, departed.

Not long after this, it chanced while our noble king was making war in France that James, King of Scotland,[5] falsely breaking his oath invaded England with a great army and did much hurt upon the borders. Whereupon on the sudden every man was appointed according to his ability to be ready with his men and furniture[6] at an hour's

---

1 *portion* Dowry.
2 *against* Before.
3 *zonne* Son; *Christ's benison* Christ's blessing, benediction; *zold all our kine* Sold all our cattle.
4 *chuld have zold* Would have sold.
5 *our noble king* Henry VIII; *James, King of Scotland* King James IV (1473–1513) invaded England in 1513 after Henry VIII left England to accompany the English forces invading France. The Scots suffered a disastrous defeat at the Battle of Flodden Field (9 September 1513), in which James and many of his nobles died.
6 *furniture* Armor.

warning, on pain of death. Jack of Newbury was commanded by the justices to set out six men, four armed with pikes and two calivers, and to meet the Queen in Buckinghamshire,[1] who was there raising a great power to go against the faithless king of Scots.

When Jack had received this charge, he came home in all haste and cut out a whole broadcloth for horsemen's coats, and so much more as would make up coats for the number of a hundred men. In short time, he had made ready fifty tall men well-mounted in white coats and red caps with yellow feathers, demi-lances in their hands, and fifty men on foot with pikes, and fifty shot[2] in white coats also, every man so expert in the handling of his weapon, as few better were found in the field. Himself likewise in complete armour on a goodly barbed horse,[3] rose foremost of the company with a lance in his hand and a fair plume of yellow feathers in his crest, and in this sort he came before the justices, who at the first approach did not a little wonder what he should be.

At length, when he had discovered what he was, the justices and most of the gentlemen gave him great commendation for this his good and forward mind showed in this action. But some other, envying here at,[4] gave words that he showed himself more prodigal than prudent, and more vainglorious than well-advised, seeing that the best nobleman in the country would scarce have done so much, and no marvel, quoth they, for such a one would call to his remembrance that the King had often occasions to urge his subjects to such charges, and therefore would do at one time as they be able to do at another. But Jack of Newbury, like the stork in the springtime, thinks the highest cedar too low for him to build his nest in, and ere the year be half done, may be glad to have his bed in a bush.

These disdainful speeches, being at last brought to Jack of Newbury's care, though it grieved him much, yet patiently put them up 'til time convenient. Within awhile after, all the soldiers in Berkshire,

---

1 *justices* Justices of the peace, inferior magistrates appointed to deal with lesser crimes and perform other local administrative functions, such as marshaling troops in times of war; *calivers* Pistols; *the Queen* Katherine of Aragon (1485–1536). Henry VIII would have their marriage annulled in 1533; *Buckinghamshire* County approximately fifty miles north of Newbury.

2 *demi-lances* Lances with short shafts; *fifty shot* Fifty soldiers armed with muskets.

3 *barbed horse* Horse armored with barbs.

4 *some ... at* Some others, envying what Jack had done.

Hampshire, and Wilshire[1] were commanded to show themselves before the Queen at Stony, Stratford, where her Grace, with many lords, knights, and gentlemen, were assembled with ten thousand men. Against Jack should go to the Queen,[2] he caused his face to be smeared with blood, and his white coat in like manner.

When they were come before her Highness, she demanded (above all the rest) what those white coats were?

Whereupon Sir Henry Englefield,[3] who had the leading of the Berkshire men, made answer: "May it please your Majesty to understand that he which rideth foremost there is called Jack of Newbury, and all those gallant men in white are his own servants, who are maintained all the year by him, who he at his own cost hath set out in this time of extremity to serve the King against his vaunting foe, and I assure your Majesty, there is not, for the number, better soldiers in the field."

"Good Sir Henry," quoth the Queen, "bring the man to me that I may see him," which was done accordingly. Then Jack with all his men alighted[4] and on their knees fell before the Queen. Her Grace said "Gentlemen, arise," and putting forth her lily white hand, gave it him to kiss.

"Most gracious Queen," quoth he, "gentleman I am none, nor the son of a gentleman, but a poor clothier, whose lands are his looms, having no other rents but what I get from the backs of little sheep. Nor can I claim any cognizance but a wooden shuttle.[5] Nevertheless, most gracious Queen, these my poor servants and myself, with life and goods, are ready at your Majesty's command not only to spend our blood, but also to lose our lives in defence of our king and country."

"Welcome to me, Jack of Newbury," said the Queen, "though a clothier by trade, yet a gentleman by condition and a faithful subject in heart, and if thou chance to have any suit in court, make account

---

1 *Berkshire, Hampshire, and Wilshire* Berkshire is Newbury's county, Hampshire lies immediately to the south and extends to the coast, and Wilshire is located to the west of Berkshire.

2 *Against Jack … the Queen* Before Jack went to see the Queen.

3 *Sir Henry Englefield* The Englefields were a prominent Berkshire family. No record of Henry exists, but a Thomas Englefield was sheriff of Berkshire during Henry VIII's reign.

4 *alighted* Got off their horses.

5 *cognizance* Heraldic badge, coat of arms; *shuttle* Loom.

the Queen will be thy friend, and would to God the King had many such clothiers. But tell me, how came thy white coat besmeared with blood, and thy face so bescratched?"

"May it please your Grace," quoth he, "to understand that it was my chance to meet with a monster, who like the people Cynamolgi, had the proportion of a man but headed like a dog, the biting of whose teeth was like the poisoned teeth of a crocodile, his breath like the basilisk's,[1] killing afar off. I understand his name was Envy who assailed me invisibly, like the wicked spirit of Mogunce,[2] who flung stones at men and could not be seen, and so I come by my scratched face, not knowing when it was done."

"What was the cause this monster should afflict thee above the rest of thy company or other men in the field?"

"Although, most sovereign Queen," quoth he, "this poisoned cur snarleth at many, and that few can escape the hurt of his wounding breath, yet at this time he bent his fore against me, not for any hurt I did him, but because I surpassed him in hearty affection to my sovereign lord, and with the poor Widow offered all I had to serve my prince and country."

"It were happy for England," said the Queen, "if in every market town there was a gibbet to hang up curs of that kind, who, like Aesop's dog[3] lying in the manger, will do no good himself, nor suffer such as would to do any."

This speech being ended, the Queen caused her army to be set in order, and in warlike manner to march toward Flodden,[4] where King James had pitched his field. But as they passed with drum and trumpet, there came a post from the valiant Earl of Surrey[5] with tidings to

---

1 *Cynamolgi* Legendary dog-headed people; *basilisk* Mythical reptile whose breath or look could kill.

2 *wicked spirit of Mogunce* Legendary evil spirit who could not be seen but terrorized the city of Mainz by throwing stones at houses. The story is recorded in the fifteenth-century *Nuremburg Chronicle*.

3 *Aesop's dog* In this popular fable, a dog prevents either cattle or an ox from eating hay, even though the dog does not eat hay itself. It is often interpreted as illustrating the perverse effects of envy.

4 *Flodden* The battle at this location took place on 9 September 1513 and was an enormous defeat for the Scots.

5 *Earl of Surrey* Thomas Howard, Second Earl of Surrey (1473–1554), eldest son of Thomas Howard, Second Duke of Norfolk (1443–1524). The father led the English forces against the Scots at Flodden Field, appointing his son to lead the vanguard. As a result of their

her Grace that now she might dismiss her army, for that it had pleased God to grant the noble Earl victory over the Scots, who he had by his wisdom and valiancy vanquished in fight and slain their king in battle. Upon which news her Majesty discharged her forces and joyfully took her journey to London, with a pleasant countenance, praising God for her famous victory and yielding thanks to all the noble gentlemen and soldiers for their readiness in the action, giving many gifts to the nobility and great rewards to the soldiers. Among whom she nothing forgot Jack of Newbury, about whose neck she put a rich chain of gold, at what time he with all the rest gave a great shout, saying "God save Katherine, the noble Queen of England!"

Many noblemen of Scotland were taken prisoners in this battle, and many more slain, so that there never came a greater foil[1] to Scotland than this. For you shall understand that the Scottish king made full account to be lord of this land, watching opportunity to bring to pass his faithless and traitorous practice, which was when our king was in France, at Tournai and Thérouanne,[2] in regard of which wars, the Scots vaunted there was none left in England but shepherds and ploughmen who were not able to lead an army, having no skill in martial affairs. In consideration of which advantage, he invaded the country, boasting of victory before he had won, which was no small grief to Queen Margaret, his wife, who was eldest sister to our noble king. Wherefore, in disgrace of the Scots and in remembrance of the famous achieved victory, the commons[3] of England made this song, which to this day is not forgotten of many:

The Song

King Jamie had made a vow,
  Keep it well if he may,
That he will be at lovely London
  Upon Saint James his day.[4]

---

services, Henry VIII made the younger Howard Earl of Surrey and the father Duke of Norfolk.

1   *foil*   Defeat.
2   *Tournai and Thérouanne*   Towns captured by Henry VIII in 1513 after he invaded France as an ally of his father-in-law, King Ferdinand of Spain.
3   *commons*   Common people.
4   *Saint James his day*   25 July.

Upon Saint James his day at noon,
  At fair London will I be,
And all the lords in merry Scotland
  They shall dine there with me.

Then bespoke good Queen Margaret,
  The tears fell from her eye,
"Leave off these wars, most noble King,
  Keep your fidelity."

"The water runs swift and wondrous deep,
  From bottom unto the brim,
My brother Henry hath good men enough,
  England is hard to win."

"Away," quoth he, "with this silly fool,
  In prison fast let her lie,
For she is come of English blood
  And for these words she shall die."

With that bespake Lord Thomas Howard,
  The Queen's chamberlain that day,
"If that you put Queen Margaret to death,
  Scotland shall rue it alway."

Then in a rage King Jamie did say,
  "Away with this foolish mome,[1]
He shall be hanged, and the other burned,
  So soon as I come home."

At Flodden Field the Scots came in,
  Which made our English men fain,
At Bramstone Green this battle was seen,
  There was King Jamie slain.

---

1   *mome*   Foolish, carping critic.

Then presently the Scots did fly,
 Their cannon they left behind,
Their ensigns gay were won all away,
 Our soldiers did beat them blind.

To tell you plain, twelve thousand were slain,
 That to the fight did stand,
And many prisoners took that day,
 The best in all Scotland.

That day made many a fatherless child,
 And many a widow poor,
And many a Scottish gay lady
 Sat weeping in her bower.

Jack with a feather was lapped all in leather,
 His boastings were all in vain.
He had such a chance with a new Morris dance
 He never went home again.

Chapter 3: How Jack of Newbury went to receive the King as he went a progress[1] into Berskhire, and how he made him a banquet in his own house.

About the tenth year of the king's reign, his Grace made his progress into Berkshire, against which time[2] Jack of Newbury clothed thirty tall fellows, being his household servants, in blue coats, faced with sarcenet, every one having a good sword and buckler on his shoulder, himself in a plain russet coat, a pair of white kersey breeches, without welt or guard, and stockings of the same piece sowed to his slops, which had a great codpiece, whereon he stuck his pins.[3] Who, knowing the King would come over a certain meadow near adjoining

---

1 *went a progress* Went on a progress, a royal journey usually undertaken with a very large entourage.
2 *against which time* At which time.
3 *faced with sarcenet* Lined with sarcenet, a very fine silk material; *buckler* Small, round shield; *kersey* Coarse cloth; *welt or guard* Trimming or ornamentation; *slops ... pins* Wide, baggy pants; the codpiece was often a padded cushion ornamented with pins.

to the town, got himself thither with all his men, and repairing to a certain ant-hill, which was in the field, took up his seat there, causing his men to stand round about, the same with their swords drawn.[1]

The King coming near the place with the rest of his nobility, and seeing them stand with their drawn weapons, sent to know the cause. Garter king at arms[2] was the messenger, who spake in this sort: "Good fellows, the King's Majesty would know to what end you stand here with your swords and bucklers prepared to fight?"

With that, Jack of Newbury started up and made this answer: "Herald," quoth he, "return to his Highness, it is poor Jack of Newbury, who being scant marquis of a mole hill, is chosen Prince of Ants, and here I stand with my weapons and guard about me to defend and keep these my poor and painful[3] subjects from the force of the idle butterflies, their sworn enemies, lest they should disturb this quiet commonwealth, who this summer season are making their winter's provision."

The messenger returning, told his Grace that it was one Jack of Newbury that stood there with his men about him to guard (as they say) a company of ants from the furious wrath of the Prince of Butterflies. With this news, the King heartily laughed, saying, "Indeed, it is no marvel he stand so well prepared, considering what a terrible tyrant he hath to deal withal. Certainly, my lords," quoth he, "this seems to be a pleasant fellow, and therefore we will send to talk with him."

The messenger being sent, told Jack he must come speak with the King.

Quoth he, "his Grace hath a horse, and I am on foot, therefore will him to come to me. Beside that, while I am away, our enemies might come and put my people in hazard, as the Scots did England while our king was in France."

"How dares the lamb be so bold with the lion?" quoth the herald.

"Why," quoth he, "if there be a lion the field, here is never a cock to fear him,[4] and tell his Majesty he might think me a very bad gover-

---

1   *with their swords drawn*   A shocking image, as drawing a sword before the monarch would have been considered an act of rebellion.

2   *Garter king at arms*   The King's senior military officer, serving here as a herald.

3   *return to*   Return this answer to;   *scant marquis*   Poor marquis, a nobleman of the second rank, below a duke and above a count;   *painful*   Full of cares.

4   *here is … fear him*   There is no cock to be frightened of; according to legend, lions were afraid of cocks.

nor that would walk aside upon pleasure and leave my people in peril. Herald," quoth he, "it is written, he that hath a charge must look to it, and so tell thy lord, my King."

The message being done, the King said: "My lords, seeing it will be no other, we will ride up to the emperor of the ants that is so careful in his government." At the king's approach, Jack of Newbery and his servants put up all their weapons, and with a joyful cry flung up their caps in token of victory.

"Why, how now, my masters?" quoth the King, "is your wars ended? Let me see where is the lord general of this great camp?"

With that, Jack of Newbury with all his servants fell on their knees, saying "God save the King of England, whose sight hath put our foes to flight and brought peace to the poor labouring people!"

"Trust me," quoth our King, "here be pretty fellows to fight against butterflies. I must commend your courage that dares withstand such mighty giants."

"Most dread Sovereign," quoth Jack, "not long ago, in my conceit,[1] I saw the most provident nation of the Ants summoned their chief peers to a parliament, which was held in the famous city, Dry Dusty, the one and thirtieth day of September, whereas, by their wisdoms, I was chosen their king. At what time also many bills of complaint were brought in against divers ill members in the commonwealth, among whom the Mole was attainted of high treason to their state, and therefore was banished forever from their quiet kingdom. So was the Grasshopper and the Caterpillar, because they were not only idle, but also lived upon the labours of other men. Amongst the rest, the Butterfly was very much misliked, but few durst say anything to him because of his golden apparel, who, through sufferance grew so ambitious and malapert that the poor Ant could no sooner get an egg into her nest but he would have it away, and especially against Easter,[2] which at length was misliked. This painted Ass took snuff in the nose and assembled a great many other of his own coat, by windy wars to

---

1   *conceit* Allegory. Compare with the excerpt from Holinshed's description of the reaction to the Amicable Grant, when the "captain" of the protesters also uses allegory to make his point (see Appendix 5).

2   *the Butterfly* Cardinal Thomas Wolsey (1473–1530), Henry VIII's right-hand man, much despised for his avarice and pride; *could no sooner ... Easter* No sooner would earn money but Wolsey would take it away; the reference to Easter is not clear.

root these painful people[1] out of the land, that he himself might be seated above them all."

("These were proud butterflies," quoth the King.)

"Whereupon I with my men," quoth Jack, "prepared ourselves to withstand them 'til such time as your Majesty's royal presence put them to flight."

"I perceive," quoth Cardinal Wolsey, "that you being King of Ants, do carry a great grudge to the butterflies."

"Aye," quoth Jack, "we be as great foes as the fox and the snake are friends, for the one of them being subtle, loves the other for his craft. But now I intend to be no longer a prince because the majesty of the king hath eclipsed my glory, so that looking like the peacock on my black feet[2] makes me abase my vainglorious feathers and humbly yield unto his Majesty all my sovereign rule and dignity, both of life and goods, casting up my weapons at his feet, to do any service wherein his Grace shall command me."

"God a mercy, good Jack," quoth the King, "I have often heard of thee, and this morning I mean to visit thy house."

Thus the King with great delight rode along until he came to the town's end, where a great multitude of people attended to see his Majesty, where also Queen Katherine with all her train[3] met him. Thus with great rejoicing of the commons, the King and Queen passed along to this jolly clothier's house, where the good wife of the house with threescore maidens attending on her presented the king with a bee hive[4] most richly gilt with gold, and all the bees therein were also of gold curiously made by art, and out of the top of the same hive sprung a flourishing green tree which bore golden apples, and at the root thereof lay divers serpents, seeking to destroy it, whom Prudence and Fortitude trod under their feet, holding this inscription in their hands:

Lo, here presented to your royal sight
The figure of a flourishing commonwealth

---

1 *took snuff in the nose* Was insulted (by the resistance to his avarice); *root these painful people* Get rid of these careworn people.

2 *looking ... feet* Proverbial expression about how the peacock's ugly feet punctures its pride in its feathers.

3 *train* Followers, entourage.

4 *threescore* Sixty; *bee hive* Conventional symbol for the state's political organization, although one subject to radically different interpretations.

Where virtuous subjects labour with delight
And beat the drones to death which live by stealth.
   Ambition, Envy, Treason loathsome serpents be
   Which seek the downfall of a fruitful tree.

But Lady Prudence with deep, searching eye
Their ill-intended purpose doth prevent,
And noble Fortitude standing always nigh[1]
Dispersed their power prepared with bad intent.
   Thus are they foiled that mount by means unmeet,[2]
   And so like slaves are trodden under feet.

The King favourably accepted this emblem, and receiving it at the woman's hands, willed Cardinal Wolsey to look thereon, commanding it should be sent to Windsor Castle.[3] This Cardinal was at that time Lord Chancellor and a wonderful proud prelate, by whose means great variance was set betwixt the King of England and the French King, the Emperor of Almaine,[4] and divers other princes of Christendom, whereby the traffic of those merchants was utterly forbidden, which bred a general woe through England, especially among clothiers, insomuch that having no sale for their cloth, they were fain to put away many of their people which wrought for them, as hereafter more at large shall be declared.

Then was his Majesty brought into a great hall, where four long tables stood ready covered, and passing through that place, the King and Queen came into a fair and large parlour hung about with goodly tapestry, where was a table prepared for his Highness and the Queen's Grace. All the floor where the King sat was covered with broadcloths[5] instead of green rushes. These were choice pieces of the finest wool of an azure colour, valued at an hundred pound a cloth, which afterward was given to his Majesty.

---

1 *nigh* Near.

2 *mount by means unmeet* Rise by unjust or inappropriate means.

3 *at* From; *Windsor Castle* Royal residence in Berkshire, approximately forty miles due east of Newbury.

4 *Lord Chancellor* England's highest judicial officer, second only in rank to the royal family and the Archbishop of Canterbury; *wonderful* Wonderfully; *Almaine* Germany.

5 *broadcloths* Cloths used as carpets.

The King being set with the chiefest of his council about him, after a delicate dinner, a sumptuous banquet was brought in, served all in glass, the description whereof were too long for me to write and you to read. The great hall was also filled with lords, knights, and gentlemen, who were attended by no other but the servants of the house. The ladies of honour and gentlewomen of the court were all seated in another parlour by themselves, at whose table the maidens of the house did wait in decent sort. The servingmen by themselves,[1] and the pages and footmen by themselves, upon who the prentices did attend most diligently. During the King's abiding in this place, there was no want of delicates: Rhenish wine, claret wine, and sack was as plentiful as small ale. Then from the highest to the lowest, they were served in such sort as no discontent was found any way, so that great commendation redounded unto the goodman[2] of the house.

The Lord Cardinal that of late found himself galled by the Allegory of the Ants spoke in this wise[3] to the King: "If it would please your Highness," quoth he, "but to note the vainglory of these artificers,[4] you should find no small cause of dislike in many of their actions. For an instance, the fellow of this house, he hath not stuck this day to undo himself only to become famous by receiving of your Majesty. Like Herostratus the Shoemaker, that burned the temple of Diana only to get himself a name,[5] more than for any affection he bears to your Grace, as may well be proved by this. Let there be but a simple subsidy levied upon them for the assistance of your Highness's wars, or any other weighty affairs of the commonwealth and state of the realm, though it be not the twentieth part of their substance, they will so grudge and repine that it is wonderful, and like people desperate, cry out, 'They be quite undone!'"[6]

---

1   *by themselves* Were by themselves.

2   *goodman* Master of the household.

3   *wise* Way.

4   *artificers* Craftsmen, those who make things requiring skill. In this instance, the term is used with strong class bias.

5   *Herostratus ... a name* According to Pedro Mexía's *The Forest* (Deloney's main source for learned references), Herostratus was a "lewd person" who burned the Temple of Diana so that he would be famous. Lawlis notes that Deloney adds the detail of Herostratus being a shoemaker.

6   *Let there be ... undone* Deloney's Cardinal draws on the very real resistance to the taxes imposed by Henry, although blamed on Wolsey, to support his French wars. See the excerpt from *Holinshed's Chronicle* (Appendix 5).

"My Lord Cardinal," quoth the Queen, "under correction of my lord the King, I durst lay an hundred pound[1] Jack of Newbury was never of that mind, nor is not at this instant. If ye ask him, I warrant he will say so. Myself had proof thereof at the Scottish invasion, at what time this man, being seized[2] but at six men, brought at his own cost an hundred and fifty into the field."

"I would I had moe[3] such subjects," said the King, "and many of so good a mind."

"Ho, ho Harry," quoth Will Somer, "then had not Empson and Dudley[4] been chronicled for knaves or sent to the Tower for treason."

"But then they had not known the pain of imprisonment," quoth our King, "who with their subtlety grieved many others."

"But their subtlety was such that it broke their necks!" quoth Will Somers.

Whereat the King and Queen, laughing heartily, rose from the table. By which time, Jack of Newbury had caused all his folks to go to their work that his Grace and all the nobility might see it, so indeed the Queen had requested. Then came his Highness, where he saw an hundred looms standing in one room and two men working in every one, who pleasantly sung in this sort:

The Weaver's Song

When Hercules did use to spin,[5]
　　And Pallas[6] wrought upon the loom,
Our trade to flourish did begin

1　*under correction ... King* Unless the King corrects me;　*an hundred pound*　One hundred pounds.

2　*seized*　Legally charged with bringing.

3　*moe*　More.

4　*Will Somer*　Henry VIII's court fool (d. 1559);　*Empson and Dudley*　Sir Richard Empson (c. 1450–1510) and Edmund Dudley (c. 1462–1510), councilors for Henry VII who were blamed for the financial oppression of the king's last years. Immediately after Henry VIII's accession to the throne, they were accused of treason, sent to the Tower, and executed.

5　*When Hercules ... spin*　According to legend, Hercules was commanded by the gods to serve the queen of Lydia, Omphale, for killing her son after he stole Hercules' cattle. Omphale dressed Hercules as a woman and humiliated him by forcing him to perform work usually associated with women. Deloney takes this derogatory story and turns it into a source of pride.

6　*Pallas*　Athena.

While conscience went not selling broom.[1]
Then love and friendship did agree
To keep the band of amity.

When princes' sons kept sheep in field,
   And queens made cakes of wheaten flour,
Then men to lucre did not yield,
      Which brought good cheer to every bower.
         Then love and friendship did agree
         To hold the bands of amity.

But when that giants, huge and high,
   Did fight with spears like weaver's beams,
Then they in iron beds did lie
      And brought poor men to hard extremes.[2]
         Yet love and friendship did agree
         To hold the bands of amity.

Then David took his sling and stone,
   Not fearing great Goliath's strength.
He pierced his brains and broke the bone
      Though he were fifty foot of length.
         For love and friendship &c.

But while the Greeks besieged Troy,
   Penelope apace did spin,
And weavers wrought with mickle[3] joy,
      Though little gains were coming in.
         For love and friendship &c.

---

1   *While conscience ... broom*   Selling brooms was considered the lowest possible form of employment, so the line means "before the general corruption of morals set in."
2   *But when ... extremes*   These stanzas conflate two episodes in the Hebrew Bible: the Israelite defeat of King Og, the last of the giants, whose "bedstead was a bedstead of iron" (Deuteronomy 3.11) and David's defeat of the Philistine, Goliath, whose spear "was like a weaver's beam" (1 Samuel 17.7). Deloney associates Og's reign with the oppression of the poor.
3   *mickle*   Much.

Had Helen[1] then sat carding wool
    (whose beauteous face did breed such strife),
She had not been Sir Paris's trull,[2]
    Nor caused so many lose their life.
        Yet we by love did still agree, &c.

Or had King Priam's wanton son,[3]
    Been making quills with sweet content,
He had not then his friends undone,
    When he to Greece a-gadding went.
        For love and friendship did agree, &c.

The cedar trees endure more storms
    Than little shrubs that sprout on high,
The weavers live more void of harms
    Than princes of great dignity,
        While love and friendship doth agree, &c.

The shepherd sitting in the field
    Doth tune his pipe with heart's delight,
When princes watch with spear and shield
    The poor man soundly sleeps all night.
        While love and friendship doth agree, &c.

Yet this by proof is daily tried,
    For God's good gifts we are ingrate,[4]
And no man through the world so wide
    Lives well contented with his state.
        No love and friendship we can see
        To hold the bands of amity.

"Well sung, good fellows!" said our king, "Light hearts and merry minds live long without grey hairs."

---

1   *Helen*   Beautiful wife of the Greek hero Menelaus. When she was taken to Troy, the Greeks sailed there to get her back, starting the Trojan War. The legends give contradictory accounts as to whether she went willingly or was abducted by Paris.

2   *trull*   Whore, slut.

3   *King Priam's wanton son*   Paris.

4   *ingrate*   Ungrateful.

"But" (quoth Will Somers), "seldom without red noses."[1]

"Well," said the King, "there is an hundred angels to make good cheer withal, and look that every year once you make a feast among yourselves, and frankly (every year) I give you leave to fetch four bucks out of Donington Park without any man's let[2] or controlment."

"O I beseech your Grace" (quoth Will Somers), "let it be with a condition."

"What is that?" said our king.

"My liege," quoth he, "that although the keeper will have the skins, that they may give their wives the horns."[3]

"Go to," said the Queen, "thy head is fuller of knavery than thy purse is of crowns."

The poor workmen humbly thanked his Majesty for his bountiful liberality, and ever since it hath been a custom among the weavers, every year presently after Bartholomewtide,[4] in remembrance of the King's favour, to meet together and make a merry feast. His Majesty came next among the spinner and carder who were merrily a-working, whereat Will Somers fell into a great laughter.

"What ails the fool to laugh?" said the King.

"Marry," quoth Will Somers, "to see these maidens get their living, as bulls do eat their meat."[5]

"How is that?" said the Queen.

"By going still backward," quoth Will Somers, "and I will lay a wager that they that practise so well being maids to go backward will quickly learn ere long to fall backward."

"But sirra," said the Cardinal, "thou didst fall forward when thou brokest thy face in Master Kingsmill's cellar."[6]

"But you, my lord, sat forward," quoth Will Somers, "when you sat in the stocks at Sir Amias Paulet's."[7]

---

1 *red noses* Caused by drinking alcohol.

2 *Donington Park* Royal deer park approximately one hundred miles north of Newbury; *let* Interference.

3 *horns* Sign of cuckoldry.

4 *Bartholomewtide* 24 August.

5 *bulls ... meat* According to legend, bulls ate while walking backward.

6 *But ... cellar* The story being referenced is no longer extant.

7 *But you ... Paulet's* When Wolsey was a young man and a fellow of Magdalen College, Oxford University, he got into trouble with Sir Amias Paulet (d. 1538). According to George Cavendish, Wolsey's servant and first biographer, Paulet "took an occasion of displeasure against him, upon what ground I know not. But, sir, by your leave, he was so bold to set the

Whereat there was greater laughing than before. The King and Queen and all the nobility heedfully beheld these women, who for the most part were very fair and comely creatures, and were all attired alike from top to toe. Then (after due reverence) the maidens in dulcet manner chanted out this song, two of them singing the ditty, and all the rest bearing the burden:[1]

The Maiden's Song[2]

It was a knight in Scotland born,
    Follow my love, leap over the strand,
Was taken prisoner and left forlorn,
    Even by the good Earl of Northumberland.

Then was he cast in prison strong,
    Follow, my love, leap over the strand,
Where he could not walk nor lie along,
    Even by the good Earl of Northumberland.

And is in sorrow thus he lay,
    Follow, my love, come over the strand,
The Earl's sweet daughter walked that way,
    And she the fair flower of Northumberland.

And loud to her this knight did cry,
    Follow, my love, come over the strand,
The salt tears standing in his eye,
    And she the fair flower of Northumberland.

"Fair Lady," he said, "take pity on me,"
    Follow, my love, come over the strand,
"And let me not in prison die,
    And you the fair flower of Northumberland."

---

schoolmaster by the feet [Wolsey in the stocks] during his pleasure." Wolsey did not forget this slight, and when he became Chancellor, he confined Paulet to London for five or six years. Wolsey let Paulet return home only after "placing Wolsey's badges prominently over the door of a new gateway built in the Middle Temple," thereby demonstrating Wolsey's superiority.

1 *bearing the burden* Singing the chorus.
2 *The Maiden's Song* Traditional ballad; the version recorded in *Jack of Newbury* appears to be the earliest.

"Fair Sir, how should I take pity on thee,"
    Follow, my love, come over the strand,
"Thou being a foe to our country,
    And I the fair flower of Northumberland?"

"Fair Lady, I am no foe," he said,
    Follow, my love, come over the strand,
"Through thy sweet love here was I stayed,
    For thee the fair flower of Northumberland?"

"Why shouldst thou come here for love of me,"
    Follow, my love, come over the strand,
"Having wife and children in thy country,
    And I the fair flower of Northumberland?"

"I swear by the blessed trinity,"
    Follow, my love, come over the strand,
"I have no wife nor children I,
    Nor dwelling at home in merry Scotland."

"If courteously you will set me free,"
    Follow, my love, come over the strand,
"I vow that I will marry thee,
    So soon as I come in fair Scotland."

"Thou shalt be a Lady of castles and towers,"
    Follow, my love, come over the strand,
"And sit like a queen in princely bowers,
    When I am at home in fair Scotland."

Then parted hence this lady gay,
    Follow, my love, come over the strand,
And got her father's ring away
    To help this sad knight into fair Scotland.

Likewise much gold she got by sleight,
    Follow, my love, come over the strand,
And all to help this forlorn knight,
    To wend¹ from her father to fair Scotland.

---

1   *wend*   Leave.

Two gallant steeds both good and able,
    Follow, my love, come over the strand,
She likewise took out of the stable,
    To ride with this knight into fair Scotland.

And to the jailor she sent this ring,
    Follow, my love, come over the strand,
The knight from prison forth to bring,
    To wend with her into fair Scotland.

A gallant steed he did bestride,
    Follow, my love, come over the strand,
And with lady away did ride,
    And she the fair flower of Northumberland.

They rode 'til they came to a water clear,
    Follow, my love, come over the strand,
"Good sir, how should I follow you here,
    And I the fair flower of Northumberland?"

"The water is rough and wonderful deep,"
    Follow, my love, come over the strand,
"And on my saddle I shall not keep,
    And I the fair flower of Northumberland."

"Fear not the ford, fair lady," quoth he,
    Follow, my love, come over the strand,
"For long I cannot stay for thee,
    And thou the fair flower of Northumberland."

The lady pricked her wanton[1] steed,
    Follow, my love, come over the strand,
And over the river swam with speed,
    And she the fair flower of Northumberland.

From top to toe all wet was she,
    Follow, my love, come over the strand,
"This have I done for love of thee,
    And I the fair flower of Northumberland."

---

1 *pricked* Spurred; *wanton* Lively, but with obvious sexual overtones.

Thus rode she all one winter's night,
  Follow, my love, come over the strand,
'Til Edinburgh they saw in sight,
  The chiefest town in all Scotland.

"Now choose," quoth he, "thou wanton flower,"
  Follow, my love, come over the strand,
"Where thou wilt be my paramour,[1]
  Or get thee home to Northumberland."

"For I have wife and children five,"
  Follow, my love, come over the strand,
"I'll have thy horse, go thou on foot,
  Go get thee home to Northumberland."

"O false and faithless knight," quoth she,
  Follow, my love, come over the strand,
"And canst thou deal so bad with me,
  And I the fair flower of Northumberland?"

"Dishonour not a lady's name,"
  Follow, my love, come over the strand,
"But draw thy sword and end my shame,
  And I the fair flower of Northumberland."

He took her from her stately steed,
  Follow, my love, come over the strand,
And left her there in extreme need,
  And she the fair flower of Northumberland.

Then sat she down full heavily,
  Follow, my love, come over the strand,
At length two knights came riding by,
  Two gallant knights of fair England.

She fell down humbly on her knee,
  Follow, my love, come over the strand,
Saying, "Courteous knights, take pity on me,
  And I the fair flower of Northumberland."

---

1 *paramour* Lover, mistress.

"I have offended my father dear,"
  Follow, my love, come over the strand,
"And a false knight that brought me here,
  From the good Earl of Northumberland."

They took her up behind them then,
  Follow, my love, come over the strand,
And brought her to her father's again,
  And he the good Earl of Northumberland.

All you fair maidens, be warned by me,
  Follow, my love, come over the strand,
Scots were never true, nor never will be,
  To lord, to lady, nor fair England.
    FINIS

After the King's Majesty and the Queen had heard this song sweetly sung by them, he cast them a great reward, and so, departing hence, went to the fulling-mills[1] and dye house, where a great many also were hard at work. And his Majesty, perceiving what a great number of people were by this one man set on work, both admired and commanded him, saying further, that no trade in all the land was so much to be cherished and maintained as this, which, quoth he, may well be called "the life of the poor." And as the King returned from this place with intent to take horse and depart, there met him a great many of children in garments of white silk fringed with gold, their heads crowned with golden bays, and about their arms each one had a scarf of green sarcenet fast tied, in their hands they bore silver bows, and under their girdles, golden arrows.

The foremost of them represented Diana, goddess of chastity, who was attended upon by a train of beautiful nymphs, and they presented to the King four prisoners. The first was a stern and grisly woman, carrying a frowning countenance and her forehead full of wrinkles, her hair as black as pitch, and her garments all bloody, a great sword she had in her hand all stained with purple gore. They called her Bellona, goddess of wars, who had three daughters: the first of them was a tall woman, so lean and ill-favoured that her cheek bones were ready

---

1 *fulling-mills* Fulling is the process by which wool cloth is cleaned and thickened.

to start out of the skin, of a pale and deadly colour, her eyes sunk into her head, her legs so feeble that they could scantly carry the body. All along her arms and hands through the skin you might tell the sinews, joints, and bones. Her teeth were very strong and sharp withal. She was so greedy that she was ready with her teeth to tear the skin from her own arms. Her attire was black, and all torn and ragged. She went bare-footed and her name was Famine. The second was a strong and lusty woman, with a look pitiless, and unmerciful countenance. Her garments were all made of iron and steel, and she carried in her hand a naked weapon, and she was called the Sword. The third was also a cruel creature. Her eyes did sparkle like burning coals, her hair was like a flame, and her garments like burning brass. She was so hot that none could stand near her, and they called her name Fire.

After this, they retired again, and brought unto his Highness two other personages, their countenance was princely and amiable, their attire most rich and sumptuous. The one carried in his hand a golden trumpet, and the other a palm tree, and these were called Fame and Victory, whom the goddess of chastity charged to wait upon this famous prince[1] forever. This done, each child after other with due reverence gave unto his Majesty a sweet-smelling gillyflower, after the manner of the Persians,[2] offering something in token of loyalty and obedience. The King and Queen, beholding the sweet favour and countenance of these children, demanded of Jack of Newbury whose children they were? Who answered: "It shall please your Highness to understand that these are the children of poor people that do get their living by picking of wool, having scant a good meal once in a week."

With that, the King began to tell[3] his gillyflowers, whereby he found that there was 96 children. "Certainly," said the Queen, "I perceive God gives as fair children to the poor as to the rich, and fairer many times, and though their diet and keeping be but simple, the blessing of God doth cherish them. Therefore," said the Queen, "I will request to have two of them to wait in my chamber."

"Fair Katherine," said the King, "thou and I have jumped in one opinion, thinking these children fitter for the court than the country."

---

1 *famous prince* Henry VIII.

2 *after ... Persians* According to Thucydides, it was the custom to give presents to the Persian king rather than to receive presents from him.

3 *tell* Count.

Whereupon he made choice of a dozen more: four he ordained to be pages to his royal person, and the rest he sent to universities, allotting to every one a gentleman's living. Divers of the noblemen did in like sort entertain some of those children into their services so that (in the end) not one was left to pick wool, but all were provided for, that their parents never needed to care for them. And God so blessed them, that each of them came to be men of great account and authority in the land, whose posterities remain to this day worshipful and famous.

The King, Queen and nobles being ready to depart, after great thanks and gifts given to Jack of Newbury, his Majesty would have made him a knight, but he meekly refused it, saying "I beseech your Grace, let me live a poor clothier among my people, in whose maintenance I take more felicity than in all the vain tilts of gentility, for these are the labouring ants whom I seek to defend, and these be the bees which I keep who labour in this life, not for ourselves, but for the glory of God, and to do service to our dread sovereign."

"Thy knighthood need be no hindrance of thy faculty," quoth the King.

"O my dread Sovereign," said Jack, "honour and worship may be compared to the Lake of Lethe,[1] which makes men forget themselves that taste thereof, and to the end I may still keep in mind from whence I came, and what I am, I beseech your Grace let me rest in my russet coat a poor clothier to my dying day."

"Seeing then," said the King, "that a man's mind is a kingdom to himself, I will leave thee to the riches of thy own content, and so farewell."

The Queen's Majesty, taking her leave of the good wife with a princely kiss, gave her in token of remembrance a most precious and rich diamond set in gold, about the which was also curiously set six rubies and six emeralds in one piece, valued at nine hundred marks, and so her Grace departed.

But in this mean space,[2] Will Somers kept company among the maids, and betook himself to spinning as they did, which among them was held as a forfeit of a gallon of wine, but William by no

---

1   *Lake of Lethe*   According to Greek mythology, the river Lethe is one of five rivers in Hades, and the souls of the dead drink its waters to forget their former lives.

2   *in this mean space*   Meanwhile.

means would pay it except they would take it out in kisses, rating every kiss at a farthing.

"This payment we refuse for two causes," quoth the maidens, "the one, for that we esteem not kisses at so base a rate, and the other, because in so doing we should give as much as you."

Chapter 4: How the maidens served Will Somers for his sauciness.

The maidens consented[1] together, seeing Will Somers was so busy both with their work and in his words, and would not pay his forfeiture, to serve him as he served. First, therefore, they bound him hand and foot, and set him upright against a post, tying him thereto, which he took in ill part, notwithstanding he could not resist them. And because he let his tongue run at random, they set a fair gag in his mouth, such a one as he could not for his life put away, so that he stood as one gaping for wind.[2] Then one of them got a couple of dog's droppings and, putting them in a bag, laid them in soak in a basin of water, while the rest turned down the collar of his jerkin and put an host[3] cloth about his neck instead of a fine towel. Then came the other maid with a basin and water in the same, and with the perfume in the pudding-bag,[4] flapped him about the face and lips 'til he looked like a tawny Moor, and with her hand washed him very orderly. The smell being somewhat strong, Will could by no means abide it, and for want of other language,[5] cried "Ah ha ha." Fain he would have spit, and could not, so that he was fain to swallow down such liquor as he never tasted the like.

When he had a pretty while been washed in this sort, at the length he crouched down upon his knees, yielding himself to their favour, which the maidens perceiving, pulled the gag out of his mouth. He

---

1 *consented* Conferred.
2 *gaping for wind* Gasping for breath.
3 *in soak* Soaking; *jerkin* Close-fitting jacket with a collar; *host* Hot.
4 *perfume in the pudding-bag* Dog feces in the bag; a pudding bag is a bag in which a pudding is boiled. According to the OED, this instance is the first recorded usage of the term.
5 *for want of other language* Because he is gagged.

had no sooner the liberty of his tongue, but that he cursed and swore like a devil. The maids that could scant[1] stand for laughing at last asked how he liked his washing?

"Washing?" quoth he, "I was never thus washed, nor ever met with such barbers since I was born. Let me go," quoth he, "and I will give you whatsoever you will demand," wherewith he cast them an English crown.[2]

"My," quoth one of the maids, "you are yet but washed, but we will shave you ere you go."

"Sweet maids," quoth he, "pardon my shaving, let it suffice that you have washed me. If I have done a trespass to your trade, forgive it me, and I will never hereafter offend you."

"Tush," said the maids, "you have made our wheels cast their bands and bruised the teeth of our cards[3] in such sort as the offence may not be remitted without great penance. As for your gold, we regard it not. Therefore, as you are perfumed fit for the dogs, so we enjoin you this night to serve all our hogs, which penance, if you will swear with all speed to perform, we will let you loose."

"O," quoth Will, "the huge elephant was never more fearful of the silly sheep[4] than I am of your displeasures. Therefore, let me loose, and I will do it with all diligence."

Then they unbound him and brought him among a great company of swine, which when Will had well viewed over, he drave[5] out of the yard all the sows. "Why, how now?" quoth the maids "what mean you by this?"

"Mary," quoth Will, "these be all sows, and my penance is but to serve the hogs."

"It is true," quoth they. "Have you overtaken us in this sort? Well, look there be not one hog unserved, we would advise you."

---

1 *scant* Scarcely.

2 *English crown* Gold coin worth five shillings, a relatively small amount of money.

3 *made our wheels ... cards* Broke our spinning wheels and damaged the cards for preparing wool.

4 *the huge elephant ... sheep* In his chapter on "the amity and enmity of sundry things," Mexía observes that "the monstrous and huge elephant ... trembleth at the presence and sight of a sheep."

5 *drave* Drove.

Will Somers stripped up to his sleeves very orderly, and clapped an apron about his motley hosen,[1] and taking a pail served the hogs handsomely. When he had given them all meat, he said thus:

My task is duly done,
My liberty is won.
The hogs have eat their crabs,
Therefore, farewell ye drabs.[2]

"Nay, soft, friend," quoth they, "the veriest hog of all hath yet had nothing."

"Where the devil is he," said Will, "that I see him not?"

"Wrapped in a motley jerkin!" quoth they. "Take thy self by the nose and thou shalt catch him by the snout."

"I was never so very a hog," quoth he, "but I would always spare from my own belly to give to a woman."

"If thou do not," say they, "eat, like the prodigal child,[3] with thy fellow hogs, we will so shave thee as thou shalt dearly repent thy disobedience."

He, seeing no remedy, committed himself to their mercy, and so they let him go. When he came to the court, he showed to the King all his adventure among the weavers' maidens, whereat the King and Queen laughed heartily.

---

1 *motley hosen* Motley hose, multicolored long stockings or leggings; fools or jesters wore multicolored, or motley, costumes.

2 *drabs* Slovenly women of loose morals.

3 *prodigal child* In the parable of the Prodigal Son, a young man, having spent his inheritance, becomes a poor laborer and eats the same food he serves to the swine (Luke 15.15).

*Chapter 5: Of the pictures which Jack of Newbury had
in his house, whereby he encouraged his servants
to seek for fame and dignity.*

In a fair large parlour which was wainscotted about, Jack of Newbury had fifteen fair pictures[1] hanging, which were covered with curtains of green silk, fringed with gold, which he would often show to his friends and servants. In the first was the picture of a shepherd before whom kneeled a great king named Viriat, who sometime governed the people of Portugal.

"See here," quoth Jack, "the father, a shepherd, the son a sovereign. This man ruled in Portugal and made great wars against the Romans, and after that invaded Spain, yet in the end was traitorously slain."

"The next was the portraiture of Agathocles, which for his surpassing wisdom and manhood was created King of Sicilia and maintained battle against the people of Carthage. His father was a poor potter, before whom he also kneeled. And it was the use of this king that whensoever he made a banquet, he would have as well vessels of earth as of gold set upon the table, to the intent he might always bear in mind the place of his beginning, his father's house, and family."

"The third was the picture of Iphicrates, an Athenian born, who vanquished the Lacedemonians[2] in plain and open battle. This man was captain general to Artaxerxes, King of Persia, whose father was notwithstanding a cobbler, and there likewise pictured. Eumenes was also a famous captain to Alexander the Great, whose father was no other than a carter."

"The fourth was the similitude of Aelius Pertinax, sometime[3] Emperor of Rome, yet was his father but a weaver, and afterward, to give example to others of low condition, to bear minds of worthy men, he

---

1   *wainscotted* Trimmed with wood paneling;   *fifteen fair pictures* The source for this list of worthies who descended from base or non-aristocratic families is Chapter 18 of Pedro Mexía's *The Forest*, "That men born of base condition should not leave by all means possible to attempt to reach and aspire unto honor with certain examples serving to that purpose." While Deloney does not include every example, he follows Mexía's order and very lightly adapts the original descriptions. The portraits, however, are Deloney's invention.
2   *Lacedemonians* Spartans.
3   *sometime* Once.

caused the shop to be beautified with marble curiously cut,[1] wherein his father before him was wont to get his living."

"The fifth was the picture of Dioclesian that so much adorned Rome with his magnifical[2] and triumphant victories. This was a most famous emperor, although no other than the son of a bookbinder."

"Valentinian stood the next, painted most artificially,[3] who also was crowned emperor, and was but the son of a poor rope-maker, as in the same picture was expressed, where his father was painted by him using his trade."

"The seventh was the Emperor Probus, whose father being a gardener, was pictured by him holding a spade."

"The eighth was of Marcus Aurelius,[4] whom every age honoreth. He was so wise and prudent an emperor, yet was he but a cloth-weaver's son."

"The ninth was the portraiture of the valiant Emperor Maximinus, the son of a blacksmith, who was there painted as he was wont to work at the anvil."

"In the tenth table[5] was painted the Emperor Galerus, who at the first was but a poor shepherd."

"Next to this picture was placed the pictures of two popes of Rome, whose wisdom and learning advanced them to that dignity. The first was the lively counterfeit of Pope John the twenty-two, whose father was a shoemaker. He, being elected pope, increased their rents and patrimony greatly."[6]

"The other was the picture of Pope Sixtus, the fourth of that name, being a poor mariner's son."

"The thirteenth picture was of Lamusius, King of Lombardy, who was no better than the son of a common strumpet, being painted like a naked child walking in water, and taking hold of the point of a lance, by the which he hung fast and saved himself. The reason whereof is this after his lewd mother was delivered of him, she unnaturally threw

---

1 *curiously cut* Skillfully or artistically sculpted.
2 *magnifical* Magnificent.
3 *artificially* Artistically.
4 *Marcus Aurelius* Like several others in this list, a Roman Emperor. Marcus Aurelius ruled from 161–180 CE; he is the author of a classic work of Stoicism, *Meditations*.
5 *table* Painting.
6 *increased ... greatly* Increased his family's wealth greatly.

him into a deep, stinking ditch, wherein was some water. By hap,[1] King Agilmond passed that way, and found this child almost drowned, who, moving him somewhat with the point of his lance, the better to perceive what he was, the child (though newly born), took hold thereof with one of his pretty hands, not suffering it to slide or slip away again. Which thing the king considering, being amazed at the strange force of this young, little infant, caused it to be taken up and carefully to be fostered, and because the place where he found it was called Lama, he named the child Lamusius, who after grew to be so brave a man and so much honoured of Fortune, that in the end he was crowned King of the Lombards, who lived there in honour. And in his succession after him, even unto the time of the unfortunate King Albovina, when all came to ruin, subversion and destruction."[2]

"In the fourteenth picture, Primislas, King of Bohemia, was most artificially drawn, before whom there stood a horse without bridle or saddle in a field where husbandmen were at plough. The cause why this king was thus painted," quoth Jack, "was this: At that time, the king of the Bohemians died without issue, and great strife being among the nobility for a new king. At length, they all consented that a horse would be let in the field, without bridle or saddle, having all determined with a most assured purpose to make him their king before whom this horse rested. At what time it came to pass, that the horse first stayed himself before this Primislas, being a simple creature[3] who was then busy driving the plough. They presently made him their sovereign, who ordered himself and his kingdom very wisely. He ordained many good laws, he compassed[4] the city of Prague with strong walls, besides many other things, meriting perpetual laud and commendations."

"The fifteenth was the picture of Theophrastus, a philosopher, a counsellor of kings, and companion of nobles, who was but son of a tailor."

"Seeing then, my good servants, that these men have been advanced to high estate and princely dignities by wisdom, learning, and

---

1 *By hap* By chance.
2 *unfortunate ... destruction* Alboinus, sixth-century king of Lombardy, was killed by his wife because he forced her to drink from a cup made from her father's skull after he had slain him in battle.
3 *being a simple creature* Who was a simple man.
4 *compassed* Surrounded, built.

diligence, I would wish you to imitate the like virtues that you might attain the like honours, for which of you doth know what good fortune God hath in store for you? There is none of you so poorly born but that men of baser birth have come to great honours. The idle hand shall ever go in a ragged garment, and the slothful live in reproach, but such as do lead a virtuous life, and govern themselves discretely, shall of the best be esteemed and spend their days in credit."

Chapter 6: How all the clothiers in England joined together, and with one consent, complained to the king of their great hindrance sustained for want of traffic into other countries, whereupon they could get no sale for their cloth.

By means of the wars our King had with other countries, many merchant strangers were prohibited for[1] coming to England, and also our own merchants (in like sort) were forbidden to have dealing with France or the Low Countries. By means whereof, the clothiers had most of their cloth lying on their hands, and that which they sold was at so low rate[2] that the money scarcely paid for the wool and workmanship. Whereupon they thought to ease themselves by abating the poor workmen's wages, and when that did not prevail, they turned away their people—weavers, shearmen, spinners and carders—so that where there was a hundred looms kept in one town, there was scant fifty, and he that kept twenty, put down ten. Many a poor man, for want of work, was hereby undone with his wife and children, and

---

1   *By means of the wars … countries*   From 1508 to 1529, when Cardinal Wolsey fell from power, Henry VIII involved himself numerous times in the wars between France and the Holy Roman Empire. These ventures were horrifically expensive (the 1512–14 French invasion may have cost over one million pounds, ten times the government's revenue), and wreaked havoc on trade; according to W.G. Hoskins, "Not only open warfare, but incessant rumours of wars and fears of impending closure of overseas markets equally brought trade to a standstill at times, notably in the early 1520s." Henry VIII paid for his foreign adventures through various "loans" (he never paid them back), benevolences, and subsidies that caused a great deal of anger, resentment, and at times, outright defiance of royal authority. The "Amicable Grant" (1525) sparked the most serious resistance (see Holinshed's narration in the Contexts section). While these tensions generally inform this chapter, Deloney bases his narrative on Henry's short-lived 1528 war against the Holy Roman Empire. Protests from both English and continental merchants quickly pushed the belligerents into declaring an eight month truce;   *strangers* Foreigners;   *for*   From.
2   *so low rate*   At such a low price.

it made many a poor widow to sit with a hungry belly. This bred great woe in most places in England.[1] In the end, Jack of Newbury intended, in the behalf[2] of the poor, to make a supplication to the King, and to the end he might do it the more effectually, he sent letters to all the chief clothing towns in England to this effect:

The Letter

Well beloved friends and brethren,
Having a taste of the general grief, and feeling, in some measure, the extremity of these times, I fell into consideration by what means we might best expel these sorrows and recover our former commodity. When I had well thought thereon, I found that nothing was more needful therein than a faithful unity among ourselves. This sore of necessity can no way be cured but by concord, for like as the flame consumes the candle, so men through discord waste themselves. The poor hate the rich because they will not set them to work, and the rich hate the poor because they seem burdenous.[3] When Belinus and Brennus were at strife, the Queen their mother in their greatest fury persuaded them to peace by urging her conception of them in one womb, and mutual cherishing of them from their tender years,[4] so let our art of clothing, which like a kind mother hath cherished us with the excellency of her secrets, persuade us to an unity. Though our occupation be decayed, let us not deal with it as men do by their old shoes, which after they have long born them out of the mire, do in the end fling them on the dunghill,

---

1   *This bred ... England*   According to *Holinshed's Chronicles*, "By this means the trade of merchandise was in manner for let here in England and namely the clothes lay on their hands, whereby the commonwealth suffered great decay, and great numbers of spinners, carders, tuckers, and such other that lived by cloth-working remained idle, to their great impoverishment."

2   *in the behalf*   On behalf.

3   *burdenous*   Burdensome.

4   *When Belinus and Brennus ... tender years*   Brothers Belinus and Brennus, legendary kings of Britain, fought against one another, causing Brennus to flee England for Gaul (present day France). He returned with an army, but, according to *Holinshed's Chronicles*, before the two met in battle, "by the intercession of their mother that came betwixt them, and demeaned herself in all motherly order, and most loving manner towards them both, they fell to an agreement, and were made friends or ever they parted asunder."

or as the husbandman[1] doth by his bees, who for their honey burns them.

Dear friends, consider that our trade will maintain us if we will uphold it, and there is nothing base but that which is basely used. Assemble therefore yourselves together, and in every town tell the number of those that have their living by means of this trade, note it in a bill, and send it to me. And because suits in court are like winter nights—long and wearisome—let there be in each place a weekly collection made to defray charges. For I tell you, noblemen's secretaries and cunning lawyers have slow tongues and deaf ears which must daily be nointed with the sweet oil of angels.[2] Then let two honest, discrete men be chosen, and sent out of every town to meet me at Blackwell Hall in London, on All Saints Eve,[3] and then we will present our humble petition to the King. Thus I bid you heartily farewell.

Copies of this letter being sealed, they were sent to all the clothing towns of England, and weavers both of linen and woolen gladly received them, so that when all the bills were brought together, there were found of the clothiers, and those they maintained, threescore thousand[4] and six hundred persons. Moreover, every clothing town, sending up two men to London, they were found to be an hundred and twelve persons, who in very humble sort fell down before his Majesty, walking in St. James his park,[5] and delivered unto him their petition.

The King, presently perusing it, asked if they were all clothiers? Who answered (as it were one man) in this sort: "We are, most gracious King, all poor clothiers, and your Majesty's faithful subjects."

"My lords," quoth the King, "let these men's complaint be thoroughly looked unto and their grief redressed, for I account them in the number of the best commonwealth's men.[6] As the clergy for the

---

1 *husbandman* Farmer.
2 *nointed* Anointed; *angels* Gold coins.
3 *Blackwell Hall* Center for the sale of wool and cloth, situated next to the Guildhall, where London's civic administration had its home; *All Saints Eve* 31 October.
4 *threescore thousand* Sixty thousand.
5 *St. James his park* Royal park in London, west of the densely populated city center.
6 *thoroughly looked unto* Thoroughly looked into; *for I account them ... men* For I consider them among the best men in the commonwealth.

soul, the soldier for defence of his country, the lawyer to execute justice, the husbandman to feed the belly, so is the skilful clothier no less necessary for the clothing of the back, who we may reckon among the chief yeomen[1] of our land. And as the crystal sight of the eye is tenderly to be kept from harms because it gives to the whole body light, so is the clothier, whose cunning hand provides garments to defend our naked parts from the winter's nipping frost. Many more reasons there are which may move us to redress their griefs, but let it suffice that I command to have it done."

With that, his Grace delivered the petition to the Lord Chancellor, and all the clothiers cried, "God save the King!" But as the King was ready to depart, he suddenly turned about, saying, "I remember there is one Jack of Newbury, I muse he had not his hand in this business, who professed himself to be a defender of true labourers."

"Then," said the Duke of Somerset,[2] "It may be his purse is answerable for his person."

"Nay," quoth the Lord Cardinal, "all his treasure is little enough to maintain wars against the butterflies."

With that, Jack showed himself unto the King and privately told his Grace of their grief anew.[3] To whom his Majesty said, "Give thy attendance at the Council Chamber, where thou shalt receive an answer to thy content." And so his Highness departed.

Finally, it was agreed that the merchants should freely traffic one with another, and that proclamation thereof should be made as well on the other side of the sea as in our land.[4] But it was long before this

---

1 *yeomen* According to William Harrison's description of England's class structure (see Appendix 6), yeomen are non-aristocrats who nonetheless own land that yields at least six pounds a year in income.

2 *Duke of Somerset* It is not clear who, if anybody, Deloney has in mind. The peerage was vacant between 1500 and 1525, when Henry VIII gave the title to his bastard son, Henry Fitzroy. The boy, however, was six years old at the time. Deloney may be relying on the memory of Edward Seymour (c. 1500–52), who made himself Duke of Somerset when he became Lord Protector to the young Edward VI, as Seymour was known for his concern for the poor and for using legislation to achieve social justice.

3 *told ... anew* Repeated their complaints.

4 *it was agreed ... land* According to *Holinshed's Chronicles*, Henry VIII consented to a truce because of the potential damage to the cloth trade: "But yet, the king wisely considering with other of his council what damage should ensue thereby unto his subjects, and specially to the merchants and clothiers, would not consent so easily to the purpose of the Frenchmen" to continue fighting. It is worth noting that Holinshed's source, Edward Hall's *Union of the Two Noble and Illustre Familes of Lancaster and York* (1548), commonly known as *Hall's*

was effected by reason the Cardinal, being Lord Chancellor, put off the matter from time to time. And because the clothiers thought it best not to depart before it was ended, they gave their daily attendance at the Cardinal's house, but spent many days to no purpose. Sometimes they were answered, "my Lord was busy, and could not be spoke withal," or else he was asleep and they durst not wake him, or at his study and they would not disturb him, or at his prayers and they durst not displease him. And still one thing or another stood the way to hinder them. At last, Patch, the Cardinal's fool, being, by their often repair thither, well acquainted with the clothiers, came unto them and said, "What, have you not spoken with my Lord yet?"

"No, truly," quoth they, "we hear say he is busy and we stay 'til his Grace be at leisure."

"It is true," said Patch, and with that in all haste he went out of the hall and at last came in again with a great bundle of straw on his back.

"Why, how now, Patch?" quoth the gentlemen, "what wilt thou do with that straw?"

"Mary," quoth he, "I will put it under these honest men's feet, lest they should freeze ere they find my Lord at leisure." This made them all to laugh and caused Patch to carry away his straw again.

"Well, well," quoth he, "if it cost you a groat's worth of faggots[1] at night, blame not me."

"Trust me," said Jack of Newbury, "if my Lord Cardinal's father[2] had been no hastier in killing of calves than he is in dispatching of poor men's suits, I doubt he had never worn a miter." Thus he spake betwixt themselves softly,[3] but yet not so softly but that he was overheard by a flattering fellow that stood by, who made it known to some of the gentlemen, and they straight certified[4] the Cardinal thereof.

The Cardinal, who was of a very high[5] spirit, and a lofty, aspiring mind, was marvellously displeased at Jack of Newbury, wherefore, in

---

Chronicle, is much more attentive to how the economic fortunes of the lowest ultimately affect the monarchy's finances: the King considered "that if the merchants lost, the poorer sort should lese [lose], and at length he should lose his customs. Wherefore leaving the glory of war, he took mercy on his subjects and concluded to take a peace for a time."

1 *faggots* Bundles of kindling.
2 *my Lord Cardinal's father* Wolsey's father was a butcher.
3 *softly* Quietly.
4 *certified* Informed, assured.
5 *high* Proud.

his rage, he commanded and sent the clothiers all to prison because the one of them should not sue for the other's releasement.[1] Four days lay these men in the Marshalsea,[2] 'til at last they made their humble petition to the King for their release. But some of the Cardinal's friends kept it from the King's sight. Notwithstanding, the Duke of Somerset, knowing thereof, spake with the Lord Cardinal about the matter, wishing he should speedily release them, lest it bred him some displeasure, "for you may perceive," quoth the Duke, "how highly the King esteems men of that faculty."[3]

"Sir," quoth the Cardinal, "I doubt not but to answer their imprisonment well enough, being persuaded that none would have given me such a quip but an heretic, and I dare warrant you, were this Jack of Newbury well examined, he would be found to be infected with Luther's spirit, against whom our King hath of late written a most learned book, in respect whereof the Pope's holiness hath entitled his Majesty, *Defender of the Faith*.[4] Therefore, I tell you such fellows are fitter to be faggots for fire than fathers of families. Notwithstanding, at your Grace's request, I will release them."

Accordingly, the Cardinal sent for the clothiers before him to Whitehall,[5] his new-built house by Westminster, and there bestowing his blessing upon them, said, "Though you have offended me, I pardon you. For as Stephen[6] forgave his enemies that stoned him, and our Saviour those sinful men that crucified him, so do I forgive you that high trespass committed in disgrace of my birth, for herein do

---

1   *sent the clothiers ... releasement*   Sent all the clothiers to prison so that nobody would be left to sue for the others' release. Wolsey's sending the clothiers to prison is Deloney's invention. In fact, according to Hall, Wolsey forced the merchants to buy the clothier's products, much to the merchants' dismay, since "in all places our vent [sale] is stopped and forbidden," and when the clothiers "heard that the Cardinal took their part, they waxed proud."

2   *Marshalsea*   Prison in Southwark (near the Globe) used for debtors, religious offenders, and those accused or convicted of sedition.

3   *faculty*   Occupation.

4   *our King ... the Faith*   In 1520, Henry VIII published a defense of Catholicism, the *Assertion of the Seven Sacraments*, for which Pope Leo X granted Henry the title indicated. Henry VIII split from Rome and created an independent, English church not because he had theological differences with Catholicism, but in order to divorce his first wife, Katherine of Aragon. Throughout his reign, Henry VIII firmly opposed Protestantism, and as Wolsey indicates, heresy was punished by fire.

5   *sent for ... Whitehall*   Sent for the clothiers to appear before him at Whitehall, Wolsey's palace located next to St. James Park and Westminster, known until 1532 as York Place.

6   *Stephen*   Early Christian martyr. See Acts 6-7.60.

men come nearest unto God, in showing mercy and compassion. But see hereafter you offend no more. Touching your suit, it is granted, and tomorrow shall be published through London."

This being said, they departed, and according to the Cardinal's words, their business was ended. The Steelyard merchants, joyful thereof, made the clothiers a great banquet, after which each man departed home, carrying tidings of their good success, so that in short space, clothing again was very good, and poor men as well set on work as before.

Chapter 7: How a young Italian merchant, coming to Jack of Newbury's house, was greatly enamoured of one of his maidens, and how he was served.

Among other servants which Jack of Newbury kept, there were in his house threescore maidens, which every Sunday waited on his wife to church and home again,[1] who had divers offices. Among other,[2] two were appointed to keep the beams and weights, to weigh out wool to the carders and spinners, and to receive it in again by weight. One of them was a comely maiden, fair and lovely, born of wealthy parents and brought up in good qualities. Her name was Joan. So it was that a young, wealthy Italian merchant, coming oft from London thither to bargain for cloth (for at that time clothiers had their cloth bespoken,[3] and half paid for aforehand). This Master Benedict fell greatly enamoured of this maiden, and therefore offered much courtesy to her, bestowing many gifts on her, which she received thankfully, and albeit his outward countenance showed his inward affection, yet Joan would take no knowledge[4] thereof. Half the day sometime would he sit by her as she was weighing wool, often sighing and sobbing to himself, yet saying nothing, as if he had been tongueless, like the men of Coromandel,[5] and the loather to speak, for that he could speak but

---

1   *waited on his wife ... again* Accompanied his wife to church and home again.

2   *Among other* Among other duties.

3   *bespoken* Ordered ahead of time

4   *take no knowledge* Not acknowledge.

5   *Coromandel* Southwest coast of India. In addition to *The Forest*, Deloney also relied on the *Polyhistor* by the third-century CE Latin grammarian and historian Solinus. This book was written, as the title for the 1576 translation has it, "for the benefit and recreation of all sorts of

bad English. Joan, on the other side, that well perceived his passions did, as it were, triumph over him,[1] as one that were bondslave to her beauty, and although she knew well enough before that she was fair, yet did she never so highly esteem of her self as at this present, so that when she heard him either sigh, sob, or groan, she would turn her face in a careless sort, as if she had been born (like the women of Taprobana)[2] without ears.

When Master Benedict saw she made no reckoning of his sorrows, at length he blabbered out this broken English, and spoke to her in this sort: "Mettressa Joan, be me tra and fa, me love you wod[3] all mine heart, and if you no shall love me again, me know me shall die, sweet Metressa love a me, and by my fa and tra you shall lack nothing. First me will give you de silk for make you a frog.[4] Second de fin camree for make you ruffles, and de tird shall be for make fin hankercher,[5] for wipe your nose."

She, mistaking his speech, began to be choleric,[6] wishing him to keep that bodkin to pick his teeth. "Ho, ho Mettressa Joan," quoth he, "be Got,[7] you are angry. Oh, Mettressa Joan, be not chafe with your friene[8] for nothing."

"Good sir," quoth she, "keep your friendship for them that care for it, and fix your love on those than can like you. As for me, I tell you plain, I am not minded to marry."

"O, 'tis no matter for marry, if you come to my chamber, beshit[9] my bed, and let me kiss you."

The maid, though she was very much displeased, yet at these words should not forbear laughing for her life.

---

persons." There is no reference to Coromandel in either text, but Solinus mentions that in "the furthest part of all the east are nations of monstrous shape.... Some have no tongues, but use beckonings and gestures instead of speech."

1 *Joan ... him* Joan, on the other hand, perceived perfectly well that his passions did triumph over him.

2 *Taprobana* Island in the Indian Ocean. According to Pliny, the inhabitants are not born without ears, but live "exceedingly long without malady or infirmity."

3 *be me tra and fa* By my truth and faith; *wod* With.

4 *frog* Frock.

5 *fin camree* Fine cambric; *fin hankercher* Fine handkerchief.

6 *choleric* Angry.

7 *be Got* By God.

8 *chafe* Angry; *friene* Friend.

9 *beshit* Besit, but the hapless Benedict obviously mispronounces the word, causing Joan's mirth.

"Ah ah, Mettressa Joan, me is very glad to see you merry. Hold, Mettressa Joan, hold your hand, I say, and there is four crown because you laugh on me."

"I pray you, Sir, keep your crowns, for I need them not."

"Yes, be Got you shall have them, Mettressa Joan, to keep in box for you."

She that could not well understand his broken language mistook his meaning in many things, and therefore willed him not to trouble her any more. Notwithstanding, such was his love toward her that he could not forbear her company, but made many journeys thither for her sake. And as a certain spring in Arcadia makes men to starve that drink of it, so did poor Benedict, feeding his fancy on her beauty, for when he was in London, he did nothing but sorrow, wishing he had wings like the monsters of Tartaria[1] that he might fly to and fro at his pleasure.

When any of his friends did tell her of his ardent affection toward her, she wished them to rub him with the seat of a mule to assuage his amorous passion, or to fetch him some of the water in Boetia[2] to cool and extinguish the heat of his affection, "for," quoth she, "let him never hope to be helped by me."

"Well," quoth they, "before he saw thy alluring face, he was a man reasonable and wise, but is now a stark fool, being by thy beauty bereft of wit, as if he drunk of the river Cea, and like bewitching Circe,[3] thou hast certainly transformed him from a man to an ass. There are stones in Pontus," quoth they, "that the deeper they be laid in the water, the fiercer they burn,[4] unto the which, fond lovers may fitly be

---

1   *certain spring ... drink of it*   From *The Forest*'s chapter on miraculous lakes and fountains: "[Classical authorities remind] us of another [spring] in Arcadia, of which whoso drinketh, starveth immediately";   *monsters of Tartaria*   Likely recalling Solinus' description of Tartary (today, the vast area of northern and central Asia) as uninhabitable, even though it "abounds in gold and precious stones," because "griffons possess all, a most fierce kind of fowl, and cruel beyond all cruelness." Solinus does not mention wings.

2   *rub him ... water in Boetia*   Deloney takes these "cures" from *The Forest*'s chapter on remedies for love.

3   *Circe*   In Greek myth, a demi-goddess who transformed men into beasts. In Homer's *Odyssey*, Ulysses agrees to stay on her island for a year after freeing his men from her spell, which had turned them into swine.

4   *stones ... burn*   From *The Forest*: "In the isle of Cea, as recordeth Pliny, there was a fountain of which whoso drank once became forthwith stupid and insensible, of no more feeling or wit than an ass.... There is also in Pontus a river in which are found certain stones that will

compared, who the more they are denied, the hotter is their desire. But seeing it is so, that he can find no favour at your hands, we will show him what you have said, and either draw him from his dumps,[1] or leave him to his own will."

Then spake one of the weavers that dwelled in the town, and was a kinsman to this maid. "I muse," quoth he, "that Master Benedict will not be persuaded, but like the moth, will play with the flame that will scorch his wings. Methinks he should forbear to love, or learn to speak, or else woo such as can answer him in his language, for I tell you that Joan my kinswoman is no taste[2] for an Italian."

These speeches were told to Benedict with no small addition. When our young merchant heard the matter so plain, he vowed to be revenged of the weaver and to see if he could find any more friendship of his wife.[3] Therefore, dissembling his sorrow and covering his grief, with speed he took his journey to Newbury, and pleasantly saluted Mistress Joan, and having his purse full of crowns, he was very liberal to the workfolks, especially to Joan's kinsman, insomuch that he got his favour many times to go forth with him, promising him very largely to do great matters, and to lend him a hundred pound, wishing him to be a servant no longer. Beside, he liberally bestowed on his wife many gifts, and if she washed him but a band,[4] he would give her an angel. If he did but send her child for a quart of wine, he would give him a shilling for his pains. The which his courtesy changed the weaver's mind, saying he was a very honest gentleman, and worthy to have one far better than his kinswoman.

This pleased Master Benedict well to hear him say so, notwithstanding, he made light of the matter, and many times when the weaver was at his master's at work, the merchant would be at home with his wife, drinking and making merry. At length, time bringing acquaintance, and often conference breeding familiarity, Master Benedict began somewhat boldly to jest with Gillian, saying that her sight and sweet countenance had quite reclaimed his love from Joan, and that she only was the mistress of his heart, and if she would lend

---

burn ... and by how much the more they be covered in the water, so much the better and sooner burn they."

1 *dumps* Depression.

2 *is no taste* Either "has not taste for" or "is not appropriate for."

3 *if he could ... his wife* If he could seduce the weaver's wife.

4 *washed him but a band* Washed for him a very small article of clothing.

him her love, he would give her gold from Arabia, orient pearls from India, and make her bracelets of precious diamonds. "Thy garments shall be of the finest silk that is made in Venice, and thy purse shall be stuffed with angels. Tell me thy mind, my love, and kill me not with unkindness, as did thy scornful kinswoman, whose disdain almost cost me my life."

"O Master Benedict, think not the wives of England can be won by rewards, or enticed with fair words, as children are with plums. It may be that you, being merrily disposed, do speak this to try my constancy. Know then that I esteem more the honour of my good name than the sliding wealth[1] of the world."

Master Benedict, hearing her say so, desired her, that considering it was love which forced his tongue to bewray his heart's affection, that yet she would be secret, and so for that time took his leave.

When he was gone, the woman began to call her wits together, and to consider of her poor estate, and withal, the better to note the comeliness of her person and the sweet favour of her face, which when she had well thought upon, she began to harbour new thoughts and to entertain contrary affections, saying: "Shall I content myself to be wrapped in sheep's russet that may swim in silks and sit all day carding for a groat, that may have crowns at my command? No," quoth she, "I will no more bear so base a mind, but take fortune's favours while they are to be had. The sweet rose doth flourish but one month, nor women's beauties but in young years; as the winter's frost consumes the summer flowers, so doth old age banish pleasant delight. O glorious gold!" quoth she, "how sweet is thy smell! How pleasing is thy sight! Thou subduest princes and overthrows kingdoms, then how should a silly woman withstand thy strength?" Thus she rested, meditating on preferment, minding to hazard her honesty to maintain herself in bravery, even as occupiers[2] corrupt their consciences to gather riches.

Within a day or two, Master Benedict came to her again, on whom she cast a smiling countenance. He, perceiving that, according to his old custom, sent for wine, and very merry they were. At last, in the midst of their cups, he cast out his former question, and after farther conference, she yielded, and appointed a time when he should come

---

1   *sliding wealth*   Wealth sliding away, i.e., impermanent.

2   *in bravery*   In fine clothing;   *occupiers*   Unscrupulous merchants or traders.

to her, for which favour he gave her half a dozen portugals.[1] Within an hour or two after, entering into her own conscience, bethinking how sinfully she had sold her self to folly, began thus to expostulate.

"Good Lord," quoth she, "shall I break that holy vow which I made in marriage and pollute my body which the Lord hath sanctified? Can I break the commandment of my God, and not rest accursed? Or be a traitor to my husband and suffer no shame? I heard once my brother read in a book that Bucephalus, Alexander's steed, being a beast, would not be backed by any but the emperor,[2] and shall I consent to any but my husband? Artemisia, being a heathen lady, loved her husband so well that she drunk up his ashes, and buried him in her own bowels?[3] And should I, being a Christian, cast my husband out of my heart? The women of Rome were wont to crown their husbands' heads with bays in token of victory, and shall I give my husband horns in token of infamy? An harlot is hated of all virtuous people, and shall I make myself a whore? O my God, forgive me my sin," quoth she, "and cleanse my heart from these wicked imaginations." And as she was thus lamenting, her husband came home. At whose sight her tears were doubled, like a river whose stream is increased by showers of rain. Her husband, seeing this, would needs know the cause of her sorrow, but a great while[4] she would not show him, casting many a piteous look upon him, and shaking her head. At last she said, "O my dear husband, I have offended against God and thee, and made such a trespass by my tongue as hath cut a deep scar in my conscience and wounded my heart with grief like a sword. Like Penelope,[5] so have I been wooed, but like Penelope, I have not answered."

"Why, woman," quoth he, "what is the matter? If it be but the bare offence of the tongue, why shouldst thou so grieve? Considering that

---

1 *portugals* Gold coins.

2 *Bucephalus ... emperor* The story of Alexander and this horse is from Plutarch's *Lives*, famously translated into English by Sir Thomas North in 1579. In Plutarch, however, Alexander understands that the horse is frightened of his shadow and so only seems wild. There is nothing about the horse that will only allow an emperor to ride him.

3 *Artemisia ... bowels* Artemisia's grief for her husband, Mausolus, not only led her to drink her husband's ashes, but to create a sepulcher so grand it became known as one of the Seven Wonders of the World, giving us the term "mausoleum."

4 *but a great while* For a long time.

5 *Penelope* Wife of Ulysses, who fended off suitors during her husband's twenty year absence.

women's tongues are like lambs' tails, which seldom stand still. And the wise man sayeth, where much talk is, must needs be some offence. Women's beauties are fair marks for wandering eyes to shoot at. But as every archer hits not the white, so every wooer wins not his mistress' favour. All cities that are besieged are not sacked, nor all women to be misliked that are loved. Why, wife, I am persuaded thy faith is more firm, and thy constancy greater, to withstand lovers' alarums than that any other but myself should obtain the fortress of thy heart."

"O sweet husband," quoth she, "we see the strongest tower at length falleth down by the cannon's force, though the bullets be but iron. Then how can the weak bulwark of a women's breast make resistance when the hot cannons of deep, persuading words are shot off with golden bullets, and every one as big as a portuguese?"[1]

"If it be so, wife, I may think myself in a good case, and you to be a very honest woman. As Mars and Venus danced naked together in a net, so I doubt,[2] you and some knave have played naked together in a bed. But in faith, you quean,[3] I will send thee to salute thy friends without a nose, and as thou hast sold thy honesty, so will I sell thy company."

"Sweet husband, though I have promised, I have performed nothing. Every bargain is not effected, and therefore, as Judas brought again the thirty silver plates,[4] for the which he betrayed his master, so repenting my folly, I'll cast him again his gold, for which I should have wronged my husband."

"Tell me," quoth her husband, "what he is?"

"It is Master Benedict," quoth she, "which for my love hath left the love of our kinswoman, and hath vowed himself forever to live my servant."

"O dissembling Italian!" quoth he, "I will be revenged on him for this wrong. I know that any favour from Joan, my kinswoman, will make him run like a man bitten with[5] a mad dog. Therefore, be ruled by me, and thou shalt see me dress him in his kind." The woman was very well pleased, saying she would be there that night.

---

1 *portuguese* I.e., portugal coin.

2 *Mars and Venus ... net* In the *Odyssey*, Homer recounts the story of Vulcan trapping his wife, Venus, and her lover Mars in bed with a net; *so I doubt* So I have no doubt.

3 *quean* Woman of loose morals; prostitute.

4 *Judas ... plates* See Matthew 27.3–10.

5 *with* By.

"All this works well with me," quoth her husband, "and to supper will I invite Joan, my kinswoman, and in the mean space make up the bed in the parlour very decently."

So the good man went forth, and got a sleepy drench from the potecary's,[1] the which he gave to a young sow which he had in his yard, and in that evening laid her down in the bed in the parlour, drawing the curtains 'round about. Suppertime being come, Master Benedict gave his attendance, looking for no other company but the good wife. Notwithstanding, at the last minute, Joan came in with her kinsman, and sat down to supper with them. Master Benedict, musing at their sudden approach, yet nevertheless glad of Mistress Joan's company, passed the suppertime with many pleasant conceits, Joan showing herself that night more pleasant in his company than at any time before. Therefore, he gave the goodman great thanks.

"Good Master Benedict, little do you think how I have travelled in your behalf to my kinswoman, and much ado I had to bring the peevish wench into any good liking of your love. Notwithstanding, by my great diligence and persuasions, I did at length win her good will to come hither, little thinking to find you here, or any such good cheer to entertain her, all which I see is fallen out for your profit. But trust me, all the world cannot alter her mind, nor turn her love from you. In regard whereof, she hath promised me to lie this night in my house for the great desire she hath of your good company, and in requital of all your great courtesies showed to me, I am very well content to bring you to her bed. Marry, this you must consider, and so she bade me tell you, that you should come to bed with as little noise as you could, and tumble nothing that you find, for fear of her best gown and her hat, which she will lay hard by the bedside, next her best partlet,[2] and in so doing you may have company with her all night, but say nothing in any case 'till you be abed."

"O," quoth he, "Mater Ian, be Got Mater Ian, me will not spoil her clothes for a tousand pound, ah, me love Mattress Jone more than my wife."[3]

---

1 *drench* Medicinal, soporific, or poisonous potion; *potecary* Apothecary.

2 *partlet* Collar or ruff.

3 *O ... my wife* "O, Master Ian, by God Master Ian, me [I] will not spoil her clothes for a thousand pounds, ah, me love Mistress Joan more than my wife."

Well, supper being done, they rose from the table. Master Benedict, embracing Mistress Joan, thanked her for her great courtesy and company, and then the goodman and he walked into town, and Joan hied her home to her master's, knowing nothing of the intended jest. Master Benedict thought every hour twain[1] 'til the sun was down and that he were abed with his beloved. At last he had his wish, and home he came to his friend's house.

"O Mater Ian," quoth he, "'tis no matter for light, me shall find Metres[2] Joan will enough in the dark."

And entering in the parlour, groping about, he felt a gown and hat. "O Metres Joan," quoth he, "here is your gown and hat, me shall no hurt for a tousand pound."

Then, kneeling down by the bed's side, instead of Mistress Joan, he saluted the sow in this sort:[3]

O my love and my delight, it is thy fair face that hath wounded my heart, thy grey sparkling eyes, and thy lily-white hands, with the comely proportion of thy pretty body that made me in seeking thee to forget myself, and to find thy favour lose my own freedom. But now is the time come wherein I shall reap the fruits of a plentiful harvest. Now, my dear, from thy sweet mouth let me suck the honey balm of thy breath, and with my hand stroke those rosy cheeks of thine, wherein I have took such pleasure. Come with thy pretty lips and entertain me into thy bed with one gentle kiss (why speakest thou not, my sweetheart?), and stretch out thy alabaster arms to enfold thy faithful friend. Why should ill-pleasing sleep close up the crystal windows of thy body so fast, and bereave thee of thy fine, lordly attendants, wherewith thou was wont to salute thy friends? Let it not offend thy gentle ears that I thus talk to thee. If thou hast vowed not to speak, I will not break it, and if thou wilt command me to be silent, I will be dumb, but thou needest not fear to speak thy mind, seeing the cloudy night concealeth everything.

---

1 *twain* Two; i.e., every hour seemed like two hours.
2 *Metres* Mistress.
3 *he saluted ... sort* Deloney departs from imitating Italian-inflected English in this speech to the pig, which Benedict thinks is Joan.

By this time, Master Benedict was unready,[1] and slipped into bed, where the sow lay swathed in a sheet, and her head bound in a great linen cloth. As soon as he was laid, he began to embrace his new bedfellow, and laying his lips somewhat near her snout, he felt her draw her breath very short.

"Why, how now, love?" quoth he. "Be you sick? Mistriss Joan, your breath be very strong, have you no cacke[2] abed?"

The sow, feeling herself disturbed, began to grunt and keep a great stir, whereat Master Benedict (like a madman) ran out of bed, crying "De deveil! De devil!" The goodman of the house, being purposely provided, came rushing in with half a dozen of his neighbours, asking what was the matter.

"Poh me," quoth Benedict, "here be the great devil! Cry ho, ho, ho, bee Gossen, I tink dee play the knave wid me, and me will be revenged on you."[3]

"Sir," quoth he, "I know you love mutton and thought pork nothing unfit, and therefore provided you a whole sow, and as you like this entertainment, spend Portugals. Walk, walk, Berkshire maids will be no Italian strumpets, nor the wives of Newbury their bawds."

"Berkshire dog," quoth Benedict, "owlface, shack, hang dou and dy wife, have it not be for me love to sweet Mestress Joan, I will no come in your houz.[4] But farewell 'til I cash you, I shall make your hog nose bud."[5]

The goodman and his neighbours laughed aloud, away went Master Benedict, and for very shame departed from Newbury before day.

---

1 *unready* Probably a misprint for "ready."

2 *cacke* While Benedict likely means "cake," which presumably would improve "Joan's" breath, there is also a pun here on "cack," an Elizabethan term for feces.

3 *"Poh me ... you"* "Poor me," quoth Benedict, "here is the great devil! Cry ho, ho, ho, by God! I think you play the knave with me, and me [I] will be revenged on you."

4 *shack* Idle, disreputable person, vagabond; *hang dou and dy wife* Thank you and your wife; *houz* House.

5 *cash* Catch; *bud* Bleed.

Chapter 8: How Jack of Newbury, keeping a very good house, both for his servants and relief of the poor, won great credit thereby, and how one of his wife's gossips found fault therewith.

"Good morrow, gossip, now by my truly I am glad to see you in health. I pray you, how doth Master Winchcomb? What, never a great belly yet? Now fie, by my fa[1] your husband is waxed idle."

"Trust me, gossip," sayeth Mistress Winchcomb, "a great belly comes sooner than a new coat, but you must consider we have not been long married. But truly, gossip, you are welcome. I pray you, sit down, and we will have a morsel of something by and by."

"Nay, truly, gossip, I cannot stay," quoth she, "indeed, I must be gone, for I did but even step in to see how you did."

"You shall not choose but stay a while," quoth Mistress Winchcomb, and with that a fair napkin was laid upon the little table in the parlour, hard by the fire side, whereon was set a fine, cold capon, with a great deal of other cheer, with ale and wine plenty.

"I pray you, gossip, eat, and I beshrew[2] you if you spare," quoth the one.

"I thank you heartily, gossip," sayeth the other. "But hear you, gossip, I pray you tell me, doth your husband love you well and make much of you?"

"Yes, truly, I thank God," quoth she.

"Now, by my truth," said the other, "it were a shame for him if he should not, for though I say it before your face, though he had little with you, yet you were worthy to be as good a man's wife as his."

"Trust me, I would not change my John for my Lord Marquess," quoth she. "A woman can be but well, for I live at heart's ease and have all things at will, and truly, he will not see me lack anything."

"God's blessing on his heart," quoth her gossip, "it is a good hearing. But I pray you, tell me, I heard say your husband is chosen for our burgess[3] in the parliament house, is it true?"

"Yes, verily," quoth his wife, "I wis[4] it is against his will, for it will be no small charges unto him."

---

1 *fa* Faith.
2 *beshrew* Wish for bad things to happen to you, but meant playfully.
3 *burgess* Representative.
4 *wis* Know.

"Tush, woman, what talk you of that? Thanks be to God, there is never a gentleman in all Berkshire that is better able to bear it. But hear you, gossip, shall I be so bold to ask you one question more?"

"Yes, with all my heart," quoth she.

"I heard say that your husband would now put you in your hood and silk gown. I pray you, is it true?"

"Yes, in truth," quoth Mistress Winchcomb, "but far against my mind, gossip. My French hood[1] is bought already, and my silk gown is a-making. Likewise, the goldsmith hath brought home my chain and bracelets. But I assure you, gossip, if you will believe me, I had rather go an hundred miles than wear them, for I shall be so ashamed that I shall not look upon any of my neighbours for blushing."

"And why, I pray you?" quoth her gossip. "I tell you, dear woman, you need not be anything abashed or blush at the matter, especially seeing your husband's estate is able to maintain it. Now, trust me, truly, I am of opinion you will become it[2] singular well."

"Alas," quoth Mistress Winchcomb, "having never been used to such attire, I shall not know where I am, nor how to behave myself in it, and beside, my complexion is so black[3] that I shall carry but an ill-favoured countenance under a hood."

"Now, without a doubt," quoth her gossip, "you are to blame to say so. Beshrew my heart if I speak it to flatter, you are a very fair and well-favoured young woman as any is in Newbury. And never fear your behaviour in your hood, for I tell you true, as old and withered as I am myself, I could become a hood well enough, and behave myself as well in such attire as any other whatsoever, and I would not learn of never a one of them all. What, woman, I have been a pretty wench in my days, and seen some fashions. Therefore, you need not to fear, seeing both your beauty and comely personage deserves no less than a French hood, and be of good comfort. At the first possible,[4] folks will gaze something at you, but be not you abashed for that. It is better they should wonder at your good fortune than lament at your misery. But when they have seen you two or three times in that attire, they

---

1   *French hood*   Type of hood that covered the ears but exposed the top of the head. Introduced into England by Anne Boleyn, French hoods had gone out of style by 1580.

2   *you will become it*   The jewels will become you.

3   *black*   Dark.

4   *At the first possible*   The first time people see you.

will afterward little respect it, for every new thing at the first seems rare, but being once a little used, it grows common."

"Surely, gossip, you say true," quoth she, "and I am but a fool to be so bashful. It is no shame to use God's gifts for your credits, and well might my husband think me unworthy to have them if I would not wear them, and though I say it, my hood is a fair one as any woman wears in this country, and my gold chain and bracelets are none of the worst sort, and I will show them you[1] because you shall give your opinion upon them." And therewithal she stepped into her chamber and fetched them forth.

When her gossip saw them, she said, "Now, beshrew my fingers, but these are fair ones indeed. And when do you mean to wear them, gossip?"

"At Whitsuntide,"[2] quoth she, "if God spare me life."

"I wish that well you may wear them," said her gossip, "and I would I were worthy to be with you when you dress yourself, it should be never the worse for you. I would order the matter so that you should set everything about you in such sort as never a gentlewoman of them all should stain you."[3]

Mistress Winchcomb gave her great thanks for her favour, saying that if she needed her help, she would be bold to send for her.

Then began her gossip to turn her tongue to another tune, and now to blame her for her great housekeeping. And thus she began, "Gossip, you are but a young woman, and one that hath had no great experience of the world. In my opinion, you are something too lavish in expenses. Pardon me, good gossip, I speak but for good will, and because I love you, I am the more bold to admonish you. I tell you plain, were I the mistress of such a house, having such large allowance as you have, I would save twenty pound a year that you spend to no purpose."

"Which way might that be?" quoth Mistress Winchcomb. "Indeed, I confess I am but a green housewife, and one that hath but small trial

---

1   *show them you*   Show them to you.

2   *Whitsuntide*   Holiday celebrating the possession of the Apostles and others by the Holy Ghost, causing them to "to speak with other tongues, as the Spirit gave them utterance" (Acts 2.4).

3   *and I would I ... stain you*   Convoluted, but the sense is clear: Were I worthy to be with you when you dressed yourself, it would never be the worse for you. I would make you look so beautiful that you would not be shamed before any gentlewoman.

in the world. Therefore, I should be very glad to learn anything that were for my husband's profit and my commodity."[1]

"Then listen to me," quoth she, "you feed poor folks with the best of the beef and the finest of the wheat, which in my opinion is a great oversight. Neither do I hear of any knight in this country that doth it. And to say the truth, how were they able to bear that port which they do, if they saved it not by some means?[2] Come hither, and I warrant you that you shall see but brown bread on the board. If it be wheat and rye mingled together, it is a great matter and the bread highly commended. But most commonly they[3] eat either barley bread or rye mingled with pease and such like coarse grain, which is doubtless but of small price, and there is no other bread allowed except at their own board. And in like manner for their meat. It is well known that necks and points of beef is their ordinary fare, which because it is commonly lean, they seethe therewith now and then a piece of bacon or pork,[4] whereby they make their pottage fat, and therewith drives out the rest with more content. And thus must you learn to do. And beside that, the midriffs of the oxen, and the cheeks, the sheep's heads, and the gathers,[5] which you give away at your gate, might serve them well enough, which would be a great sparing to your other meat, and by this means you would save in the year much money whereby you might the better maintain your hood and silk gown. Again, you serve your folks with such superfluities that they spoil in manner as much as they eat. Believe me, were I their dame, they should have things more sparingly, and then they would think it more dainty."

"Trust me, gossip," quoth Mistress Winchcomb, "I know your words in many things to be true, for my folks are so corn fed that we have much ado to please them in their diet. One doth say this is too salt, and another sayeth this is too gross, this is too fresh, and that too fat, and twenty fault they will find at their meals. I warrant you, they make such parings of their cheese and keep such chipping of their

---

1   *commodity*   Good, benefit.
2   *how were they able ... means?*   How were the knights able to spend on luxuries if they did not find some way of cutting back expenses elsewhere?
3   *they*   The poor.
4   *seethe ... pork*   Braise with a small amount of very fatty meat, such as bacon or fatback pork. This technique remains common today.
5   *gathers*   Organs.

bread that their very orts[1] would serve two or three honest folks to their dinner."

"And from whence, I pray you, proceeds that," quoth her gossip, "but of too much plenty? But ifaith,[2] were they my servants, I would make them glad of the worst crumb they cast away, and thereupon. I drink to you, and I thank you for my good cheer with all my heart."

"Much good may it do you, good gossip," said Mistress Winchcomb, "and I pray you when you come this way, let us see you."

"That you shall verily," quoth she, and so away she went.

After this, Mistress Winchcomb took occasion to give her folks shorter commons and courser meat than they were wont to have, which at length being come to the goodman's[3] ear, he was very much offended therewith, saying, "I will not have my people thus pinched of their victuals. Empty platters make greedy stomachs, and where scarcity is kept, hunger is nourished, and therefore, wife, as you love me let me have no more of this doings."

"Husband," quoth she, "I would they should have enough, but it is a sin to suffer and a shame to see the spoil they make. I could be very well content to give them their belly's full and that which is sufficient, but it grieves me, to tell you true, to see how coy they are, and the small care they have in wasting of things. And I assure you, the whole town cries shame of it, and it hath bred me no small discredit for looking no better to it. Trust me no more, if I was not checked in my own house about this matter,[4] when my ears did burn to hear what was spoken."

"Who was it that checked thee? I pray thee, tell me. Was it not your old gossip, dame dainty, mistress trip and go?[5] I believe it was."

"Why, man, if it were she, you know she hath been an old housekeeper, and one that hath known the world, and that she told me was for good will."

"Wife," quoth he, "I would not have thee to meddle with such light-brained housewives, and so I have told thee a good many times, and yet I cannot get you to leave her company."

---

1   *orts*   Scraps.

2   *ifaith*   In faith.

3   *goodman*   Her husband, Jack.

4   *if I was not checked ... matter*   If someone did not rebuke me about how I run my household.

5   *mistress trip and go*   The exact meaning is unclear, but the phrase is obviously an insult.

"Leave her company? Why, husband, so long as she is an honest woman, why should I leave her company? She never gave me hurtful counsel in all her life, but hath always been ready to tell me things for my profit, though you take it not so. Leave her company? I am no girl, I would you should well know, to be taught company I should keep. I keep none but honest company, I warrant you. Leave her company, ketha?[1] Alas, poor soul, this reward she hath for her good will. I wis I wis, she is more your friend than you are your own."

"Well, let her be what she will," said her husband, "but if she come any more in my house, she were as good no. And therefore, take this for a warning, I would advise you," and so away he went.

Chapter 9: How a Draper in London, who owed Jack of Newbury much money, became a bankrout,[2] whom Jack of Newbury found carrying a porter's basket on his neck, and how he set him up again at his own cost, which draper afterward became an Alderman of London.

There was one Randall Pert, a draper, dwelling in Watling Street,[3] that owed Jack of Newbury five hundred pounds at one time, who in the end fell greatly to decay in so much that he was cast in prison and his wife with her poor children turned out of doors. All his creditors, except Winchcomb, had a share of his goods, never releasing him out of prison so long as he had one penny to satisfy them. But when this tidings was brought to Jack of Newbury's ear, his friends counselled him to lay his action[4] against him.

"Nay," quoth he, "if he be not able to pay me when he is at liberty, he will never be able to pay me in prison, and therefore, it were as good for me to forbear my money without troubling him, as to add more sorrow to his grieved heart, and be never the nearer.[5] Misery is trodden down by many, and once brought low, they are seldom or

---

1   *ketha?*   Quotha, say you?
2   *bankrout*   Bankrupt.
3   *Watling Street*   Street in central London, near St. Paul's Cathedral, where many wealthy drapers lived.
4   *lay his action*   Sue him for debt.
5   *it were as good ... nearer*   It would be better to forbear demanding my money from him than adding more sorrow to his grieved heart, and be no nearer to clearing his debt to me.

never relieved. Therefore, he shall rest for me untouched, and I would to God he were clear of all other men's debts, so that I gave him mine to begin the world again."[1]

Thus lay the poor draper a long time in prison, in which space his wife, which before for daintiness, would not foul her fingers nor turn her head aside, for fear of hurting the set of her neckenger, was glad to go about and wash bucks[2] at the Thames side, and to be a char-woman in rich men's houses. Her soft hand was now hardened with scouring, and instead of gold rings upon her lily fingers, they were now filled with chaps, provoked by the sharp lee[3] and other drudgeries.

At last, Master Winchcomb, being (as you heard) chosen against[4] the Parliament a burgess for the town of Newbury, and coming up to London for the same purpose, when he was alighted at his inn, he left one of his men there to get a porter to bring his trunk up to the place of his lodging. Poor Randall Pert, which lately before was come out of prison, having no other means of maintenance, became a porter to carry burdens from one place to another, having an old ragged doublet and a torn pair of breeches, with his hose out at the heels and a pair of old broke slip-shoes[5] on his feet, a rope about his middle instead of a girdle, and on his head an old greasy cap, which had so many holes in it that his hair started through it, who, as soon as he heard one call for a porter, made answer straight: "Here, master, what is it that you would have carried?"

"Mary," quoth he, "I would have this trunk born to the Spread Eagle at Ivy Bridge."[6]

"You shall, master," quoth he, "but what will you give me for my pains?"

"I will give thee two pence."

---

1   *gave ... again*   Forgave his debt to me so that he could start anew.

2   *neckenger*   Neckerchief; *bucks* Buckets, meaning, wash very dirty clothes. She has become a laundress.

3   *lee*   Lye.

4   *against*   For, as.

5   *slip-shoes*   Slippers.

6   *Spread Eagle at Ivy Bridge*   Ivy Bridge Lane is just south of Covent Garden in Westminster, then well outside central London, and a very wealthy part of town. While no record exists of an inn by this name at this location, "The Spread Eagle" was apparently a popular designation for inns and buildings. In 1600, John Milton, Sr., the poet's father, bought a house bearing this name, located on Bread Street.

"A penny more, and I will carry it," said the porter. And so, being agreed, away he went with his burden 'til he came to the Spread Eagle, where on a sudden, espying Master Winchcomb standing, he cast down the trunk and ran away as hard as ever he could.

Master Winchcomb, wondering what he meant thereby, caused his man to run after him and to fetch him again. But when he saw one pursue him, he ran then the faster, and in running here he lost one of his slip-shoes, and there another. Ever looking behind him, like a man pursued with a deadly weapon, fearing every twinkling of an eye to be thrust through. At least, his breech, being tied but with one point,[1] what with the haste he made and the weakness of the thong, fell about his heels, which so shackled him that down he fell in the street, all along sweating and blowing, being quite worn out of breath. And so, by this means, the serving-man overtook him, and taking him by the sleeve, being as windless as the other, stood blowing and puffing a great while ere they could speak one to another.

"Sirra," quoth the serving-man, "you must come to my master. You have broken his trunk all to pieces by letting it fall."

"O for God's sake," quoth he, "let me go! For Christ's sake, let me go! Or else Master Winchcomb of Newbury will arrest me, and then I am undone forever."

Now, by this time, Jack of Newbury had caused his trunk to be carried into the house, and then he walked along to know what the matter was. But when he heard the porter say that he would arrest him, he wondered greatly, and having quite forgot Pert's favour,[2] being so greatly changed by imprisonment and poverty, he said, "wherefore should I arrest thee? Tell me, good fellow, for mine own part, I know no reason for it."

"O Sir," quoth he, "I would to God I knew none neither!"

Then asking him what his name was, the poor man, falling down on his knees, said, "Good Master Winchcomb, bear with me and cast me not into prison. My name is Pert, and I do not deny but I owe you five hundred pound, yet for the love of God, take pity upon me!"

When Master Winchcomb heard this, he wondered greatly at the man, and did as much pity his misery, though as yet he made it not known, saying, "Passion of my heart, man, thou wilt never pay me

---

1 *breech* Breeches, pants; *point* Knot.
2 *favour* Looks, face.

thus. Never think being a porter to pay five hundred pound debt. But this hath your prodigality brought you to, your thriftless neglecting of your business, that set more by your pleasure than your profit." Then, looking better upon him, he said, "What, never a shoe to thy foot, hose to thy leg, band to thy neck, nor cap to thy head? O Pert, this is strange, but wilt thou be an honest man, and give me a bill of thy hand of my money?"

"Yes, sir, with all my heart," quoth Pert.

"Then come to the scrivener's,"[1] quoth he, "and dispatch it, and I will not trouble thee."

Now, when they were come thither, with a great many following them at their heels, Master Winchcomb said, "Hearest thou, scrivener? This fellow must give me a bill of his hand for five hundred points. I pray thee, make it as it should be."

The scrivener, looking upon the poor man, and seeing him in that case, said to Master Winchcomb, "Sir, you were better to let it be a bond,[2] and have some sureties bound him."

"Why, scrivener," quoth he, "does thou think this is not a sufficient man of himself for five hundred pounds?"

"Truly, sir," quoth the scrivener, "if you think him so, you and I am of two minds."

"I'll tell thee what," quoth Master Winchcomb, "were it not that we are all mortal, I would take his word as soon as his bill or bond, the honesty of a man is all."

"And we in London," quoth the scrivener, "do trust bonds far better than honesty. But sir, when must this money be paid?"

"Marry, scrivener, when this man is Sheriff of London."

At that word, the scrivener and the people standing by laughed heartily, saying, "In truth, sir, make no more ado but forgive it him, as good to do the one as the other."

"Nay, believe me," quoth he, "not so, therefore do as I bid you."

Whereupon the scrivener made the bill to be paid when Randall Pert was Sheriff of London, and thereunto set his own hand[3] for a

---

1 *scrivener* A scrivener created legal documents, often concerning loans and real estate. Many engaged in lending as well, and while scriveners did not enjoy a high reputation, some (such as John Milton's father) became very wealthy.

2 *bond* Legal note promising a penalty if the money is not paid back as agreed.

3 *hand* Signature.

witness, and twenty person more that stood by set their hands like-wise. Then he asked Pert what he should have for carrying his trunk.

"Sir," quoth he, "I should have three pence, but seeing I find you so kind, I will take but two pence at this time."

"Thanks, good Pert," quoth he, "but for thy three pence, there is three shillings, and look thou come to me tomorrow morning betimes."

The poor man did so, at what time Master Winchcomb had provided him out of Birchin Lane[1] a fair suit of apparel. Merchant-like, with a fair black cloak, and all other things fit to the same. Then he took him a shop in Canwick Street[2] and furnished the same shop with a thousand pounds worth of cloth. By which means, and other favours that Master Winchcomb did him, he grew again into great credit, and in the end, became so wealthy that while Master Winchcomb lived he was chosen Sheriff, at what time he paid five hundred pounds every penny, and after, died an alderman of the city.[3]

Chapter 10: How Jack of Newbury's servants were revenged of their dame's tattling gossip.

Upon a time it came to pass, when Master Winchcomb was far from home and his wife gone abroad, that Mistress Many-Better, dame Tittle-Tattle, Gossip Pint-Pot, according to her old custom, came to Mistress Winchcomb's house, perfectly knowing of the goodman's absence and little thinking the good wife was from home. Where, knocking at the gate, Tweedle stepped out and asked who was there. Where hastily opening the wicket, he suddenly discovered the full proportion of this foul beast, who demanded if their mistress were within.

"What, Mistress Frank!" quoth she, "In faith, welcome! How have you done a great while? I pray you, come in."

---

1   *Birchin Lane*   Street known for second-hand clothing stalls.
2   *took him a shop*   Set him up in a shop;   *Canwick Street*   Candlewick Street, home to many drapers and weavers.
3   *died an alderman of the city*   While many characters in *Jack of Newbury* are based on reality, "Randall Pert" is not. Nobody by that name was either a sheriff or an alderman of London.

"Nay, I cannot," quoth she. "Notwithstanding, I did call to speak a word or two with your mistress. I pray you, tell her that I am here."

"So I will," quoth he, "so soon as she comes in."

Then said the woman, "What, is she abroad? Why then, farewell, good Tweedle."

"Why, what haste, what haste, Mistress Frank!" quoth he, "I pray you stay and drink ere you go. I have a cup of new sack will do your old belly no hurt."

"What," quoth she, "have you new sack already? Now, by my honesty, I drunk none this year, and therefore I do not greatly care if I take a taste before I go," and with that she went into the wine cellar with Tweedle, where first he set before her a piece of powdered beef as green as a leek.[1] And then, going into the kitchen, he brought her a piece of roasted beef hot from the spit.

Now, certain of the maidens of the house and some of the young men, who had long before determined to be revenged of this prattling housewife, came into the cellar one after another, one of them bringing a great piece of a gambon[2] of bacon in his hand, and every one bade Mistress Frank welcome. And first, one drank to her, and then another, and so the third, the fourth, and the fifth, so that Mistress Frank's brains waxed as mellow as a pippin at Michaelmas[3] and so light that sitting in the cellar she thought the world ran round. They, seeing her to fall into merry humours, whetted her on in merriment as much as they could, saying, "Mistress Frank, spare not, I pray you, but think yourself as welcome as any woman in Newbury, for we have cause to love you because you love our mistress so well."

"Now, assure," quoth she (lisping in her speech,[4] her tongue waxing somewhat too big for her mouth), "I love your mistress well indeed, as if she were my own daughter."

"Nay, but hear you," quoth they, "she begins not to deal well with us now."

---

1 *powdered beef* Salted beef; *as green as a leek* The connection is not entirely clear, but as Thomas Middleton writes in *The Owles Almanacke*, "surely there will be very good agreement betwixt powdered beef and the spring," suggesting an association with growth and renewal. I am grateful to Rachel Lauden for this information.

2 *gambon* Side.

3 *pippin* Sweet apple; *Michaelmas* Feast of St. Michael on 29 September, marking the end of the harvest season.

4 *lisping in her speech* Slurring her words (because she is drunk).

"No, my lamb," quoth she, "why so?"

"Because," quoth they, "she seeks to bar us of our allowance, telling our master that he spends too much in housekeeping."

"Nay then," quoth she, "your mistress is an ass and a fool, and though she go in her hood, what care I? she is but a girl to me. Twittle twattle, I know what I know. Go to, drink to me. Well, Tweedle, I drink to thee with all my heart. Why, thou whoreson, when wilt thou be married? O, that I were a young wench for thy sake. But 'tis no matter. Though I be a poor woman, I am a true woman. Hang, dogs, I have dwelt in this town these thirty winters."

"Why then," quoth they, "you have dwelt here longer than our master."

"Your master?" quoth she, "I knew your master a boy,[1] when he was called Jack of Newbury. Aye, Jack, I knew him called 'plain Jack,' and your mistress, now she is rich and I am poor, but 'tis no matter, I knew her a draggle-tail girl,[2] mark ye."

"But now," quoth they, "she takes upon her lustily,[3] and hath forgot what she was."

"Tush, what will you have of a green thing," quoth she. "Here I drink to you, so long as she goes where she list a-gossiping, and 'tis no matter, little said is soon amended. But hear you, my masters, though Mistress Winchomb[4] go in her hood, I am as good as she, I care not who tell it to her. I spend not my husband's money in cherries and codlings.[5] Go to, go to, I know what I say well enough. I am sure I am not drunk. Mistress Winchcomb? Mistress? No, Nan Winchcomb, I will call her name, plain Nan. What, I was a woman when she was sa-reverence,[6] a paltry girl, though now she goes in her hood and chain of gold. What care I for her? I am her elder, and I know more of her tricks. Nay, I warrant you, I know what I say. 'Tis no matter, laugh at me and spare not. I am not drunk, I warrant." And with that, being scant able to hold open her eyes, she began to nod and to spill

---

1   *a boy*   When he was a boy.

2   *I knew her a draggle-tail girl*   I knew her when she was a girl whose clothes were filthy or dragged through dirt, indicating poverty.

3   *she takes upon her lustily*   She eagerly takes on airs.

4   *Winchomb*   Mistress Frank likely mispronounces the name, another indication of drunkenness

5   *codlings*   Apples; cherries and codlings were considered luxurious fruits.

6   *sa-reverence*   Save your reverence, a phrase indicating low social origins.

the wine out of the glass, which they perceiving, let her alone, going out of the cellar 'til she was sound asleep, and in the mean space they devised how to finish this piece of knavery. At least, they consented to lay her forth at the backside of the house, half a mile off, even at the foot of a stile,[1] that whosoever came next over might find her. Notwithstanding, Tweedle stayed hard by to see the end of this action.

At last comes a notable clown from Greenham,[2] taking his way to Newbury, who, coming hastily over the stile, stumbled at the woman and fell down clean over her. But in the starting up, seeing it was a woman, cried out, "Alas, alas!"

"How now, what is the matter?" quoth Tweedle.

"O," quoth he, "here lies a dead woman."

"A dead woman!" quoth Tweedle. "That's not so, I trow."[3] And with that he tumbled her about. "Bones of me," quoth Tweedle, "it's a drunken woman, and one of the town,[4] undoubtedly! Surely it is great pity she should lie here."

"Why? Do you know her?" quoth the clown.

"No, not I," quoth Tweedle, "nevertheless, I will give thee half a groat and take in thy basket and carry her throughout the town, and see if anybody know her."

Then said the other, "Let me see the money, and I will. For by the mass, che[5] earned not half a groat this great while."

"There it is," quoth Tweedle.

Then the fellow put her in basket, and so lifted her upon his back. "Now, by the mass, she stinks vilely of drink or wine, or something, but tell me, what shall I say when I come into the town?" quoth he.

"First," quoth Tweedle, "I would have thee, so soon as ever thou canst, go to the town's end, with lusty voice, to cry 'O yes,'[6] and then say, 'Who knows this woman, who?' And though possible some will say, 'I know her,' and 'I know her,' yet do not thou set her down 'til thou comest to the market cross, and there use the like words. And if any be so friendly to tell thee where she dwells, then just before her

---

1 *stile* Ladder allowing passage over a fence.
2 *clown* Lower-class person; *Greenham* Suburb of Newbury.
3 *trow* Believe.
4 *one of the town* Prostitute.
5 *che* I.
6 *O yes* Oyez, a call for attention by a public crier or court official.

door, cry so again. And if thou perform this bravely, I will give thee half a groat more."

"Master Tweedle," quoth he, "I know you well enough. You dwell with Master Winchcomb, do not? Well, if I do it not in the nick,[1] give me never a penny." And so, away he went 'til he came to the town's end, and he cries out as boldly as any bailiff's man, "O yes, who knows this woman, who?"

Then said the drunken woman in the basket, her head falling first on one side and then on the other side, "Who co[2] me, who?"

Then said he again, "Who knows this woman, who?"

"Who co me, who?" quoth she, and look how oft he spake the one, she spake the other, saying still "Who co me, who co me, who?" Whereat all the people in the street fell into such a laughing that the tears ran down again.

At last one made answer, saying, "Good fellow, she dwells in the Northbrook Street, a little beyond Master Winchcomb's."

The fellow hearing that, goes down thither in all haste, and there in the hearing of a hundred people, cries "Who knows this woman, who?" Whereat her husband comes out, saying, "Marry, that do I too well, God help me."

Then said the clown, "if you know her, take her, for I know her not but for a drunken beast."

And as her husband took her out of the basket, she gave him a sound box on the ear, saying, "What, you queans, do you mock me?" and so was carried in.

But the next day, when her brains were quiet and her head cleared of these foggy vapours, she was so ashamed of herself that she went not forth of her doors a long after, and if anybody did say unto her, "Who co me, who?" she would be so mad and furious that she would be ready to draw her knife and to stick them, and scold as if she strove for the best game at the cucking-stools.[3] Moreover, her prattling to Mistress Winchcomb's folks of their mistress made her on the other side to fall out with her in such short that she troubled them no more, either with her company or her counsel.

---

1 *in the nick* In the nick of time, quickly or immediately.
2 *co* Knows.
3 *cucking-stools* Disorderly women were punished by being tied to a chair, exposed to ridicule, and dunked in water.

Chapter 11: How one of Jack of Newbury's maidens became a lady.

At the winning of Morlesse in France, the noble Earl of Surrey, being at that time Lord High Admiral of England, made many knights, among the rest was Sir George Rigley brother to Sir Edward Rigley, and sundry other,[1] whose valours far surpassed their wealth, so that when peace bred a scarcity in their purses that their credits grew weak in the city, they were enforced to ride into the country, where at their friends' houses they might have favourable welcome without coyne[2] or grudging. Among the rest, Jack of Newbury, that[3] kept a table for all comers, was never lightly without many such guests, where they were sure to have bold welcome and good cheer, and their mirth no less pleasing than their meat was plenty. Sir George, having lyen long at board in this brave yeoman's[4] house, at length fell in liking of one of his maidens, who was as fair as she was fond.

This lusty wench he so allured with hope of marriage that at length she yielded him her love, and therewithal bent her whole study to work his content.[5] But in the end, she so much contented him that it wrought altogether her own discontent. To become high, she laid herself so low that the knight suddenly fell over her, which fall became the rising of her belly. But when this wanton perceived herself to be with child, she made her moan unto the knight, say-

---

1   *At the winning ... other*   In July 1522, a fleet under the command of the Lord Admiral, Thomas Howard, Second Earl of Surrey, besieged and sacked the coastal town of Morlaix, Henry VIII having become allied with the Holy Roman Emperor, Charles V, against France. Why this incident captured Deloney's attention is unclear, but two factors may have influenced his decision. To finance this venture, Henry VIII forced yet another "loan" from London's economic elite, which may have gratified the poor but did nothing to soothe class tensions, as described by Hall: "The poor men were content with this payment and said, 'Let the rich churls pay, for they may well.'" Also, Morlaix "was very rich, and specially of linen cloth," so Surrey's conquest would have benefitted the English cloth trade by removing a competitor. While Hall and others record that Surrey knighted Edward Rigley and others "for their hardiness and noble courage," George Rigley (like Randall Pert) is Deloney's invention.

2   *city* London; *without coyne* "Coyne" refers to the custom of forcing people to billet the military, a practice that caused great resentment. Deloney means that their friends did not object to providing Rigley and others with food and shelter.

3   *that* Who.

4   *lyen* Laid; *yeoman* Wealthy, non-aristocratic person who owns land (Jack's current designation since he refused Henry VIII's offer of a knighthood).

5   *work his content* Make him happy.

ing, "Ah, Sir George, now is the time to perform your promise or to make me a spectacle of infamy to the whole world forever. In the one, you shall discharge the duty of a true knight, but in the other, show yourself a most perjured person. Small honour will it be to boast in the spoil of poor maidens whose innocencie[1] all good knights ought to defend."

"Why, thou lewd, paltry thing," quoth he. "Comest thou to father thy bastard upon me? Away, ye dunghill carrion, away! Hear you, good housewife, get you among your companions, and lay your litter where you list. But if you trouble me anymore, trust me, thou shalt dearly abye[2] it." And so, bending his brows like the angry god of war, he went his ways, leaving the child-breeding wench to the hazard of her fortune, either good or bad.

The poor maiden, seeing herself for her kindness thus cast off, shed many tears of sorrow for her sin, inveighing with many bitter groans against the unconstancy of love-alluring men. And in the end, when she saw no other remedy, she made her case known unto her mistress, who, after she had given her many checks and taunts, threatening to turn her out of doors, she opened the matter to her husband.

So soon as he heard thereof, he made no more to do but presently posted to London after Sir George and found him at my Lord Admiral's.[3] "What, Master Winchcomb," quoth he, "you are heartily welcome to London, and I thank you for my good cheer. I pray you, how doth your good wife, and all our friends in Berkshire?"

"All well and merry, I thank you, good Sir George," quoth he. "I left them in health and hope they do so continue. And trust me, sir," quoth he, "having earnest occasion to come up to talk with a bad debtor, in my journey it was my chance to light in company of a gallant widow, a gentlewoman she is of wondrous good wealth, whom grisly death hath bereft of a kind husband, making her a widow ere she had been half a year a wife. Her land, Sir George, is well worth a hundred pound a year as one penny, being as fair and comely a creature as any of her degree in our whole country. Now sir, this is the worst: by the reason that[4] she doubts herself to be with child, she hath

---

1   *innocencie*   Innocence.
2   *abye*   Suffer for.
3   *my Lord Admiral's*   Thomas Howard, Earl of Surrey's house.
4   *by the reason that*   Because.

vowed not to marry these 12 months. But because I wish you well and the gentlewoman no hurt, I came of purpose from my business to tell you thereof. Now, Sir George, if you think her a fit wife for you, ride to her, woo her, win her, and wed her."

"I thank you, good Master Winchcomb," quoth he, "for your favour ever toward me, and gladly would I see this young widow, if I wist where."[1]

"She dwell not half a mile from my house," quoth Master Winchcomb, "and I can send for her at any time, if you please."

Sir George, hearing this, thought it was not best to come there, fearing Joan would father a child upon him, and therefore, said he had no leisure to come from my Lord.[2] "But," quoth he, "would I might see her in London, on the condition it cost me twenty nobles."

"Tush, Sir George," quoth Master Winchcomb, "delay in love is dangerous, and he that will woo a widow must take time by the forelock[3] and suffer none other to stop before him, lest he leap without the widow's love. Notwithstanding, seeing now I have told you of it, I will take my gelding and get me home. If I hear of her coming to London, I will send you word, or perhaps come myself. 'Til then, adieu good Sir George."

Thus parted Master Winchcomb from the knight, and being come home, in short time he got a fair taffeta gown and a French hood for his maid, saying, "Come, ye drab, I must be fain to cover a foul fault with a fair garment, yet all will not hide your great belly. But if I find means to make you a lady, what wilt thou say then?"

"O Master," quoth she, "I shall be bound while I live to pray for you."

"Come then, minion,"[4] quoth her mistress, "and put you on this gown and French hood, for seeing you live lien[5] with a knight, you must needs be a gentlewoman."

The maid did so, and being thus attired, she was set on a fair gelding, and a couple of men sent with her up to London. And being well instructed by her master and dame what she should do, she took her

---

1   *wist where*   If I knew where she lived.
2   *father a child upon him*   Claim him as the father of her child;   *my Lord*   Surrey.
3   *take time by the forelock*   Seize the opportunity.
4   *minion*   Person kept for sexual purposes.
5   *lien*   Lay.

journey to the city in the term time, and lodged at the Bell in the Strand.[1] And Mistress Loveless must be her name, for so her master had warned her to call herself, neither did the men who waited on her know the contrary, for Master Winchcomb had borrowed them of their master to wait upon a friend of his to London because he could not spare any of his own servants at that time. Notwithstanding, they were appointed, for the gentlewoman's credit, to say they were her own men. This being done, Master Winchcomb sent Sir George a letter, that the gentlewoman which he told him of was now in London, lying at the Bell in the Strand, having great business at the term.[2]

With which news, Sir George's heart was on fire 'til such time as he might speak with her. Three or four times went he thither, and still she would not be spoken withal, the which close keeping of herself made him the more earnest in his suit.

At length, he watched her so narrowly that finding her going forth in an evening,[3] he followed her, she having one man before and another behind. Carrying a very stately gait[4] in the street, it drave him into the greater liking of her, being the more urged to utter his mind.

And suddenly stepping before, he thus saluted her: "Gentlewoman, God save you, I have often been at your lodging and could never find you at leisure."

"Why, sir," quoth she (counterfeiting her usual speech), "have you any business with me?"

"Yes, fair widow," quoth he, "as you are a client to the law, so am I a suitor for your love, and may I find you so favourable to let me plead my own case at the bar of your beauty, I doubt not but to unfold so true a tale as I trust will cause you to give sentence on my side."

"You are a merry gentleman," quoth she, "but for my own part I know you not. Nevertheless, in a case of love, I will be no let[5] to your

---

1   *term time*   Period when the courts were in session;   *the Strand*   Street running next to the Thames from the Temple Bar (the barrier between London and the liberty of Westminster, England's political center) to Charing Cross. Originally occupied by bishops and the nobility, the street became increasingly commercial over the course of the late sixteenth and seventeenth centuries.

2   *having great business at the term*   Despite their supposedly having no legal standing, women, including if not especially widows, frequently used the courts to enforce their rights.

3   *narrowly*   Closely;   *in an evening*   One evening.

4   *Carrying a very stately gait*   Walking in a very stately, elegant manner.

5   *let*   Obstacle.

suit, though perhaps I help you little therein. And therefore, sir, if it please you to give attendance at my lodging, upon my return from the Temple,[1] you shall know more of my mind." And so they parted.

Sir George, receiving hereby some hope of good hap, stayed for his dear at her lodging door, whom, at her coming, she friendly greeted, saying, "Surely, sir, your diligence is more than the profit you shall thereby, but I pray you, how shall I call your name?"

"George Rigley," quoth he, "I am called, and for some small deserts I was knighted in France."

"Why then, Sir George," quoth she, "I have done you too much wrong to make you thus dance attendance on my worthless person. But let me be so bold to request you to tell me how you came to know me. For my own part, I cannot remember that ever I saw you before."

"Mistress Loveless," said Sir George, "I am well acquainted with a good neighbour of yours called Master Winchcomb, who is my very good friend, and to say the truth, you were commended unto me by him."

"Truly, Sir George," said she, "you are so much the better welcome. Nevertheless, I have made a vow not to love any man for this twelvemonth's space. And therefore, Sir, 'til then I would wish you to trouble yourself no further in this matter 'til that time be expired. And then, if I find you be not entangled to[2] any other, and that by trial I find out the truth of your love, for Master Winchcomb's sake your welcome shall be as good as any other gentleman's whatsoever."

Sir George, having received this answer, was wondrous woe,[3] cursing the day that ever he meddled with Joan, whose time of deliverance would come long before a twelvemonth were expired, to his utter shame and overthrow of his good fortune, for by that means should he have Master Winchcomb his enemy and therewithal the loss of this fair gentlewoman. Wherefore to prevent this mischief, he sent a letter in all haste to Master Winchcomb, requesting him most earnestly to come up to London, by whose persuasions he hoped straight to finish the marriage. Master Winchcomb fulfilled his request, and then presently was the marriage solemnized at the Tower of London, in presence of many gentlemen of Sir George's friends. But when he

---

1   *the Temple*   Area around the royal courts.
2   *entangled to*   Involved with.
3   *wondrous woe*   Wondrously woeful, unhappy.

found it was Joan, whom he had gotten child, he fretted and fumed, stamped and stared like a devil.

"Why," quoth Master Winchcomb, "what needs all this? Came you to my table to make my maid your strumpet? Had you no man's house to dishonour but mine? Sir, I would you should well know, that I account the poorest wench in my house too good to be your whore, were you ten knights. And seeing you took pleasure in making her your wanton, take it no scorn to make her your wife. And use her well too, or you shall hear of it. And hold thee, Joan," quoth he, "there is a hundred pounds for thee. And let him not say thou comest to him a beggar."

Sir George, seeing this, and withal casting in his mind what friend Master Winchcomb might be to him, taking his wife by the hand, gave her a loving kiss and Master Winchcomb great thanks. Whereupon he willed him for two years space to take his diet and his lady's at his house, which, the knight accepting, rode straight with his wife to Newbury. Then did the mistress make curtsy to the maid, saying, "You are welcome, Madame," giving her the upper hand in all places. And thus they lived afterward in great joy, and our king, hearing how Jack had matched Sir George, laughing heartily thereat, gave him a living forever, the better to maintain my lady, his wife.

FINIS

In Context

1. Thomas Deloney, "The Queen's Visiting of the Camp at Tilbury with Her Entertainment There" (1588)

After the English victory over the Spanish Armada in 1588, Deloney contributed to the outpouring of nationalist sentiment three celebratory songs, one of which is reprinted here. As the ballad demonstrates, Deloney both shared and contributed to the wave of patriotism following the victory.

To the tune of "Wilson's Wild."

Within the year of Christ our Lord
   A thousand and five hundreth full:
And eighty-eight by just record,
   The which no man may disannul.
And in the thirtieth year remaining
   Of good Queen Elizabeth's reigning.
A mighty power there was prepared
   By Philip, then the king of Spain
Against the maiden Queen of England,
   Which in peace before did reign.

Her royal ships to sea she sent
   To guard the coast on every side:
And seeing how her foes were bent,[1]
   Her realm full well she did provide.
With many thousands so prepared
   As like was never erst[2] declared.
Of horsemen and of footmen plenty,
   Whose good hearts full well is seen
In the safeguard of their country
   And the service of our Queen.

---

1 *how her foes were bent* What her foes intended.
2 *erst* Before.

In Essex faire that fertile soil
    Upon the hill of Tilbury
To give our Spanish foes the foil[1]
    In gallant camp they now do lie,
Where good orders is ordained,
    And true justice eke[2] maintained
For the punishment of persons
    That are lewd or badly bent
To see a sight so strange in England,
    T'was our gracious Queen's intent.

And on the eight of August she
    From fair Saint James[3] took her way
With many lords of high degree
    In princely robes and rich array.
And to a barge[4] upon the water,
    Being King Henry's[5] royal daughter,
She did go with trumpets sounding
    And with dubbing[6] drums apace,
Along the Thames, that famous river,
    For to view the camp a space.[7]

When she as far as Gravesend[8] came,
    Right over against that pretty town,
Her royal grace with all her train
    Was landed there with great renown.
The lords and captains of her forces,
    Mounted on their gallant horses,
Ready stood to entertain her,
    Like martial men of courage bold.

---

1 *To give our Spanish foes the foil* To defeat our Spanish foes.
2 *eke* Also.
3 *fair Saint James* Saint James Park.
4 *to a barge* Into a barge.
5 *King Henry* King Henry VIII.
6 *dubbing* Beating.
7 *a space* Over a short space of time.
8 *Gravesend* Town in northwest Kent on the south side of the Thames estuary, very close to the river's mouth. Tilbury is on the opposite bank.

"Welcome to the camp, dread sovereign!"
    Thus they said, both young and old.

The bulwarks strong that stood thereby,
    Well guarded with sufficient men,
Then flags were spread courageously,
    Their cannons were discharged then.
Each gunner did declare his cunning,
    For joy conceived of her coming.
All the way her Grace was riding
    On each side stood armed men,
With muskets, pikes, and good calivers,
    For her Grace's safeguard then.

The Lord General of the field
    Had there his bloody ancient borne,[1]
The Lord Marshal's colours[2] eke,
    Was carried there all rent and torn,
The which with bullets was so burned
    When in Flanders[3] he sojourned.
Thus in warlike wise they marched,
    Even as soft as foot could fall,
Because her Grace was fully minded
    Perfectly to view them all.

Her faithful soldiers great and small,
    As each one stood within his place,
Upon their knees began to fall
    Desiring God to save her Grace.
For joy whereof her eyes was filled
    That the water down distilled.
"Lord bless you all, my friends," she said,
    "But doe not kneel so much to me."

---

1   *ancient borne*   Carried his flag or ensign.
2   *colours*   Also a flag.
3   *Flanders*   Protestant province in the Netherlands that in 1579 joined the rebellion against Spain. Elizabeth declined official involvement, and so the "Lord Marshal" fought for the Protestant cause on his own.

Then sent she warning to the rest,
    They should not let such reverence be.

Then casting up her princely eyes
    Unto the hill with perfect sight,
The ground all covered she espies,
    With feet of armed soldiers bright.
Whereat her royal heart so leaped
    On her feet upright she stepped.
Tossing up her plume of feathers
    To them all as they did stand.
Cheerfully her body bending,
    Waving of her royal hand.

Thus through the camp she passed quite,
    In manner as I have declared.
At Master Rich's[1] for that night
    Her Grace's lodging was prepared.
The morrow after her abiding,
    On a princely palfrey riding
To the camp she came to dinner
    With her lords and ladies all.
The Lord General went to meet her
    With his guard of yeomen tall.

The sergeant trumpet with his mace,
    And nine with trumpets after him,
Bare-headed went before her Grace
    In coats of scarlet colour trim.
The king of heralds, tall and comely,
    Was the next in order duly.[2]
With the famous arms[3] of England,
    Wrought with rich, embroidered gold,
On finest velvet, blue and crimson,
    That for silver can be sold.

---

1   *Master Rich's*   Arderne Hall, at the time rented by a Thomas Rich.
2   *in order duly*   In due order.
3   *arms*   Coat of arms.

With maces of clean beaten gold
    The Queen's two sergeants then did ride,
Most comely men for to behold,
    In velvet coats and chain's beside.
The Lord General then came riding,
    And Lord Marshal hard[1] beside him.
Richly were they both attired
    In princely garments of great price,
Bearing still their hats and feathers
    In their hands in comely wise.[2]

Then came the Queen on prancing steed,
    Attired like an angel bright,
And eight brave footmen at her feet,
    Whose jerkins were most rich in sight.
Her ladies likewise of great honour,
    Most sumptuously did wait upon her,
With pearls and diamonds brave adorned,
    And in costly cales[3] of gold:
Her guard in scarlet then rid[4] after,
    With bows and arrows stout and bold.

The valiant captains of the field,
    Mean space themselves in order set:[5]
And each of them with spear and shield
    To join in battle did not let.[6]
With such a warlike skill extended
    As the same was much commended.
Such a battle pitched in England,
    Many a day hath not been seen.
Thus they stood in order waiting
    For the presence of our Queen.

---

1   *Lord Marshal* Sir John Norris (c. 1547–97); *hard* Near.
2   *in comely wise* In a comely (appropriate) fashion.
3   *cales* Cauls, richly adorned head-dresses or hair-nets.
4   *rid* Rode.
5   *Mean space themselves in order set* Meanwhile set themselves in due order.
6   *did not let* Did not prevent, i.e., were eager to join in battle.

At length her Grace most royally
   Received was and brought again
Where she might see most loyally
   This noble host and warlike train,
How they came marching all together,
   like a wood in winter's weather.
With the strokes of drummers sounding,
   And with trampling horses, then
The earth and air did sound like thunder
   To the ears of every man.

The warlike army then stood still,
   And drummers left their dubbing sound
Because it was our prince's[1] will,
   To ride about the army round.
Her ladies she did leave behind her,
   And her guard, which still did mind her.
The Lord General[2] and Lord Marshal,
   Did conduct her to each place,
The pikes, the colours and the lances
   At her approach fell down apace.

And then bespake our noble Queen:
   "My loving friends and countrymen,
I hope this day the worst is seen
   That in our wars ye shall sustain.
But if our enemies do assail you,
   Never let your stomachs fail you.
For in the midst of all your troupe,
   We ourselves will be in place
To be your joy, your guide and comfort,
   Even before our enemy's face."

---

1 *prince* According to the OED, starting in about 1560, the term "prince" referred to all
   monarchs regardless of gender.
2 *Lord General* Probably Robert Dudley, Earl of Leicester (1532–88). He arranged
   Elizabeth's visit to the Tilbury camp.

This done, the soldiers all at once
   A mighty shout or cry did give,
Which forced from the azure skies,
   An echo loud from thence to drive,
Which filled her grace with joy and pleasure,
   And riding then from them by leisure,
With trumpets sound most loyally,
   Along the court of guard she went,
Who did conduct her Majesty
   Unto the Lord Chief General's tent.

Where she was feasted royally
   With dainties of most costly price,
And when that night approached nigh,
   Her Majesty with sage advice.
In gracious manner then returned
   From the camp where she sojourned.
And when that she was safely set
   Within her barge, and passed away,
Her farewell then the trumpets sounded,
   And the cannons fast did play.

2. from "An Exhortation Concerning Good Order and Obedience to Rulers and Magistrates," *Certain Sermons or Homilies to Be Declared and Read by All Persons, Vicars, or Curates, every Sunday in Their Churches, where They Have Cure*[1] (1547)

During the reign of Edward VI, the leaders of the Anglican Church, alarmed at the clergy's ignorance, decided to create a book of sermons, one of which had to be read every Sunday. While most of the sermons concern purely theological matters, the "Exhortation" (better known as the "Homily on Obedience") shows how religious doctrine could be invoked to justify and maintain the political status quo by depicting the social hierarchy as stable, unchanging, and divinely authorized— the opposite of the ideology Deloney promotes in *Jack of Newbury*.

---

1   *Cure* Spiritual care or responsibility.

Almighty God hath created and appointed all things in Heaven, earth, and waters in a most excellent and perfect order. In Heaven, he hath appointed distinct orders and states of archangels and angels. In earth, he hath assigned kings, princes, with other governors under them, all in good and necessary order. The water above is kept and raineth down in due time and season. The sun, moon, stars, rainbow, thunder, lightning, clouds and all birds of the air do keep their order. The earth, trees, seeds, plants, herbs, corn, grass and all manner of beasts keep them in their order. All the parts of the whole year, as winter, summer, months, nights and days, continue in their order. All kinds of fishes in the sea, rivers and waters, with all fountains, springs, yea, the seas themselves, keep their comely course and order. And man himself also hath all his parts, both within and without, as soul, heart, mind, memory, understanding, reason, speech, with all and singular corporal members of his body, in a profitable, necessary and pleasant order. Every degree of people, in their vocation, calling and office, hath appointed to them their duty and order. Some are in high degree, some in low, some kings and princes, some inferiors and subjects, priests and laymen, masters and servants, fathers and children, husbands and wives, rich and poor, and every one have need of other: so that in all things is to be lauded and praised the goodly order of God, without the which, no house, no city, no commonwealth can continue and endure. For where there is no right order, there reigneth all abuse, carnal liberty, enormity, sin and Babylonical confusion.[1]

Take away kings, princes, rulers, magistrates, judges and such states of God's order, no man shall ride or go by the highway unrobbed; no man shall sleep in his own house or bed unkilled; no man shall keep his wife, children, and possessions in quietness. All things shall be common, and there must needs follow all mischief and utter destruction, both of souls, bodies, goods, and commonwealths.

But blessed be God, that we in this realm of England feel not the horrible calamities, miseries, and wretchedness which all they undoubtedly feel and suffer that lack this godly order. And praised be God that we know the great, excellent benefit of God showed towards us in this behalf. God hath sent us his high gift, our most dear sover-

---

1 *carnal liberty* Sexual license; *Babylonical confusion* Likely a reference to both the linguistic chaos following God's destruction of the Tower of Babel (Genesis 11.1-9) and to Roman Catholicism, which Protestant polemics often referred to as Babylon.

eign lord, King Edward VI,[1] with godly, wise, and honourable council, with other superiors and inferiors in a beautiful order. Wherefore, let us subjects do our bounden duties, giving hearty thanks to God and praying for the preservation of this godly order. Let us all obey even from the bottom of our hearts all their godly proceedings, laws, statutes, proclamations, and injunctions, with all other godly orders. Let us consider the Scriptures of the Holy Ghost,[2] which persuade and command us all obediently to be subject first and chiefly to the King's Majesty, supreme head over all; and next, to his honourable Council, and to all other noblemen, magistrates, and officers, which by God's goodness be placed and ordered. For almighty God is the only author and provider of this forenamed state and order, as it is written of God in the Book of the Proverbs: "Through me kings do reign; through me counsellors make just laws; through me do princes bear rule and all judges of the earth execute judgment: I am loving to them that love me."[3]

Here let us mark well and remember that the high power and authority of kings, with their making of laws, judgments, and officers, are the ordinances not of man, but of God, and therefore is this word "through me" so many times repeated. Here is also well to be considered and remembered that this good order is appointed of God's wisdom, favour, and love, specially for them that love God, and therefore he sayeth, "I love them that love me." Also, in the Book of Wisdom, we may evidently learn that a king's power, authority, and strength is a great benefit of God, given of his great mercy to the comfort of our great misery. For thus we read there spoken to kings: "Hear, O ye kings, and understand; learn, ye that be judges of the ends of the earth; give ear, ye that rule the multitudes: for the power is given you of the Lord, and the strength from the Highest."[4] Let us learn also here by the infallible word of God that kings and other supreme and higher officers are ordained of God, who is most highest, and therefore they are here diligently taught to apply themselves to knowledge and wisdom necessary for the ordering of God's people to their gov-

---

1 *King Edward VI* Edward VI (1537–53) and the Lord Protector, Edward Seymour (1500–52), were strongly Protestant.

2 *Scriptures of the Holy Ghost* The Bible, supposedly inspired by the Holy Ghost.

3 *Through me … love me* Proverbs 8.15–17.

4 *Hear … Highest* Book of Wisdom 6.1–3 (the Book of Wisdom is not part of the Protestant bible, but one of the Apocrypha).

ernance committed. And they be here also taught by almighty God that they should reknowledge themselves to have all their power and strength not from Rome, but immediately of God most highest.[1]

We read in the Book of Deuteronomy that all punishment pertaineth to God by this sentence: "Vengeance is mine, and I will reward."[2] But this sentence we must understand to pertain also unto the magistrates, which do exercise God's room[3] in judgment and punishing by good and godly laws here in earth. And the places of Scripture which seem to remove from among all Christian men judgment, punishment, or killing ought to be understand[4] that no man, of his own private authority, may be judge over other, may punish, or may kill. But we must refer all judgment to God, to kings and rulers, and judges under them, which be God's officers, to execute justice and by plain words of Scripture have their authority and use of the sword granted from God, as we are taught by St. Paul, the dear and elect apostle of our saviour Christ, whom we ought diligently to obey even as we would obey our saviour Christ, if he were present. Thus St. Paul writeth to the Romans:

> Let every soul submit himself unto the authority of the higher powers, for there is no power but of God; the powers that be, be ordained of God.
>
> Whosoever, therefore, resisteth the power, resisteth the ordinance of God, but they that resist shall receive to themselves damnation. For rulers are not fearful to them that do good, but to them that do evil. Wilt thou be without fear of the power? Do well then, and so shalt thou be praised of the same: For he is the minister of God for thy wealth.[5] But and if thou do that which is evil, then fear, for he beareth not the sword for naught, for he is the minister of God, to take vengeance on him that doth evil.[6]

---

1   *reknowledge* Acknowledge;   *not from Rome ... highest*   Monarchs derive their authority not from the Pope, but from God.
2   *Vengeance ... reward*   Deuteronomy 32.35.
3   *God's room*   God's space, authority.
4   *understand*   Understood.
5   *wealth*   Happiness or prosperity (according to the OED, this usage died out after 1600).
6   *Let every soul ... evil*   Romans 13.1–5.

Wherefore ye must needs obey, not only for fear of vengeance, but also because of conscience; And even for this cause pay ye tribute, for they are God's ministers, serving for the same purpose.

Here let us all learn of St. Paul, the elect vessel of God, that all persons having souls—he excepteth none, nor exempteth none, neither priest, apostle, nor prophet, sayeth St. Chrysostom[1]—do owe of bounden duty, and even in conscience, obedience, submission, and subjection to the high powers, which be constituted in authority by God, forasmuch as they be God's lieutenants, God's presidents, God's officers, God's commissioners, God's judges, ordained of God himself, of whom only they have all their power and all their authority. And the same St. Paul threateneth no less pain than everlasting damnation to all disobedient persons, to all resisters against this general and common authority, forasmuch as they resist not man, but God, not man's device and invention, but God's wisdom, God's order, power, and authority.[2]

And here, good people, let us all mark diligently that it is not lawful for inferiors and subjects in any case[3] to resist the superior powers, for St. Paul's words be plain, that whosoever resisteth shall get to themselves damnation: for whosoever resisteth, resisteth the ordinance of God. Our saviour Christ himself and his apostles received many and diverse injuries of the unfaithful and wicked men in authority, yet we never read that they, or any of them, caused any sedition or rebellion against authority. We read oft that they patiently suffered all troubles, vexations, slanders, pangs and pains, and death itself obediently, without tumult or resistance. They committed their cause to him that judgeth righteously, and prayed for their enemies heartily and earnestly. They knew that the authority of the powers was God's ordinance, and therefore, both in their words and deeds, they taught ever obedience to it and never taught, nor did the contrary. The wicked judge, Pilate, said to Christ, "Knowest thou not that I have power to crucify thee and have power also to loose thee?" Jesus answered, "Thou couldst have no power at all against me, except it

---

1 *Chrysostom* John Chrysostom (c. 347–407), Bishop of Constantinople and one of the Church Fathers. The citation is to Chrysostom's commentary, *In Epistolam ad Romanos* (On the Epistle to the Romans).

2 *forasmuch as they resist ... authority* See Romans 13.2.

3 *in any case* In any situation or example.

were given thee from above."[1] Whereby Christ taught us plainly that even the wicked rulers have their power and authority from God. And therefore it is not lawful for their subjects by force to resist them, although they abuse their power, much less than it is lawful for subjects to resist their godly and Christian princes which do not abuse their authority, but use the same to God's glory and to the profit and commodity of God's people.

The holy apostle St. Peter commandeth servants to be obedient to their masters, not only if they be good and gentle, but also if they be evil and froward,[2] affirming that the vocation and calling of God's people is to be patient and of the suffering side. And there he bringeth in the patience of our saviour Christ to persuade obedience to governors, yea, although they be wicked and wrong doers. But let us now hear St. Peter himself speak, for his own words certify best our conscience. Thus he uttereth them in his first Epistle:

> Servants, obey your masters with fear, not only if they be good and gentle, but also if they be froward.
>
> For it is thankworthy, if a man for conscience toward God suffereth grief and suffereth wrong undeserved,
>
> For what praise is it, when ye be beaten for your faults, if ye take it patiently? But when ye do well, if you then suffer wrong and take it patiently, then is there cause to have thank[3] of God;
>
> For hereunto verily were ye called. For so did Christ suffer for us, leaving us an example that we should follow his steps.[4]

All these be the very words of St. Peter.

St. David also teacheth us a good lesson in this behalf, who was many times most cruelly and wrongfully persecuted of King Saul and many times also put in jeopardy and danger of his life by King Saul

---

1 *Knowest ... from above* John 19.10–11.
2 *froward* Contrary, unreasonable.
3 *thank* Thanks.
4 *Servants ... follow his steps* 1 Peter 2.18–21.

and his people.[1] Yet he never resisted, neither used any force or violence against King Saul, his mortal enemy, but did ever to his liege lord and master, King Saul, most true, most diligent, and most faithful service. Insomuch that when the Lord God had given King Saul into David's hands in his own cave, he would not hurt him, when he might without all bodily peril easily have slain him; no, he would not suffer any of his servants once to lay their hands upon King Saul, but prayed to God in this wise: "Lord, keep me from doing that thing unto my master, the Lord's anointed; keep me that I lay not my hand upon him, seeing he is the anointed of the Lord. For as truly as the Lord liveth, except the Lord smite him, or except his day come, or that he go down to war and in battle perish, the Lord be merciful unto me, that I lay not my hand upon the Lord's anointed."[2]

And that David might have killed his enemy, King Saul, it is evidently proved in the first Book of the Kings, both by the cutting of the lap of Saul's garment and also by the plain confession of King Saul. Also another time, as it is mentioned in the same book, when the most unmerciful and most unkind King Saul did persecute poor David, God did again give King Saul into David's hands by casting of King Saul and his whole army into a dead sleep, so that David and one Abishai with him came in the night into Saul's host where Saul lay sleeping and his spear stuck in the ground at his head. Then said Abishai unto David, "God hath delivered thine enemy into thy hands at this time; now, therefore, let me smite him once with my spear to the earth, and I will not smite him again the second time" meaning thereby to have killed him with one stroke and to have made him sure forever. And David answered, and said to Abishai, "Destroy him not, for who can lay his hands on the Lord's anointed and be guiltless?" And David said furthermore, "As sure as the Lord liveth, the Lord shall smite him, or his day shall come to die, or he shall descend into battle, and there perish. The Lord keep me from laying my hands upon the Lord's anointed. But take thou now the spear that is at his head and the cruse of water, and let us go."[3] And so he did. Here is evidently proved that we may not resist, nor in any ways hurt

---

1 *St. David ... people* See 1 Samuel 18–31 for the story of Saul's tortured relations with David.

2 *Lord, keep me ... anointed* This quote conflates 1 Samuel 24.6–7 and 26.10–11.

3 *cruse* Small jar or bottle; *casting of King Saul ... let us go* 1 Samuel 26.5–12.

an anointed king, which is God's lieutenant, vicegerent, and highest minister in that country where he is king.

But peradventure, some here would say that David in his own defence might have killed King Saul lawfully and with a safe conscience. But holy David did know that he might in no wise resist, hurt, or kill his sovereign lord and king. He did know that he was but King Saul's subject, though he were in great favour with God, and his enemy, King Saul, out of God's favour. Therefore, though he were never so much provoked, yet he refused utterly to hurt the Lord's anointed. He durst not, for offending God and his own conscience, although he had occasion and opportunity, once lay his hands upon God's high officer, the king, whom he did know to be a person reserved, for his office sake, only to God's punishment and judgment. Therefore, he prayeth so oft and so earnestly that he lay not his hands upon the Lord's anointed. And by these two examples St. David, being named in Scripture a man after God's own heart,[1] giveth a general rule and lesson to all subjects in the world not to resist their liege lord and king, not to take a sword by their private authority against their king, God's anointed, who only beareth the sword by God's authority for the maintenance of the good and for the punishment of the evil, who only by God's law hath the use of the sword at his commandment, and also hath all power, jurisdiction, regiment,[2] and coercion as supreme governor of all his realms and dominions, and that, even by the authority of God and by God's ordinances.

Yet another notable story and doctrine is in the second Book of the Kings that maketh also for this purpose. When an Amalechite, by King Saul's own consent and commandment, had killed King Saul, he went to David supposing to have had great thanks for his message that he had killed David's mortal enemy, and therefore he made great haste to tell to David the chance, bringing with him King Saul's crown that was upon his head and his bracelet that was upon his arm to persuade his tidings to be true. But godly David was so far from rejoicing at these news that immediately he rent his clothes of his back; he mourned and wept, and said to the messenger, "How is it that thou wert not afraid to lay thy hands on the Lord's anointed to destroy him?" And by and by, David made one of his servants to kill

---

1   *a man after God's own heart* 1 Samuel 13.14.
2   *regiment* Rule.

the messenger, saying, "Thy blood be on thine own head, for thy own mouth hath testified against thee, granting that thou hast slain the Lord's anointed."[1]

These examples being so manifest and evident, it is an intolerable ignorance, madness, and wickedness for subjects to make any murmuring, rebellion, resistance, commotion, or insurrection against their most dear and most dread sovereign lord and king, ordained and appointed of God's goodness for their commodity, peace, and quietness.

Yet let us believe undoubtedly, good Christian people, that we may not obey kings, magistrates, or any other, though they be our own fathers, if they would command us to do anything contrary to God's commandments. In such a case, we ought to say with the apostles, "We must rather obey God than man."[2]

But nevertheless, in that case, we may not in any wise resist violently or rebel against rulers, or make any insurrection, sedition, or tumults, either by force of arms or other ways, against the anointed of the Lord or any of his appointed officers. But we must in such case patiently suffer all wrongs and injuries, referring the judgment of our cause only to God. Let us fear the terrible punishment of almighty God against traitors or rebellious persons by the example of Korah, Dathan, and Abiram, which repined and grudged against God's magistrates and officers, and therefore the earth opened, and swallowed them up alive.[3] Other, for their wicked murmuring and rebellion, were by a sudden fire sent of God utterly consumed. Other, for their froward behaviour to their rulers and governors, God's ministers, were suddenly stricken with a foul leprosy.[4] Other were stinged to death with wonderful strange fiery serpents.[5] Other were sore plagued, so that there was killed in one day the number of fourteen thousand and

---

1   *When an Amalechite ... the Lord's anointed*   2 Samuel 1.1–16.

2   *Yet let us ... man*   This passage anticipates the arguments of the Protestant resistance theorists who went into exile when Edward's sister, the Catholic Mary Tudor, became queen in 1553. For example, Christopher Goodman (c. 1520–1603) argues in *How Superior Powers Ought to Be Obeyed of Their Subjects* (1558) that a monarch who defies God's law (i.e., Catholic monarchs) merits not just disobedience, but active resistance.

3   *repined*   Complained;   *Korah ... alive*   Leaders of a revolt against Moses who were eventually punished by God (Numbers 16.1–35).

4   *stricken with a foul leprosy*   See Numbers 12.9–10.

5   *stinged ... fiery serpents*   See Numbers 21.6.

seven hundred for rebellion against them whom God had appointed to be in authority.[1] Absalom also, rebelling against his father King David, was punished with a strange and notable death.[2]

And let no man think that he can escape unpunished that committeth treason, conspiracy, or rebellion against his sovereign lord, the king, though he commit the same never so secretly, either in thought, word, or deed; never so privily, in his privy chamber by himself, or openly communicating and consulting with other. For treason will not be hid; treason will out at the length. God will have that most detestable vice both opened and punished, for that it is so directly against his ordinance and against his high principal judge and anointed in earth. The violence and injury that is committed against authority is committed against God, the commonweal, and the whole realm, which God will have known and condignly punished, one way or other. For it is notably written of the wise man in Scripture, in the book called Ecclesiastes, "Wish the king no evil in thy thought, or speak no hurt of him in thy privy chamber, for a bird of the air shall betray thy voice, and with her feathers shall she bewray thy words."[3] These lessons and examples are written for our learning. Let us all, therefore, fear the most detestable vice of rebellion, ever knowing and remembering that he that resisteth common authority resisteth God and his ordinance, as it may be proved by many other more places of Holy Scripture.

And here let us take heed that we understand not these or such other like places which so straightly command obedience to superiors, and so straightly punisheth rebellion and disobedience to the same, to be meant in any condition of the pretenced power of the Bishop of Rome.[4] For truly the Scripture of God alloweth no such usurped power, full of enormities, abusions,[5] and blasphemies. But the true meaning of these and such places be to extol and set forth God's true ordinance and the authority of God's anointed kings, and of their officers appointed under them. And concerning the usurped power

---

1 *Other were sore plagued ... authority* Numbers 16.41–50.
2 *Absalom ... notable death* Absalom was caught in a tree while riding his mule and slain by his father's supporter Joab (2 Samuel 18.9–17).
3 *Wish ... thy words* Ecclesiastes 10.20.
4 *Bishop of Rome* The Pope.
5 *abusions* Abuses.

of the Bishop of Rome, which he most wrongfully challengeth[1] as the successor of Christ and Peter, we may easily perceive how false, feigned, and forged it is, not only in that it hath no sufficient ground in Holy Scripture, but also by the fruits and doctrine thereof. For our saviour Christ and St. Peter teacheth most earnestly and agreeably obedience to kings, as to the chief and supreme rulers in this world, next under God. But the Bishop of Rome teacheth immunities, privileges, exemptions, and disobedience, most clearly against Christ's doctrine and St. Peter's. He ought, therefore, rather to be called Antichrist and the successor of the Scribes and Pharisees than Christ's vicar, or St. Peter's successor, seeing that not only in this point, but also in other weighty matters of Christian religion, in matters of remission of sins and of salvation, he teacheth so directly against both St. Peter and against our saviour Christ, who not only taught obedience to kings, but also practiced obedience in their conversation and living. For we read that they both payed tribute to the King.[2] And also we read that the holy Virgin Mary, mother to our saviour Christ, and Joseph, who was taken for his father, at the Emperor's commandment went to the city of David, named Bethlehem, to be taxed among other and to declare their obedience to the magistrates for God's ordinance's sake.[3]

And here let us not forget the blessed Virgin Mary's obedience, for although she was highly in God's favour and Christ's natural mother, and was also great with child that same time, and so nigh her travail[4] that she was delivered in her journey, yet she gladly, without any excuse or grudging, for conscience sake did take that cold and foul winter journey, being in the mean season[5] so poor that she lay in the stable, and there she was delivered of Christ. And according to the same, lo how St. Peter agreeth, writing by express words in his first Epistle: "Submit yourselves," sayeth he, "unto kings, as unto the chief heads or unto rulers, as unto them that are sent of him for the punishment of evil doers and for laud of them that do well, for so is the will of God."[6] I need not to expound these words: they be so plain of themselves. St. Peter doth not say, "submit yourselves unto me, as

---

1   *challengeth* Claims.
2   *they both payed tribute to the King* See Matthew 22.21, 17.24–27.
3   *the holy Virgin Mary ... ordinance's sake* See Luke 2.1–5.
4   *travail* Labor.
5   *mean season* Meanwhile.
6   *laud* Praise; *Submit ... God* 1 Peter 2.13–14.

supreme head of the Church"; neither he sayeth, "submit yourselves from time to time to my successors in Rome." But he sayeth, "Submit yourselves unto your king, your supreme head, and unto those that he appointeth in authority under him." For that ye shall so show your obedience, it is the will of God. God will that you be in subjection to your head and king. That is God's ordinance, God's commandment, and God's holy will, that the whole body of every realm and all the members and parts of the same shall be subject to their head, their king, and that, as St. Peter writeth, "for the Lord's sake" and, as St. Paul writeth, "for conscience sake, and not for fear only."[1] Thus we learn by the word of God to yield to our king that is due to our king: that is, honour, obedience, payments of due taxes, customs, tributes, subsidies, love, and fear.

Thus we know partly our bounden duties to common authority. Now let us learn to accomplish the same. And let us most instantly and heartily pray to God, the only author of all authority, for all them that be in authority, according as St. Paul willeth, writing thus to Timothy in his first Epistle: "I exhort, therefore, that above all things, prayers, supplications, intercessions and giving of thanks be done for all men: for kings and for all that be in authority, that we may live a quiet and a peaceable life with all godliness and honesty, for that is good and accepted in the sight of God our saviour."[2] Here St. Paul maketh an earnest and an especial exhortation, concerning giving of thanks and prayer for kings and rulers, saying above all things, as he might say in any wise principally and chiefly, let prayer be made for kings. Let us heartily thank God for his great and excellent benefit and providence concerning the state of kings. Let us pray for them, that they may have God's favour and God's protection. Let us pray that they may ever in all things have God before their eyes. Let us pray that they may have wisdom, strength, justice, clemency, and zeal to God's glory, to God's verity, to Christian souls, and to the commonwealth. Let us pray that they may rightly use their sword and authority for the maintenance and defence of the catholic[3] faith, contained in Holy Scripture, and of their good and honest subjects, and for the fear and punishment of the evil and vicious people. Let us pray

---

1   *for conscience ... only*   Romans 13.5.
2   *I exhort ... saviour*   1 Timothy 2.1–3.
3   *catholic*   Universal, not to be confused with the Catholic Church, led by the Pope.

that they may faithfully follow the most faithful kings and captains in the Bible: David, Hezekiah, Josiah and Moses, with such other. And let us pray for ourselves, that we may live godly, in holy and Christian conversation, so we shall have God of our side.[1] And then let us not fear what man can do against us, so we shall live in true obedience, both to our most merciful king in Heaven and to our most Christian king in earth. So shall we please God, and have the exceeding benefit, peace of conscience, rest and quietness here in this world, and after this life we shall enjoy a better life, rest, peace, and the eternal bliss of Heaven, which he grant us all, that was obedient for us all, even to the death of the cross, Jesus Christ: to whom with the Father and the Holy Ghost be all honour and glory, both now and ever. Amen.

3. from "An Homily against Disobedience and Willful Rebellion" (1570)

> First published in 1570 as a response to the Northern Rebellion, this homily was included in the second edition of *The Second Tome of Homilies* (1571). This text focuses exclusively on the evils of rebellion. The "Exhortation"'s emphasis on mutuality, on each class "having need of the other," is entirely absent.

The First Part

As God the creator and Lord of all things appointed his angels and heavenly creatures in all obedience to serve and to honour his majesty, so was it his will that man, his chief creature upon the earth, should live under the obedience of his creator and Lord, and for that cause, God, as soon as he had created man, gave unto him a certain precept and law, which he (being yet in the state of innocence, and remaining in Paradise) should observe as a pledge and token of his due and bounden obedience, with denunciation of death if he did transgress and break the said law and commandment. And as God would have man to be his obedient subject, so did he make all earthly creatures subject unto man, who kept their due obedience unto man so long as man remained in his obedience unto God, in

---

1 *of* On; *let us pray … our side* Likely an allusion to Psalm 118.6.

the which obedience if man had continued still, there had been no poverty, no diseases, no sickness, no death, nor other miseries wherewith mankind is now infinitely and most miserably afflicted and oppressed. So here appears the original kingdom of God over angels and man, and universally over all things, and of man over earthly creatures which God had made subject unto him, and with all the felicity and blessed state, which angels, man, and all creatures had remained in, had they continued in due obedience unto God their King. For as long as in this first kingdom the subjects continued in due obedience to God their king, so long did God embrace all his subjects with his love, favour, and grace, which to enjoy, is perfect felicity, whereby it is evident, that obedience is the principal virtue of all virtues, and indeed the very root of all virtues, and the cause of all felicity. But as all felicity and blessedness should have continued with the continuance of obedience, so with the breach of obedience and breaking in of rebellion, all vices and miseries did withal break in, and overwhelm the world.

The first author of which rebellion, the root of all vices, and mother of all mischief, was Lucifer, first God's most excellent creature, and most bounden subject, who by rebelling against the majesty of God, of the brightest and most glorious angel is become the blackest and most foulest fiend and devil: and from the height of heaven, is fallen into the pit and bottom of hell. Here you may see the first author and founder of rebellion, and the reward thereof, here you may see the grand captain and father of rebels, who persuading the following of his rebellion against God their creator and Lord, unto our first parents Adam and Eve, brought them in high displeasure with God, wrought their exile and banishment out of Paradise, a place of all pleasure and goodness, into this wretched earth and vale of misery, procured unto them sorrows of their minds, mischief, sickness, diseases, death of their bodies, and which is far more horrible than all worldly and bodily mischief, he had wrought thereby their eternal and everlasting death and damnation, had not God, by the obedience of his son Jesus Christ repaired that which man by disobedience and rebellion had destroyed, and so of his mercy had pardoned and forgiven him: of which all and singular the premises, the holy Scriptures do bear record in sundry places....

What shall subjects do then? Shall they obey valiant, stout, wise, and good princes, and condemn, disobey, and rebel against children being their princes, or against indiscreet and evil governors? God forbid! For first, what a perilous thing were it to commit unto the subjects the judgment which prince is wise and godly, and his government good, and which is otherwise, as though the foot must judge of the head: an enterprise very heinous, and must needs breed rebellion. For who else be they that are most inclined to rebellion, but such haughty spirits? From whom springs such foul ruin of realms? Is not rebellion the greatest of all mischief? And who are most ready to the greatest mischief, but the worst men? Rebels, therefore, the worst of all subjects, are most ready to rebellion, as being the worst of all vices and farthest from the duty of a good subject. As on the contrary part, the best subjects are most firm and constant in obedience, as in the special and peculiar virtue of good subjects. What an unworthy matter were it then to make the naughtiest subjects and most inclined to rebellion and all evil, judges over their princes, over their government, and over their counsellors, to determine which of them be good or tolerable, and which be evil, and so intolerable that they must needs be removed by rebels, being ever ready as the naughtiest subjects, soonest to rebel against the best princes, specially if they be young in age, women in sex, or gentle and courteous in government, as trusting by their wicked boldness, easily to overthrow their weakness and gentleness; or at the least, so to fear the minds of such princes that they may have impunity of their mischievous doings....

4. from Pedro Mexía, *The Forest, Or Collection of Histories No Less Profitable than Pleasant and Necessary, Done Out of French into English by Thomas Fortescue* (1571)

Written by Pedro Mexía, Spanish humanist and historian (1497–1551), *Silva de varia lección* (A Miscellany of Several Lessons) was first published in 1540, and it became an international best seller, with translations into Italian (1542), French (1552), and English (1571; reprinted in 1576). The title page states that the present translation was "done out of French to English," and the voyage across three languages helps to explain the awkwardness of the prose.

Chapter 18: That men born of base condition should not leave by all means possible to attempt to reach and aspire unto honour with certain examples serving to that purpose.

Generally, we see that men descending of a noble house or family became also in time very brilliant and honourable, imitating the noblest of their birth and virtue of their ancestors. Howbeit, for that there is no law nor rule so certain which suffereth or admitteth not some kind of exception, this also may be said to fail with the others, for sometimes, the father, wise, learned, advised and honest, hath a son idle, abject, less wise and unprofitable. And yet again, admit that this rule were more certain, more infallible, and more assured than indeed it is, yet should not they that descend of poor and mean parentage leave to attempt by incessant pain and industry to aspire to the seat of virtue and honour? For that these families that this day are reputed for ancient and noble have taken their beginning and spring of virtue, nobling[1] their posterity and successors with honour. Wherefore the better to animate men to aspire to great matters, I will remember the examples of some in particular issuing out of mean and simple parentage which in the end excelled in honour and virtue.

And in the first place, Viriat, a Portugale[2] so much renowned among the historians, especially Romans, on whom he eftsoons did cruel and bloody revenge. This man was the son of a poor shepherd, and in his youth aided his father in his charge, but having his heart inclined to matters more high and of greater importance, left to keep sheep[3] and other tamed beasts, following more busily the chase of the wild and the savage, wherein he excelled in courage all others. After this the Romans invading the Spaniards, he gather and assembled certain his companions, by whose help he skirmished at times with the enemy. At times also, again for practice, with his friends, where he so valiant was, so noble and courageous, that in few days he had gathered an army sufficient with which, being entered the field, he gave battle the Romans in defence of that country,[4] which

---

1   *nobling*   Ennobling.
2   *Viriat*   Viriathus (d. c. 140 BCE) led the resistance against the Roman invasion of present-day Spain. He was assassinated, probably at Rome's behest;   *Portugale*   Portuguese.
3   *left to keep sheep*   Left the keeping of sheep to others.
4   *again*   Likely a printer error for "against";   *that country*   Spain.

wars, or rather, enmity, continued fourteen years, during which time he obtained against them sundry great and honourable victories. By means whereof he grew in honour and authority, dread[1] and feared for his prowess continually of his enemy. But in fine,[2] unkindly by treason was slain to the great discomfort and sorrow of all his army, by which he was (as duty would) most pompously buried.

Arsaces,[3] king of the Parthians, was of such base and simple parentage that no man could speak of or knew any of parents. Who, after he had withdrawn himself from the subjection and obedience of Alexander, he ordained the first kingdom that ever was among the Parthians, a people no less renowned than dread, indeed, of the Romans.[4] By means of whose only passing prowess and valiancy, all other kings his successors, for the sole memory and reverence of his name, though they never were crowned, by inheritance or succession, were called Arsiades, as the Roman emperors took also the name of Caesar for the love of great Caesar Octavian Augustus.

That excellent captain, Agathocles,[5] which for his surpassing wisdom and manhood was created king of Sicilia and maintained cruel battle against the people of Carthage was, not withstanding, of a mean family, that, as I remember, his father was a potter. Whence, he being advanced to the honour of a king, did nevertheless as often times, as he banqueted, his table to be furnished with vessels as well of clay as also of gold or silver, to the intent he still might have in mind and remember the place of his beginnings, his father's house and family.

The example also of Ptolemy[6] well serveth the purpose, being one of the most worthiest captains of Alexander, after whose death, he became king of Egypt and of Syria, such and so virtuous, that

---

1   *dread*   Dreaded.

2   *But in fine*   But in the end.

3   *Arsaces*   Arsaces I (c. third century BCE), founder of the Arsacid dynasty, which ruled Parthia (present day Iran) until 224 CE.

4   *a people ... Romans*   The syntax seems confused, but the sense is that the Parthians were both dreaded and renowned among the Romans.

5   *Agathocles*   King of Sicily from 304 to 289 BCE. In *The Prince*, Machiavelli uses Agathocles as an example of someone who comes to power through a combination of "wickedness" and "skill of mind and body."

6   *Ptolemy*   Ptolemy I Soter, (c. 367–c. 283 BCE), one of Alexander the Great's most trusted generals and his eventual successor. His father, however, was probably a nobleman, not a "common horseman."

his successors there would after him be called all "Ptolemys." This Ptolemy was the son of a gentleman that highte[1] Lac, which never had better office than that of common horseman in the camp of Alexander.

Iphicrates,[2] an Athenian, was in martial affairs very well skilled. He vanquished the Lacedaemonians in plain and open battle, and valiantly withstood the impetuosity of Epaminondas, a captain Theban, both renowned and honourable. The same he was whom Artaxerxes, King of Persia, assigned captain general over all his whole army, when he had to do or belt[3] with the Egyptians. Yet know we nevertheless, as is evidently written of him, that he was the son of none other than a poor cobbler.

I had almost passed over Eumenes, one of the most worthiest captains of Alexander, as well for his valiancy as learning and good counsel, whose life and famous gests are recorded of Plutarch and Paulus Aemilius,[4] who, concerning wealth and abundance of riches, though he were less gracious in the fight of fortune, yet was he in the policies of war second to no man, renowned and honourably by his own only demerits,[5] by no man advanced but by his only pain and travail, being the son of a poor man and, as some deem, a carter.

Among all other seigniories and honours in the world, none was there ever so great and so puissant as was that sometimes of the empire of Rome, which ordered[6] continually by such excellent personages, so ripe in virtue, so absolute and so perfect, and yet for all that sundry have there attained even unto the highest and sovereign degree of government descending of very simple and of base parentage. Elius Pertinax, Emperor of Rome, was the son of a certain artificer, his grandfather a libertine (which is to say, such as was sometimes a

---

1   *highte*   Was named.
2   *Iphicrates*   Athenian general (c. 418–c. 353 BCE) known for success in battle and reforming weaponry.
3   *belt*   Fight.
4   *Eumenes*   General under Alexander the Great (c. 362–c. 316 BCE) and secretary to both Philip II and Alexander; *gests* Deeds; *Plutarch* Greek historian (c. 46–120 CE) who became a Roman citizen and is best known for the *Parallel Lives*, a series of biographies of Greek and Roman political and mythical figures; *Paulus Aemilius* Probably Paulus Aemilius Veronensis (c. 1455–1529), Italian historian, although he wrote on French kings, not the classical world.
5   *demerits*   Merits.
6   *ordered*   Was ruled.

bondman but was again afterward for some just cause enfranchised) that notwithstanding, for his virtue and honesty was assigned by the Romans their sovereign and emperor, and afterward, to give example to others of low condition, he caused the shop to be done about[1] with marble curiously cut where his father before him wrought to get his living. Neither aspired this Elius, issued of base parentage, unto the Empire only, for Diocletian, that so much adorned Rome with his magnifical[2] and triumphant victories, was the son of none other than a common scribe or notary. Some say that his father was a bookbinder, and himself a bondman born.

Valentinian was also crowned Emperor, but was the son notwithstanding of a roper.[3] The Emperor Probus had to father a gardener.[4] The renowned Aurelius, whom every age honoureth, issued out of so obscure a family that the historiographers less agree[5] among themselves of his living and beginning. Maximinus[6] also was the son of a smith, or other some will, a carter. Marcus Julius Lucinus, also as Bonosus, by their prudent policy governed the said empire of which the first was an husbandman's son of Dacia, the other the son of a poor and stipendary[7] school master. Of this sort was there many other emperors in Rome, whom all for brevity's sake I leave to

---

1   *Elius Pertinax*   Helvius Pertinax (126–193 CE) was declared Emperor of Rome after the praetorian guards assassinated Commodus, but ruled for only 86 days before the guards assassinated him as well;   *bondman*   Slave;   *done about*   Decorated with.

2   *Diocletian*   Emperor from 284 to 305, when he voluntarily abdicated the throne, the only Roman Emperor to do so;   *magnifical*   Magnificent.

3   *Valentinian*   Probably Valentinian I (321–75), founder of the Valentinian dynasty. His inclusion is probably an error, as Valentinian's father was a patrician;   *roper*   Ropemaker.

4   *Probus*   Marcus Aurelius Probus (232–82). His parentage is uncertain. Some sources claim his father was a tribune, others say a gardener, but at some point he joined the Roman army and eventually became a general. His troops declared him Emperor in 276;   *had to father a gardener*   Probus' father was a gardener.

5   *Aurelius*   Marcus Aurelius (121–80 CE), also author of the *Meditations*, an important statement of Stoic philosophy. His family was not obscure, but distinguished;   *less agree*   Cannot agree.

6   *Maximinus*   Two Roman emperors had this name: Maximinus Thrax (c. 173–238) and Maximinus Daia (c. 270–313). Both came from non-aristocratic families.

7   *Bonosus*   Soldier (c. 281 CE) who rose through the ranks to become a general under Probus. Having allowed the Germans to burn his fleet, he tried to save his life by declaring himself emperor. He committed suicide after a lengthy struggle. This passage again demonstrates Mexía's sometimes unsure grasp of Roman history; there is no Roman emperor named "Marcus Julius Lucinus," and Bonosus never ruled. The author attributes to "Lucinus" and Bonosus the biographies of Maximinus Thrax and Maximinus Daia;   *stipendary*   Salaried.

remember, as Mauricius Justinus,[1] predecessor to Justinian. Galerus[2] also, in the beginning, [was] a shepherd.

From this haughty and supreme dignity, let us descend to the see of Rome, unto which aspired men of like condition with the others. As Pope John XXII, which was the son of a shoemaker, a Frenchman born, notwithstanding,[3] for his learning and wisdom, elected bishop, which increased their rents and patrimony busily. Pope Nicholas V, having the name tofore[4] of Thomas, was the son of a poor poulterer. Pope Sixtus IV,[5] first called Francis, by profession a friar, had to father a poor seaman or mariner. I could in this place remember many others, whom all of purpose I leave to name for that such offices are less due to nobility of blood, but rather to the learned and virtuous whatsoever. Whereof Christ himself hath left us good example, for the first that ever sat in that chair, whom also Christ himself there placed, was that good and true pastor, Saint Peter, which before laboured the seas for his living [as] a fisher, whom from thence Christ elected to be a fisher of men.[6]

Hence descending again unto kings and princes, the Romans to them chose Tarquinus Priscus[7] for their king, the son of a stranger and merchant of Corinth, and that which more was banished out of his country, who nevertheless augmented the confines of kingdom, the number as well of senators, as also then of the order of knighthood. He appointed new estates both for their service and ceremo-

---

1   *leave to remember*   Decline to remember, to list;   *Mauricius Justinus*   Justin or Justinian I (c. 482–565), originally a lowly soldier, rose through the ranks of the palace guards and was declared emperor in 518. Rome at this time had split into two, and Justinian I ruled the eastern, Byzantine half.

2   *Galerus*   Galerius (c. 260–311), originally a shepherd; nothing is known of his rise until he became emperor in 293.

3   *Pope John XXII*   Pope elected in 1316;   *son of a shoemaker … notwithstanding*   Notwithstanding his low birth and his nationality.

4   *Pope Nicholas V*   Pope elected in 1447;   *tofore*   Heretofore, before; his father was a physician, not a dealer in poultry.

5   *Pope Sixtus IV*   Pope elected in 1471. A patron of the arts, he commissioned the building of the Sistine Chapel.

6   *fisher of men*   See Matthew 4.18–19.

7   *Tarquinus Priscus*   Legendary fifth king of Rome (said to have ruled from c. 616–579 BCE). While originally from the Etruscan city of Tarquinii (not Corinth), he was far from poor. According to legend, his grandson, Sextus Tarquinius (son of Tarquin the Proud), raped Lucretia, who then committed suicide. This act led the Romans to abolish the monarchy and establish a republic.

nies to the gods, so that the people nothing at all repented them to have chosen them a stranger to their king and sovereign. Servius Tullius[1] lived also long time King of Rome. He obtained great victories and triumphed three times, reputed notwithstanding to be the son of a poor bondwoman, whence he continually held the name "Servius."[2]

The kings of Lombardy,[3] if they were not so ancient as the others of Rome, yet were they in respect no less famous than they. The third of which having to name Lamusius[4] was the son of a beggarly and common strumpet, which also being delivered at the same time of two other children, as a most wretched and beastly woman, threw them into a deep and stinking ditch in which also was some kind of water. By hap King Agelmund,[5] passing that way, found this child almost drowned in the water, and moving him softly with the end of his lance, which he at that time had present there in hand, to the end he more perfectly might feel what it was, but this child, even then newly born, feeling itself touched, taketh hold of the lance with one of his hands, not letting it slip or slide from him again. Which things the prince considering, all amazed at the strange force of this young little creature, caused it to be taken thence and carefully to be fostered, and for that the place where he found it was called Lama, he bid him thence to be named Lamasius. Which afterwards was such a one and so favoured of fortune that in the end he was crowned king of the Lombards, who lived there in honour, and his succession after him even until the times of the unfortunate King Alboin,[6] when all came to ruin, subversion and destruction.

Another matter like strange to this happened in Bohemia, whereas one Primislas,[7] the son of a ploughman, was then chosen king when he most busily was labouring the soil in the field. For at that time,

---

1   *Servius Tullius*   Legendary sixth king of Rome (reigned c. 578–535 BCE), whose mother was a slave in the royal household.

2   *bondwoman*   Slave;   *Servius*   It was commonly believed that "Servius" was derived from the Latin word "servus," meaning "slave."

3   *Lombardy*   Very wealthy area in northern Italy. Today, Milan is the capital.

4   *Lamusius*   Lamissio (c. 363–420), legendary king of Lombardy.

5   *hap*   Chance;   *King Agelmund*   Second king of Lombardy, also legendary.

6   *King Alboin*   Ruler of Lombardy (c. 530–72) whose assassination by his wife and foster-brother led to significant political turmoil.

7   *this*   The story of Lamasius;   *Primislas*   Přemysl the Ploughman (c. 9th century), legendary ruler of Bohemia.

the Bohemians, not knowing who they might choose for their king, did to pass out a horse unbridled into the fields, letting him to go whither it best liked him, having all determined with most assured purpose to make him their king before whom this horse arrested. So, it came to pass that the horse first stayed him before this Primislas, busied then in turning the glebe,[1] a simple carter. So, being forthwith confirmed (as is before) their sovereign, he ordered himself and his kingdom very wisely. He ordained many good and profitable laws, he compassed the city of Prague with walls, besides many other things, meriting perpetual laud and commendation. The great Tamburlaine also, whose famous exploits are of part above remembered, was at the first a shepherd, as we before rehearsed.[2] The valiant and virtuous captain,[3] father of Francis Sforca, whose succession and posterity, even until this our time, have been dukes continually of Milan, was born in a bad village called Cotignol, the son of a poor and needy workman. But he, naturally inclined to martial affairs, of a valiant heart and very courageous, left that his father's simple vocation, following a troop of soldiers which past through the country, and in th'end, by continuance and skilled practice proveth a most famous and renowned captain.

C. Marius, a consul Roman, issued of simple parentage, born in the village Arpinum, was nevertheless such and so politic a captain that all the world yet spaketh[4] to this day of valiancy. He seven times was chosen consul in Rome, during which time he obtained such and so great victories that he also twice (to his perpetual honour and commendation) triumphed. M.T. Cicero, the father and prince of Latin eloquence, well skilled also in every the sciences,[5] was consul in

---

1   *glebe*   Earth.

2   *Tamburlaine*   Turko-Mongol ruler, also known as Timur (1336–1405), who conquered much of Asia. Also subject of Christopher Marlowe's two-part play, *Tamburlaine the Great* (1587–88);   *we before rehearsed*   Not in the English version of this chapter.

3   *The valiant and virtuous captain*   Giacomo Attendolo (1369–1424), military commander and father of Francesco Sforza, ruler of Milan. His father was not poor, but wealthy, if rural, nobility. According to legend, Giacomo was plowing a field when a troop of mercenaries rode by, and he stole one of his father's horses to join them.

4   *C. Marius*   Gaius Marius (157–86 BCE), Roman general and statesman, elected consul for an unprecedented seven times. The claim that Marius' father was a laborer originates in Plutarch, but is likely untrue. "C." is an error;   *spaketh*   Speaketh.

5   *M.T. Cicero*   Marcus Tullius Cicero (106–43 BCE), Roman statesman and rhetorician, considered Rome's greatest prose stylist. His family was not in fact poor, although Plutarch

Rome and proconsul in Asia, and yet was also born in a simple cottage in Arpinum, by birth and parentage a very mean and abject Roman. Ventidius[1] also the son of a most simple and abject personage, was sometimes by profession a muleteer, but leaving that vocation, followed the wars of Caesar, by whose favour he obtained through his prowess and virtue, that he shortly was appointed captain of a band, and after that again under him, generally the whole army, and from thence was called to the honour of a bishop, and in fine, from thence mounted to the estate of a consul, who, waging battle to the Parthians, triumphantly conquered them and was that first that ever apparently and thoroughly quailed their courages.[2]

It should also belong in this place to remember all those that issuing from obscure race or parentage have notwithstanding by their excellency in learning been advanced to great estimation and honour. Virgil[3] was the son of none other than a potter, yet aspired he to be called the best poet among the Latins. Horace,[4] in mine opinion, excelled in poetry, no prince of birth, but much like unto th'others. Eustatius and Pampinus were the sons of two that had been bondmen, but both were manumitted.[5] Theophrastus,[6] the philosopher, had to father a tailor or butcher. Menedemus,[7] also to whom for his singular learning the Athenians erected a sumptuous image, was the son of a poor artificer.

---

records a legend that Cicero's grandfather was a blacksmith; *every the sciences* All the sciences, areas of knowledge.

1 *Ventidius* Publius Ventidius Bassus (d. c. 38 BCE), Roman general and one of Julius Caesar's protégés. His origins are obscure, but Ventidius was captured by the Roman army during one of Rome's wars against other Italian cities and forced to work as a muleteer. After enlisting in the Roman army, Ventidius quickly rose and gained Caesar's notice through his military skill.

2 *quailed their courages* Caused the Parthians to retreat in fear.

3 *Virgil* Publius Vergillius Maro (70–19 BCE), author of the *Aeneid*, among other works. One tradition claims that his father was a peasant, but the family's status cannot be confirmed.

4 *Horace* Quintus Horatius Flaccus (65–8 BCE), author of the *Odes*, among other works. While his father, a freed slave, made his living as an auctioneer, he became sufficiently wealthy to send his son to Rome and Athens for his education.

5 *Eustatius and Pampinus* The author mistakenly splits the Roman poet, Statius Publius Papinius (c. 45–96 CE), author of the *Thebaid*, into two people. While one of Statius' ancestors may have been a freed slave, his father was a successful poet and teacher; *manumitted* Freed.

6 *Theophrastus* Athenian philosopher (371–287 BCE). His family history is unknown.

7 *Menedemus* Greek philosopher (c. 345?–261? BCE). His father was a poor builder.

Besides these, we read of infinite others, whom all I pass[1] as a thing most assured and evident. By these examples, it now thus lieth manifest that of what estate soever, or condition man be born, he may if he will attain sometime to honour so that he walk still in the path of virtue,[2] which only is acquired by incessant pain and diligency, with a final consideration of Heaven, our wished city, for whoso otherwise doeth, if he indeed might possibly conquer the whole, the wide and the waste world, what advantage should he have for the same to lose the soul after this life transitory?

5. from *Holinshed's Chronicles* (1577, revised 1587) [on the reaction to the "Amicable Grant"]

> Henry VIII paid for his foreign adventures through various "loans" (he never paid them back), benevolences, and subsidies that caused a great deal of anger, resentment, and at times, outright defiance of royal authority. The "Amicable Grant" (1525) sparked the most serious resistance; it is discussed in the following excerpt from *Holinshed's Chronicles*, a massive history of England first published in 1577 and revised in 1587. The tensions involved are part of the background to Chapter 6 of *Jack of Newbury*.

The king, being determined this to make wars in France and to pass[3] the sea himself in person, his council considered that above all things great treasure and plenty of money must needs be provided. Wherefore, by the Cardinal there was devised strange commissions, and sent in the end of March into every shire, and commissioners appointed, and privy[4] instructions sent to them how they should proceed in their sittings, and order the people to bring them their purpose, which was that the sixth part of every man's substance should be paid in money or plate to the King without delay, for the furniture[5] of his war. Hereof followed such cursing, weeping, and exclamation against both King and Cardinal that pity it was to hear. And to be brief,

---

1 *whom all I pass* All of whom I pass over.
2 *so that he ... virtue* So long as he walks in the path of virtue.
3 *pass* Cross over.
4 *strange* New, novel; *privy* Secret.
5 *furniture* Funding.

notwithstanding all that could be said or done, forged, or devised by the commissioners to persuade the people to this contribution, the same would not be granted. And in excuse of their denial it was alleged that wrong was offered, and the ancient customs and laws of the realm broken, which would not any man to be charged with such payment, except it were granted by the estates of the realm in parliament assembled. The like answer was made by them of the spirituality, of whom was demanded the fourth part of their goods [....] The Cardinal travailed earnestly with the mayor and aldermen of London about the aid of money to be granted, and likewise the commissioners appointed in the shires of the realm sat upon the same, but the burthen[1] was so grievous, that it was generally denied, and the commons in every place so moved that it was like to grow to rebellion.

In Essex the people would not assemble before the commissioners in no houses, but in open places, and in Huntingtonshire diverse resisted the commissioner and would not suffer them to sit, which were apprehended and sent to the Fleet. The Duke of Suffolk,[2] sitting in commission about this subsidy in Suffolk, persuaded by courteous means the rich clothiers to assent thereto, but when they came home, and went about to discharge and put from them their spinners, carders, fullers, weavers, and other artificers, which they kept in work afore time, the people began to assemble in companies. Whereof when the Duke was advertised, he commanded the constables that every man's harness[3] should be taken from him. But when that was known, then the rage of the people increased, railing openly on the Duke, and Sir Robert Drury, and threatened them with death, and the Cardinal[4] also. And herewith there assembled together after the manner of rebels four thousand men of Lanham, Sudbury, Hadley, and other towns thereabouts, which put themselves in harness and rang the bell's alarm, and began to assemble in great number.

The Duke of Suffolk, perceiving this, began to gather such power as he could, but that this was very slender. Yet the gentlemen that were with the Duke did so much that all the bridges were broken, so that

---

1   *travailed* Worked hard;   *burthen* Burden.

2   *Duke of Suffolk* Charles Brandon (c. 1484–1545).

3   *advertised* Notified;   *harness* Arms and armor.

4   *Sir Robert Drury* Important Suffolk lawyer and landowner (c. 1456–1535) who also served as speaker of the House of Parliament;   *Cardinal* Cardinal Thomas Wolsey.

the assembly of those rebels was somewhat letted.[1] The Duke of Norfolk[2] being thereof advertised, gathered a great power in Norfolk and came towards the commons, and sending them to know their intent, received answer that they would live and die in the king's causes and be to him obedient. Hereupon he came himself to talk with them, and willing to know who was their captain, that he might answer for them all. It was told him by one John Greene, a man of fifty years of age, that Poverty was their captain, the which with his cousin, Necessity, had brought them to that doing. For whereas they and a great number of other in that country lived not not [sic] upon themselves, but upon the substantial occupiers, now that they through such payments as were demanded of them, were not able to maintain them in work, they must of necessity perish for want of sustenance.

The Duke hearing this matter, was sorry for their case, and promised them, that if they would depart home to their dwellings, he would be a mean[3] for their pardon to the King. Whereupon they were contented to depart. After this, the Duke of Norfolk and the Duke of Suffolk came to Bury, and thither resorted much people of the country in their shirts, with halters[4] about their necks, meekly desiring pardon for their offences. The Dukes so wisely demeaned themselves that the commons were appeased, and the demand of money ceased in all the realm, for well it was perceived that the commons would pay none. Then went the two Dukes to London, and brought with them the chief captains of the rebellion, which were put in the Fleet.[5] The King then came to Westminster to the Cardinal's palace, and assembled there a great council, in the which he openly protested that his mind was never to ask any thing of his commons which might be found to the breach of his laws, wherefore he willed to know by whose means the commissions were so strictly given forth to demand the sixth part of every man's goods.

The Cardinal excused himself, and said that when it was moved in council how to levy money to the King's use, the King's council, and namely, the judges, said that he might lawfully demand any sum

---

1 *letted* Prevented.
2 *Duke of Norfolk* Thomas Howard (1473–1554).
3 *mean* Means.
4 *halters* Nooses.
5 *the Fleet* London prison.

by commission, and that by the consent of the whole council it was done, and took God to witness that he never desired the hindrance of the commons, but like a true councillor devised how to enrich the King. The king indeed was much offended that his commons were thus entreated, and thought it touched his honour, that his council should attempt such a doubtful matter in his name, and to be denied both of the spirituality and temporality. Therefore he would no more of that trouble, but caused letters to be sent into all shires, that the matter should no further be talked of, and he pardoned all them that had denied the demand openly or secretly. The Cardinal, to deliver himself of the evil will of the commons, purchased by procuring and advancing of this demand, affirmed, and caused it to be bruited[1] abroad that through his intercession the king had pardoned and released all things.

Those that were in the Tower and Fleet for the rebellion in Suffolk and resisting the commissioners as well there as in Huntingtonshire and Kent were brought before the lords in the Star chamber, and there had their offences opened and showed to them, and finally, the King's pardon declared, and thereon they were delivered.

6. from William Harrison, *The Description of England*, in *Holinshed's Chronicles* (1587)

Harrison's *The Description of England*, a three-volume description of England's ancient history, geography, and social structure, prefaced both editions of the *Chronicles*.

Chapter 5: Of degrees of people in the commonwealth of England

We in England divide our people commonly into four sorts: as gentlemen, citizens or burgesses, yeomen, which are artificers, or labourers. Of gentlemen the first and chief (next the king) be the prince, dukes, marquises, earls, viscounts, and barons: and these are called gentlemen of the greater sort, or (as our common usage of speech is) lords and noblemen. And next unto them be knights, esquires, and, last of all, they that are simply called gentlemen, so that in effect our

---

1   *bruited*   Rumored.

gentlemen are divided into their conditions, whereof in this chapter I will make particular rehearsal.

The title of prince doth peculiarly[1] belong with us to the king's eldest son, who is called Prince of Wales, and is the heir apparent to the crown; as in France, the king's eldest son hath the title of "Dolphin," and is named peculiarly "Monsieur." So that the prince is so termed of the Latin word "Princeps," sith[2] he is (as I may call him) the chief or principal next the king. The king's younger sons be but gentlemen by birth (till they have received creation or donation from their father of higher estate, as to be either viscounts, earls, or dukes) and called after their names, as Lord Henry, or Lord Edward, with the addition of the word "Grace," properly assigned to the king and prince, and now also by custom conveyed to dukes, archbishops, and (as some say) to marquises and their wives.[3] ...

Moreover, as the king doth dub knights, and createth the barons and higher degrees, so gentlemen whose ancestors are not known to come in with William, Duke of Normandy (for of the Saxon races yet remaining we now make none accompt,[4] much less of the British issue) do take their beginning in England, after this manner in our times. Whosoever studieth the laws of the realm, who so abideth in the university, giving his mind to his book, or professeth physic[5] and the liberal sciences, or beside his service in the room of a captain in the wars, or good counsel given at home, whereby his commonwealth is benefited, can live without manual labour, and thereto is able and will bear the port, charge, and countenance of a gentleman, he shall for money have a coat and arms bestowed upon him by heralds (who in the charter of the same do of custom pretend antiquity and service, and many gay things) and thereunto being made so good cheap be called "master," which is the title that men give to esquires and gentlemen, and reputed for a gentleman ever after.

Which is so much the less to be disallowed of, for that the prince doth lose nothing by it, the gentleman being so much subject to taxes and public payments as is the yeoman or husbandman, which he

1 *peculiarly* Exclusively.
2 *sith* Since.
3 *The title of prince ... wives* Even though Harrison wrote this passage under Queen Elizabeth, who was preceded by Queen Mary, he does not take daughters into account.
4 *accompt* Account.
5 *physic* Medicine.

likewise doth bear the gladlier for the saving of his reputation. Being called also to the wars (for with the government of the commonwealth he meddleth little), whatsoever it cost him, he will both array and arm himself accordingly, and show the more manly courage, and all the tokens of the person which he representeth. No man hath hurt by it but himself, who peradventure will go in wider buskins than his legs will bear, or as our proverb sayeth, now and then bear a bigger sail than his boat is able to sustain....

Citizens and burgesses have next place to gentlemen, who be those that are free within the cities and are of some likely substance to bear office in the same. But these citizens or burgesses are to serve the commonwealth in their cities and boroughs, or in corporate towns where they dwell. And in the common assembly of the realm wherein our laws are made, for in the counties they bear but little sway (which assembly is called the high court of parliament), the ancient cities appoint four and the boroughs two burgesses to have voices in it, and give their consent or dissent unto such things as pass or stay there in the name of the city or borough for which they are appointed.

In this place also are our merchants to be installed, as amongst the citizens (although they often change estate with gentlemen, as gentlemen do with them, by a mutual conversion of the one into the other) whose number is so increased in these our days, that their only maintenance is the cause of the exceeding[1] prices of foreign wares, which otherwise when every nation was permitted to bring in their own commodities were far better cheap and more plentifully to be had. [...] Whereby we may see the sequel of things not always but very seldom to be such as is pretended in the beginning. The wares that they[2] carry out of the realm, are for the most part broad cloths ... likewise cottons, friezes, rugs, tin, wool, our best beer ... which, being shipped at sundry ports of our coasts, are born from thence into all quarters of the world, and there either exchanged for other wares or ready money to the great gain and commodity of our merchants. And whereas in times past their chief trade was into Spain, Portugal, France, Flanders, Dansk, Norway, Scotland, and Iceland, only now in these days, as men not contented with these journeys, they have sought out the East and West Indies, and made

---

1   *exceeding* Rising.
2   *they* English merchants.

now and then suspicious voyages not only unto the Canaries, and New Spain, but likewise into Cathay,[1] Moscovia, Tartary, and the regions thereabout, from whence (as they say) they bring home great commodities. But alas, I see not by all their travel that the prices of things are any whit abated. Certes, this enormity[2] (for so I do accompt of it) was sufficiently provided for [in] An. 9. Edward 3. by a noble estatute[3] made in that behalf, but upon what occasion the general execution thereof is stayed or not called on, in good sooth I cannot tell. This only I know: that every function and several vocation striveth with other, which of them should have all the water of commodity run into their own cistern....

The fourth and last sort of people in England are day labourers, poor husbandmen, and some retailers[4] (which have no free land) copy holders, and all artificers, as tailors, shoemakers, carpenters, brickmakers, masons, etc. As for slaves and bondmen we have none, nay, such is the privilege of our countrie by the especiall grace of God, and bounty of our princes, that if any come hither from other realms, so soon as they set foot on land they become so free of condition as their masters, whereby all note of servile bondage is utterly removed from them.... This fourth and last sort of people therefore have neither voice nor authority in the common wealth, but are to be ruled, and not to rule other. Yet they are not altogether neglected, for in cities and corporate towns, for default[5] of yeomen they are fain to make up their inquests of such manner of people. And in villages they are commonly made churchwardens, sidemen, aleconners, now and then constables, and many times enjoy the name of headboroughs.[6]

---

1   *suspicious* Suspect; *Canaries* Canary Islands; *New Spain* Mexico; *Cathay* China.

2   *enormity* Great crime.

3   *estatute* Statute made in the ninth year of Edward III's reign (1351). Parliament passed two statutes that year, one stating that foreign merchants could trade in England "without disturbance," the other outlawing the export of gold or silver. It is not immediately evident to which Harrison refers, or the relevance of the statute.

4   *retailers* Small businessmen or traders.

5   *default* Lack of.

6   *sidemen* Church assistants; *aleconners* Officers appointed by local authorities to assure the quality of beer or bread; *headboroughs* Petty constables.

7. The Norfolk Libel (1595)

This document, evidence of the extreme social distrust caused by the crop failures and the failure of the government to put an end to hoarding and price-gouging, was included among the manuscripts preserved at Hatfield House in Hertforshire, England, home of Robert Cecil, Earl of Salisbury. It is likely that Norfolk's mayor sent the libel to Robert's father, William Cecil, Lord Burghley, Queen Elizabeth's chief advisor, who kept it among his papers.

To the Mayor and justices of Norfolk,

God save our Queen Elizabeth. For seven years the rich have fed on our flesh. Bribes make you justices blind and you are content to see us famished. What are these edicts and proclamations, which are here and there scattered in the country, concerning kidders, cornmongers and those devilish cormorants, but a scabbard without the sword, for neither are those murthering malsters nor the bloody cornbuyers stayed.[1] We thought to have pressed higher to our L. Admiral, to entreat him to shut up the gate of his gain awhile and content himself with that he hath got. Sir William Paston, who might have been called "Passion" for his former pity, but now is "Paston" because he is become as hard as a stone. Woe to Hasselt who inhabits the seacoast, that noble thief! We hear a sound of the devils whispering to persuade the rich to complain of subsidies and other great charges to sue for 'out lode,' and one grant of 'out lode' in a year will sweep away all. There are 60,000 craftsmen in London and elsewhere, besides the poor country clown, that can no longer bear,[2] therefore their draught is in the cup of the Lord which they shall drink to the dregs, and some barbarous and unmerciful soldier shall lay open your hedges, reap your fields, rifle your coffers, and level your houses to the ground. Meantime give license to the rich to set open shop to sell poor men's skins. Necessity hath no law.

---

1 *kidders* Individuals who buy provisions from producers and sell them in a market; *murthering malsters* Murdering malsters, i.e., malt makers who overcharge the malt; *stayed* Prevented from overcharging the poor.
2 *bear* Endure their grievances.

8. Letter from the Lord Mayor of London to Lord Burghley Concerning Thomas Deloney (1596)

After Deloney published a ballad criticizing Elizabeth, the matter came to the attention of the highest authorities in the land. This letter contains the mayor of London's report to William Cecil, Lord Burghley, and it shows that Deloney went underground rather than face arrest and imprisonment.

My humble duty to your Lordship remembered, there was brought to my hand a certain ballad containing a complaint of the great want and scarcity of corn within this realm, which, forasmuch as it containeth in it certain vain and presumptuous matter, bringing in her Highness to speak with her people in dialogue in very fond and undecent sort, and prescribeth orders for the remedying of the dearth of corn, extracted (as it seemeth) out of the book published by your Lordship the last year, but in that vain and undiscreet manner as that thereby the poor may aggravate their grief, and take occasion of some discontentment, I thought good to call before me the printer and the party by whom it was put to print, who pretended a licence; but finding the same to be untrue, I have committed him to one of the counters, and have taken sureties of the printer himself for his appearance, if your Lordship shall think it fit to have any further punishment inflicted upon him. The maker himself, who is one Deloney, (an idle fellow, and one noted with the like before in printing a book for the silk weavers, wherein was found some like foolish and disordered matter,) I cannot yet find. A copy of the ballad I have sent to your Lordship enclosed herewithal.

And so I humbly take my leave. From London, the 25th of Julie, 1596

Your Lordship's most humble,
Stephen Slany, M

9. Depositions of Bartholomew Steere and His Associates (1596)

As discussed in the introduction, acts of rebellion to protest food shortages were not confined to London. In early fall, 1596, Bartholomew Steere of Oxfordshire tried to organize an uprising; it failed miserably, and the depositions reveal the depth of resentment against the "rich," whom the participants blamed for their misery. As the letter from Norris to the Privy Council and the Council's response indicate, the authorities took this rebellion very seriously, and while the participants were all executed, Norris at least wanted to address what he considered the cause of the violence—the abuses of the Enclosure Movement—so "that the poor may be able to live."

December 14, 1596
From Henry Lord Norris to Sir William Knollys,[1] Comptroller of the Household. I send a letter from Sir William Spencer[2] with examinations concerning an intended rising of the people in Oxfordshire. I want the Council's orders what is to be done with the offenders to prevent like attempts.

p.s.—I want your commission and some order to be taken about enclosures on the western part of the shire, where this stir began, that the poor may be able to live.

Enclosed letter: Sir W. Spencer, deputy Lieutenant to Lord Norris and Sir William Knollys, Comptroller of the Household, Lords Lieutenant of Oxfordshire. There was a rising planned at Enslow Hill of 200 or 300 seditious people, from various towns of that

---

1   *Henry Lord Norris*   Elizabethan diplomat and courtier (1525–1601). From 1585 to 1599, he and Sir William Knollys served as joint lord lieutenant for Oxfordshire and Berkshire, and so were responsible for home defense and generally keeping the peace. According to the *Oxford Dictionary of National Biography*, "In 1596 his house was targeted for attack by a group of Oxfordshire men planning a rising against enclosures. They had heard that the house was full of munitions and timed their action for St Hugh's day, when most of the local gentry would be in London to celebrate Elizabeth's accession day. The rising, however, proved abortive and Norris was made responsible for interrogating its leaders, one of whom was his own carpenter, Bartholomew Steere"; *Sir William Knollys* Courtier and member of Elizabeth's Privy Council (c. 1545–1632). As comptroller, he was responsible for running Elizabeth's household.

2   *Sir William Spencer*   Oxfordshire landowner (d. 1609), and as the letter says, deputy to Norris and Knollys.

shire, and with design of raising a rebellion. They were to spoil the neighbouring gentlemen's houses of arms and horses, and go towards London, where they expected to be joined by the apprentices. I have bound the parties concerned to appear before at the assizes,[1] but imprisoned [Bartholomew] Steere, carpenter, and Roger Ibill, miller, who persuaded many into this action. They have confessed little, but might do more, if sent for and more sharply examined.[2] I am daily apprehending others, but little can be discovered 'til Steere or Ibill confess. They met when most of the gentlemen of the shire were to appear in the King's Bench, on a suit betwixt Mr. Broome and Mr. Hoare. They are chiefly young unmarried men, and not poor.

Examinations before Sir Wm. Spencer concerning a rebellion intended in the country of Oxford, as follows:

November 23, 1596

Roger Ibill of Hampton-Gay, loader.[3] Has heard divers poor people say that there must be a rising soon, because of the high price of corn. Barth[olomew] Steere told him that there would be such a rising has had not been seen a great while, and the meeting would be at Campsfield Green. Remembers no others with whom he spoke about it.

November 25, 1596

Roger Symonds, carpenter of Hampton Gay. Was told by Steere that he need not work for his living this dear year, for there would be a merry world shortly; he tried to persuade examinate[4] to join to pull the corn out of rich men's houses, and on his refusal, left him.

November 26, 1596

Barth. Steere of Hampton-Poyle. Refuses to confess anything.

December 5, 1596

Roger Symonds further confessed that Steere, to encourage him, told him 100 men were coming from Witney, and others from other parts,

---

1   *assizes*   Judicial inquest, civil or criminal.
2   *more sharply examined*   Tortured.
3   *loader*   Ibill's occupation, one who loads heavy objects onto a cart.
4   *examinate*   Person being examined.

who were all to meet on Enslow Heath. They meant to spoil the houses of Mr. Power of Blechington, Mr. Berry, Mr. Rathbone, Mr. Fryer, Mr. Whitton, Sir Hen[ry] Lee, and Sir [William] Spencer, and Steere said he would cut off all the gentlemen's heads; thence they were to go to Lord Norris's of Rycott, who has two pieces of brass ordnance, which they were to take, and make carriages for them by taking his coaches off their wheels; also to take arms for 100 men which he had, and his horses, my Lord and Lady being both in London. Thence they were to go to London, and be joined by the apprentices. A dresser of arms, dwelling at Thame, who was said to know where all the best arms in Buckinghamshire are, was to join them. One man promised them 100 quarters[1] of corn.

John Steere of Witney. Was told of the rising by his brother Bartholomew, who said there would be 200 or 300 people not needy, from Woodstock, Bladen, Kirtleton, etc., and they would go from one rich man's house to another, and take horses, arms and victuals. Tried to persuade him against such unlawful courses, but he said he would not always live like a slave. James Bradshaw, the miller's son of Hampton, also asked him to join.

December 14, 1596

The Council to Lord Norris: We thank you for your pains in the examination of these seditious persons. We desire you to send up Bartholomew Steere, Roger Ibill, and James and Richard Bradshaw, the ringleaders of the conspiracy, by the high sheriff, and under guard, their hands pinioned and their legs bound under their horses' bellies, and allow them no conference on their way. If needful, they should be watched at night at the inns where they lodge. John Harcourt and Pudsey of Elsfield, charged with offering to be leaders, should be apprehended, examined, and sent up, under charge of your son, Sir [Henry] Norris, with their examinations or any others that may discover these mischievous purposes. All concerned should be apprehended and committed to prison, and the justice and other gentlemen and officers take special care to suppress any tumult or gathering of the people. Those gentlemen whose houses have been threatened

---

1   *quarters*   Measures of grain equal to approximately eight bushels each.

should look to their safety, and have their servants, retainers, and tenants ready in their defence. The farmer who offered to give them corn should be apprehended. We rely on your diligence for a full discovery of the plot.

January 7, 1597

Examination, in answer to interrogatories, of Bartholomew Steere, of Hampton-Gay, carpenter:

1. Was told by Jas. Bradshaw that between 40 and 60 men had been to Lord Norris, at Rycott, and had threatened to pull down the hedges and knock down gentlemen, if they could not have remedy. Knows that divers people did go to his Lordship, and petitioned for some corn to relieve their distress, and for putting down enclosures, but does not remember the time.

2. Agreed with Roger Symonds, a carpenter, Bradshaw, and other named to get up a rising, pull down the enclosures, and knock down Mr. Power and other gentlemen.

3. Settled with Bradshaw that the rising should be at Enslow Hill, having heard of a former rising there. Told Symonds that before, the risers were persuaded to go home, and were then hanged like dogs; but now, if they were once up they would never yield, but go through with it. Conferred several times with Symonds and others; Bradshaw, being a miller and travelling the country, undertook to persuade others to join.

4. Arranged for the rising as early as might be, that is, the Monday after St. Hugh's day; denies that Bradshaw told him that Mr. Pudsey was to be their leader, although he said he was a tall and lusty man.

5, 6, 7. Told Bradshaw and Symonds that after they had risen, if they had found themselves weak, they should go towards London, as he thought the apprentices there would take their part; was induced to think so by the late intended insurrection in London, when certain apprentices were hanged; Bradshaw and Symonds approved this. Told them there was armour for 100 men at Lord Norris's, and two field pieces, and that if they could get enough to join them, they would take these things.

8. At the time appointed, went with [Thomas] Horne and —— Burton to Enslow Hill, each of them being armed; there they met with Bompas, who said he knew of half a score of good fellows at Kirtleton that he could fetch to join them; they waited on the hill from 9 to 11 at night, expecting company, and none coming, they departed.

9. Nothing.

10. At the time of his first determination to get up a rising, served Lord Norris, and was a single man, and therefore stood in no need, but meant to have risen to help his poor friends, and other people who lived in misery.

11 and 12. Nothing.

13. Mr. Power has enclosed much; Mr. Frere has destroyed the whole town of Water-Eaton; Sir Wm. Spencer has enclosed common fields, and many about Banbury and other places have done the same.

14, 15, and 16. Nothing. Also,

Like examination of Jas. Bradshaw, miller:

1. Bartholomew Steere first talked to him about a rising at Hampton-Poyle in the presence of John Steere, his father, and John, his brother, when the latter said there were 100 in Witney who would go with them to throw down enclosures, and Bartholomew Steere said it would never be well until the gentry were knocked down.

2. After this, had speech with William ——, baker to Sir Wm. Spencer, who said that corn would not be cheaper until the hedges were thrown down; Sir Wm. Spencer's carter, a smith of Yarnton, and Heath, of the same place, said the same, and agreed to join in any rising for that purpose.

3, 4, 5, 6, 7, 8, and 9. Nothing.

10. At the time of his first conference with Steere, was house-hold servant to Sir Wm. Spencer, and therefore had no need to attempt such an act, being unmarried, and in a good place.

11 and 12. Nothing.

13. Power has enclosed much; confesses nothing of any other enclosures.

14, 15, 16, and 17. Nothing. Also,

January 8, 1597
Like examination of Roger Symonds, of Hampton-Gay—

1 and 2. Met Bartholomew Steere, who asked him how he did this hard year, and how he maintained his wife and children, having seven sons; told him he did so by hard work, and could hardly find them bread and water. Steere replied, "care not for work, for we shall have a merrier world shortly; there be lusty fellows abroad, and I will get more, and I will work one day and play the other," adding, that there was once a rising at Enslow Hill, when they were entreated to go down, and after were handed like dogs, but now they would never yield, but go through with it; that he knew where there was harness for 100 men; that servants were so held in and kept like dogs, that they would be ready to cut their master's throats, and that Sir Wm. Spencer had two sound fellows in his house. Made the less account of these speeches as when he went to market, he commonly heard the poor people say that they were ready to famish for want of corn, and thought they should be forced by hunger to take it out of men's houses.

Steere also said there were 100 who would come out of Witney, and that there was a mason who could make balls of wild-fire, and had a sling to fling the same, whereby he could fire houses as occasion should serve; also that there was a farmer who had 80 quarters of corn, and that poor men could not have a bushel under 4s. 2d., and their want of 2d.[1] was often the occasion of their not having any; but if they would come to him, he would sell them some at 4s.; that there was an armourer in Thame, who knew where the best armour was in Oxfordshire; that when they had risen, they would go to Lord Norris's, and get wine and beer, and take two of his brass ordnance, and set them upon coach wheels, and so proceed. Refused to go with him, and said he had always lived like an honest man, and this was the way to undo himself and family.

Discovered all this to Mr. Berry, examinate's landlord, on his return from Northampton fair, and he hardly believed it; told him John Horne and Wm. Dowley, two of his own men, talked of it, whereupon Mr. Berry examined all his servants. Horne was angry, and wished to charge examinate with the matter.

3. Steere said that when they were up, the London apprentices would join them; that they would murder Mr. Powter, as also Mr. Berry and his daughter, and spoil[2] Rabone, the yeoman, Geo. Whilton, Sir Hen. Lee, Sir Wm. Spencer, Mr. Frere, and Lord Norris, and then go to London, and that it would be only a month's work to overrun the realm; and that the poor once rose in Spain and cut down the gentry, since which they had lived merrily.

13. [sic] Admits that Mr. Power, Mr. Frere, and Sir Wm. Spencer have enclosed,

To all the rest he can say nothing. Also,

January 8, 1597

Examination of John Ibill, of Hampton-Gay. Was told by Barth. Steere that there would be a rising of the people on a Sunday night, when they would pull down the enclosures, whereby the ways were stopped, and arable lands enclosed, and lay them open again; told it to John Belcher, who admonished him how he spoke of it, as it might bring him into trouble.

---

1   *4s. ... of 2d.*   Four shillings, twopence, and their lack of twopence.
2   *spoil*   Rob.

10. A Portfolio: Images of Weaving and Cloth-Making

The following selection of images depict textile production in late medieval and early modern Europe. There is a surprising scarcity of English illustrations of cloth-making from this period; the French and Dutch cloth-making processes represented here would have been similar, but note that Jack's integrated cloth factory (described in Chapter 2) is significantly larger than anything depicted here.

French manuscript illustration of women spinning, c. 1440. British Library MS Royal 16 G V fol. 56.

Isaac van Swanenburg, *Shearing and Combing* (Het Ploten en Kammen), 1594–96.

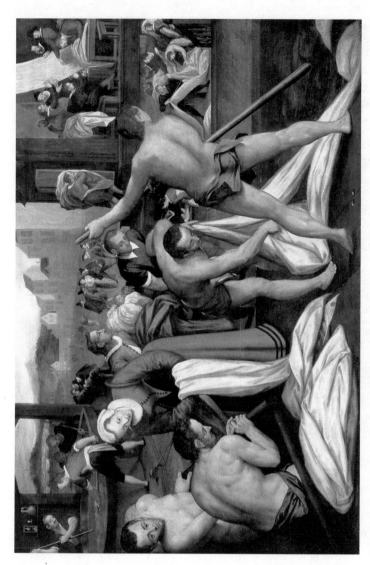

Isaac van Swanenburg, *Fulling and Dyeing* (Het Vollen en Verven), 1594–96.

Karel van Mallery, *Silk Reeling* (Haspelen van de Zijde), c. 1595.

Further Reading

Clark, Peter. "A Crisis Contained? The Condition of English Towns in the 1590s." Clark 44–66.

———, ed. *The European Crisis of the 1590s: Essays in Comparative History*. London: George Allen, 1985. Print.

Dorsinville, Max. "Design in Deloney's *Jack of Newbury*." *PMLA: Publications of the Modern Language Association of America* 88.2 (1973): 233–39. Print.

Eagleton, Terry. *The English Novel: An Introduction*. Malden, MA: Blackwell, 2005. Print.

Fleck, Andrew. "'Conveyance of History': Narrative, Chronicle, History and the Elizabethan Memory of the Henrician Golden Age." *Henry VIII and His Afterlives: Literature, Politics, and Art*. Eds. Mark Rankin and Christopher Highley. Cambridge: Cambridge University Press, 2009. 225–45. Print.

Hall, Edward. *Hall's Chronicle*, ed. Sir Henry Ellis. London, 1809. Print.

Hentschell, Roze. "Clothworkers and Social Protest: The Case of Thomas Deloney." *Comitatus: A Journal of Medieval and Renaissance Studies* 32 (2001): 43–67. Print.

Herman, Peter C. *A Short History of Early Modern England: British Literature in Context*. Oxford: John Wiley, 2011. Print.

Jordan, Constance. "The 'Art of Clothing': Role-Playing in Deloney's Fiction." *English Literary Renaissance*. 11.2 (1981): 183–93. Print.

Kewes, Paulina, Ian Archer, Felicity Heal, and Henry Summerson, eds. *The Holinshed Project*. Oxford University, 2013. Web. <http://www.cems.ox.ac.uk/holinshed/>.

Ladd, Roger A. "Thomas Deloney and the London Weavers Company." *Sixteenth Century Journal: Journal of Early Modern Studies* 32.4 (2001): 981–1001. Print.

Lawlis, Merritt E. "Introduction." *The Novels of Thomas Deloney*, ed. M.E. Lawlis. Bloomington: Indiana University Press, 1961. Xi–xxxii. Print.

Linton, Joan Pong. "Jack of Newbury and Drake in California: Domestic and Colonial Narratives of English Cloth and Manhood." *ELH* 59.1 (1992): 23–51. Print.

Manning, Roger. *Village Revolts: Social Protest and Popular Disturbances in England, 1509–1640.* Oxford: Clarendon Press, 1988. Print.

McKeon, Michael. *The Origins of the English Novel: 1600–1740.* Baltimore: The Johns Hopkins University Press, 1987. Print.

Mendelson, Sara, and Patricia Crawford. *Women in Early Modern England.* Oxford: Oxford University Press, 2000. Print.

Mustazza, Leonard. "Thomas Deloney's *Jacke of Newbury* (1596?)." *Journal of Popular Culture* 23.3 (1989): 165–77. Print.

Oldenburg, Scott. *Alien Albion: Literature and Immigration in Early Modern England.* Toronto: University of Toronto Press, 2015. Print.

Outhwaite, R.B. "Dearth, the English Crown, and the 'Crisis of the 1590s.'" Clark 23–43.

Palliser, D.M. *The Age of Elizabeth: England under the Later Tudors.* London: Longman, 1983. Print.

Power, M.J. "London and the Control of the 'Crisis' of the 1590s." *History* 70 (1985): 371–85. Print.

Sterling, Eric. "Teaching Gascoigne, Deloney, and the Emergence of the English Novel." *Teaching Early Modern English Prose.* Eds. Susannah Brietz Monta and Margaret W. Ferguson. New York: MLA, 2010. 164–74. Print.

Suzuki, Mihoko. "The London Apprentice Riots of the 1590s and the Fiction of Thomas Deloney." *Criticism* 38.2 (1996): 181–217. Print.

Tribble, Evelyn B. "'We will do no harm without swords': Royal Representation, Civic Pageantry, and the Displacement of Popular Protest in Thomas Deloney's *Jacke of Newburie.*" *Place and Displacement in the Renaissance.* Ed. Alvin Vos. Binghamton, NY: Medieval & Renaissance Texts & Studies, 1995. 147–57. Print.

Walter, John. "'A Rising of the People?': The Oxfordshire Rising of 1596." *Past and Present* 107 (1985): 90–103. Print.

Watt, Ian. *The Rise of the Novel.* Berkeley: University of California Press, 1957. Print.

From the Publisher

A name never says it all, but the word "Broadview" expresses a good deal of the philosophy behind our company. We are open to a broad range of academic approaches and political viewpoints. We pay attention to the broad impact book publishing and book printing has in the wider world; we began using recycled stock more than a decade ago, and for some years now we have used 100% recycled paper for most titles. Our publishing program is internationally oriented and broad-ranging. Our individual titles often appeal to a broad readership too; many are of interest as much to general readers as to academics and students.

Founded in 1985, Broadview remains a fully independent company owned by its shareholders—not an imprint or subsidiary of a larger multinational.

For the most accurate information on our books (including information on pricing, editions, and formats) please visit our website at www.broadviewpress.com. Our print books and ebooks are also available for sale on our site.

On the Broadview website we also offer several goods that are not books—among them the Broadview coffee mug, the Broadview beer stein (inscribed with a line from Geoffrey Chaucer's *Canterbury Tales*), the Broadview fridge magnets (your choice of philosophical or literary), and a range of T-shirts (made from combinations of hemp, bamboo, and/or high-quality pima cotton, with no child labor, sweatshop labor, or environmental degradation involved in their manufacture).

All these goods are available through the "merchandise" section of the Broadview website. When you buy Broadview goods you can support other goods too.

broadview press
www.broadviewpress.com

From the Publisher

A name never says it all, but the word "Broadview" expresses a good deal of the philosophy behind our company. We are open to a broad range of academic approaches and political viewpoints. We pay attention to the broad impact book publishing and book printing has in the wider world; we began using recycled stock more than a decade ago, and for some years now we have used 100% recycled paper for most titles. Our publishing program is internationally oriented and broad-ranging. Our individual titles often appeal to a broad readership too; many are of interest as much to general readers as to academics and students.

Founded in 1985, Broadview remains a fully independent company owned by its shareholders—not an imprint or subsidiary of a larger multinational.

For the most accurate information on our books (including information on pricing, editions, and formats) please visit our website at www.broadviewpress.com. Our print books and ebooks are also available for sale on our site.

On the Broadview website we also offer several goods that are not books—among them the Broadview coffee mug, the Broadview beer stein (inscribed with a line from Geoffrey Chaucer's *Canterbury Tales*), the Broadview fridge magnets (your choice of philosophical or literary), and a range of T-shirts (made from combinations of hemp, bamboo, and/or high-quality pima cotton, with no child labor, sweatshop labor, or environmental degradation involved in their manufacture).

All these goods are available through the "merchandise" section of the Broadview website. When you buy Broadview goods you can support other goods too.

broadview press
www.broadviewpress.com

Further Reading

Clark, Peter. "A Crisis Contained? The Condition of English Towns in the 1590s." Clark 44–66.

———, ed. *The European Crisis of the 1590s: Essays in Comparative History*. London: George Allen, 1985. Print.

Dorsinville, Max. "Design in Deloney's *Jack of Newbury*." *PMLA: Publications of the Modern Language Association of America* 88.2 (1973): 233–39. Print.

Eagleton, Terry. *The English Novel: An Introduction*. Malden, MA: Blackwell, 2005. Print.

Fleck, Andrew. "'Conveyance of History': Narrative, Chronicle, History and the Elizabethan Memory of the Henrician Golden Age." *Henry VIII and His Afterlives: Literature, Politics, and Art*. Eds. Mark Rankin and Christopher Highley. Cambridge: Cambridge University Press, 2009. 225–45. Print.

Hall, Edward. *Hall's Chronicle*, ed. Sir Henry Ellis. London, 1809. Print.

Hentschell, Roze. "Clothworkers and Social Protest: The Case of Thomas Deloney." *Comitatus: A Journal of Medieval and Renaissance Studies* 32 (2001): 43–67. Print.

Herman, Peter C. *A Short History of Early Modern England: British Literature in Context*. Oxford: John Wiley, 2011. Print.

Jordan, Constance. "The 'Art of Clothing': Role-Playing in Deloney's Fiction." *English Literary Renaissance*. 11.2 (1981): 183–93. Print.

Kewes, Paulina, Ian Archer, Felicity Heal, and Henry Summerson, eds. *The Holinshed Project*. Oxford University, 2013. Web. <http://www.cems.ox.ac.uk/holinshed/>.

Ladd, Roger A. "Thomas Deloney and the London Weavers Company." *Sixteenth Century Journal: Journal of Early Modern Studies* 32.4 (2001): 981–1001. Print.

Lawlis, Merritt E. "Introduction." *The Novels of Thomas Deloney*, ed. M.E. Lawlis. Bloomington: Indiana University Press, 1961. Xi–xxxii. Print.

Linton, Joan Pong. "Jack of Newbury and Drake in California: Domestic and Colonial Narratives of English Cloth and Manhood." *ELH* 59.1 (1992): 23–51. Print.

Manning, Roger. *Village Revolts: Social Protest and Popular Disturbances in England, 1509–1640*. Oxford: Clarendon Press, 1988. Print.

McKeon, Michael. *The Origins of the English Novel: 1600–1740*. Baltimore: The Johns Hopkins University Press, 1987. Print.

Mendelson, Sara, and Patricia Crawford. *Women in Early Modern England*. Oxford: Oxford University Press, 2000. Print.

Mustazza, Leonard. "Thomas Deloney's *Jacke of Newbury* (1596?)." *Journal of Popular Culture* 23.3 (1989): 165–77. Print.

Oldenburg, Scott. *Alien Albion: Literature and Immigration in Early Modern England*. Toronto: University of Toronto Press, 2015. Print.

Outhwaite, R.B. "Dearth, the English Crown, and the 'Crisis of the 1590s.'" Clark 23–43.

Palliser, D.M. *The Age of Elizabeth: England under the Later Tudors*. London: Longman, 1983. Print.

Power, M.J. "London and the Control of the 'Crisis' of the 1590s." *History* 70 (1985): 371–85. Print.

Sterling, Eric. "Teaching Gascoigne, Deloney, and the Emergence of the English Novel." *Teaching Early Modern English Prose*. Eds. Susannah Brietz Monta and Margaret W. Ferguson. New York: MLA, 2010. 164–74. Print.

Suzuki, Mihoko. "The London Apprentice Riots of the 1590s and the Fiction of Thomas Deloney." *Criticism* 38.2 (1996): 181–217. Print.

Tribble, Evelyn B. "'We will do no harm without swords': Royal Representation, Civic Pageantry, and the Displacement of Popular Protest in Thomas Deloney's *Jacke of Newburie*." *Place and Displacement in the Renaissance*. Ed. Alvin Vos. Binghamton, NY: Medieval & Renaissance Texts & Studies, 1995. 147–57. Print.

Walter, John. "'A Rising of the People?': The Oxfordshire Rising of 1596." *Past and Present* 107 (1985): 90–103. Print.

Watt, Ian. *The Rise of the Novel*. Berkeley: University of California Press, 1957. Print.